Lord of Her Heart

by

Sherrinda Ketchersid

SMITTEN
HISTORICAL ROMANCE
LIGHTHOUSE PUBLISHING of the CAROLINAS

LORD OF HER HEART BY SHERRINDA KETCHERSID
Published by Smitten Historical Romance
An imprint of Lighthouse Publishing of the Carolinas
2333 Barton Oaks Dr., Raleigh, NC 27614

ISBN: 978-1-946016-88-1
Copyright © 2019 by Sherrinda Ketchersid
Cover design by Elaina Lee
Interior design by Karthick Srinivasan

Available in print from your local bookstore, online, or from the publisher at:
ShopLPC.com

For more information on this book and the author visit: https://sherrinda.com

Brought to you by the creative team at Lighthouse Publishing of the Carolinas (LPCBooks.com):
Eddie Jones, Pegg Thomas, Karin Beery, Shonda Savage, Stephen Mathisen, Jenny Leo, Christy Callahan

Library of Congress Cataloging-in-Publication Data
Ketchersid, Sherrinda.
Lord of Her Heart / Sherrinda Ketchersid 1st ed.

Printed in the United States of America

PRAISE FOR *LORD OF HER HEART*

"Ketchersid unfolds a mystery with skill that draws you on and makes you turn the pages, at the same time she builds a funny and sassy relationship that makes you want to linger over every word."

~ **Mary Connealy**
Author of *High Sierra Sweethearts Series*

"In *Lord of Her Heart,* Ketchersid sets the stage for a lavish romance with rich characters, superb writing, and a fast-paced plot—a true page-turner 'til the end. Malcolm Castillon is everything a hero should be—chivalrous, handsome, and thoughtful. And his Lady Jocelyn proves to be an intelligent heroine, triumphing through obstacles with faith and humility. I highly recommend this story for any historical romance reader. A brilliant debut for 2019!"

~**Angie Dicken**
Author of *My Heart Belongs In Castle Gate, Utah*

"This unique and compelling debut will whisk you back to the days of knights and beautiful maidens and steal your heart."

~**Lynne Gentry**
Author of *The Carthage Chronicles*

"Sherrinda Ketchersid's debut novel, *Lord of Her Heart*, is an adventurous romp into the medieval world of tournaments, subterfuge, and unexpected romance. Even the most stubborn heart can be turned by the truest love. Such a story!"

~**Pepper Basham**
Author of *My Heart Belongs in the Blue Ridge*
and the *Pleasant Gap Series*

"*Lord of Her Heart* had me from page one! Sherrinda Ketchersid's debut novel satisfies on every level: a swoon-worthy hero, a kind yet sassy heroine, dashing sword fights, and a message on what it means to trust not only God but others as well. Fans of Tamara Leigh will undoubtedly enjoy this talented new author."

~Jennifer A. Davids
Author of *A Perfect Weakness* and *Brides of Ohio*

Acknowledgments

From start to finish, this book came to fruition because of the many exceptional people who helped me, supported me, and encouraged me along the way.

To my husband, John. Your belief in me never wavered, and I felt like I was a real writer because of your continual faith in me.

To my four children, Thomas, Caleb, Elyssa, and Mark, thanks for being proud of your mom, even if it is a love story with kissing.

To Dad and Mom, who allowed me time to develop a love for reading, even if it meant putting off chores. Dad, thanks for being my first reader and chopping it to bits with your gentle red pen.

To Pegg Thomas and the LPC team, who took a chance on a medieval story. Thank you from the bottom of my heart.

To Karin Beery, my incredible editor. There truly are no words to express how grateful I am for making this book the best it could be. You taught me so much about writing and were gracious in the process. Your humor, attention to detail, and words of encouragement were a gift to my heart.

To Tina Radcliffe, my mentor and friend. God used you to pull me back into writing and to push me to take a chance, to put myself out there, and to believe in myself. I wouldn't be here without you.

To my Alley Cats, who loved me, encouraged me, and cheered me on over the last eight years. I love you, ladies.

To my Writing Sisters, whose prayers and encouragement have been a blessing beyond compare.

To my critique groups, thanks for the encouragement and laughter I've found with you all.

DEDICATION

For John, my very own knight in shining armor.
Your chivalrous and sacrificial love for me takes my breath away.

CHAPTER 1

Lomkirk Abbey, England, 1198 AD

"I tire of this endless cleaning." Jocelyn Ashburne sat on the cold stone floor of the cellarium and put a hand to her aching back. Her gray woolen habit made her itch. She wanted to pull off the veil to release her damp curls from its confines. "Methinks the Reverend Mother Agatha is attempting to tire my body and mind into forgetting my desire to return home. My petition for release has been again ignored, and I know not what to do."

"Perhaps you should write to your father once more." Sister Mary, her dearest friend at the convent, scrubbed the floor, swiping at her forehead before looking up at Jocelyn. "It could be he has had much to deal with at Ramslea and has been too busy to answer."

Jocelyn dipped her rag into the bucket of rosemary-scented water and wrung it out. "I've been here four years. I know I've only heard from him a few times, but 'tisn't like him to be so silent, even with the distraction of his new wife. My father has been silent for an entire year, and I am worried." Perhaps she should scour his missives for clues to solve the mystery of his silence.

"Do you sincerely think Helen might sway his ability to make decisions?"

Jocelyn huffed and scrubbed the floor with renewed vigor. "Aye, she cares not for me and only fawned over me in the presence of Father. He was blind to everything but her beauty and charm."

"He was lonely after losing your mother. I'm sure Helen fills the void in his heart. God will provide for you. Never fear."

Would that Jocelyn had Mary's faith in God's ability to manage her return home. So far, He had been silent to her pleas. Perhaps

His lack of communication *was* His answer. Perhaps she was to have faith amid the silence of her earthly father, as well as her heavenly one.

Jocelyn and Mary scrubbed the small storeroom in the quiet, as was customary for the sisters. Prayerful in all things. 'Twas a good thing, to be sure, but Jocelyn's mind wandered back to her father. As she worked, voices drifted beneath the crack in the door. She paused. The strident voice of the abbess reached her ears.

"Tell her she must allow me more time." Parchment rustled. "She might be able to coerce me to do what she wants, but we cannot be rushed."

A male voice followed, low and timid, "Reverend Mother, she insisted the novice either take her final vows or marry quickly. There will be consequences if not done quickly."

"She doesn't realize what a stubborn fool Jocelyn is." The abbess sighed. "I may not be able to force her to take her vows, though I can most certainly find a man to marry her."

Jocelyn's heart seized, and her lungs refused to fill with air. She was to be married off? She glanced at Sister Mary whose wide eyes mirrored her own surprise.

The abbess's voice faded down the hall as Jocelyn sat in disbelief, pulse hammering in her ears. Who would plot against her? Not her father, surely. Could it be Helen? Jocelyn would not wait to find out. She had to escape. "Mary, I must get home and investigate who is behind this bribery. Perhaps 'tis connected to my father's silence." Jocelyn's trembling limbs betrayed her determination to stand.

Mary rushed to steady her, then pulled her into a warm embrace. "I can scarce believe the words uttered by our own Reverend Mother." She pulled back to look into Jocelyn's face. "We shall go directly to Mother Agatha and confront her."

"Nay!" Jocelyn startled, her reply echoing against the walls. Lowering her voice, she continued, "I love your willingness to help, but you heard the abbess. Someone is threatening her. We must plan my escape."

"But Jocelyn, you cannot travel unaided. 'Tisn't safe. You shall be accosted, or worse, find your death along the road."

Mary spoke truth. Jocelyn couldn't travel alone as a woman. She stepped out of Mary's arms, pushed back her headdress, and massaged her aching temples. How could she leave unaided? If only she were a man.

As she fiddled with her veil, an idea sparked. "I will disguise myself as a lad. Even you won't recognize me once I cut my hair and am outfitted in tunic and hose."

"Nay, Jocelyn, you cannot do this. 'Tis improper."

"Is it proper that our abbess keep me prisoner? Pushing me to take vows I do not want to take? Conspiring to force me into marriage? Nay, Mary. I shall not stay." Jocelyn drew in a deep breath and stiffened her spine, prepared for more opposition.

Mary studied Jocelyn with furrowed brows. After a moment, she blew out her cheeks. "What can I do to help?"

Wrapping Mary in a tight embrace, Jocelyn blinked against the tears of gratitude filling her eyes. "Thank you." Her mind whirled with all the possibilities for escape. Though she wanted to leave immediately, she knew a plan must be in place before she could set foot outside the convent. "Let us take time to consider the best way to escape. Between the two of us, surely we can manage a plan to outwit Moth—the abbess." Jocelyn could no longer bring herself to call the woman Mother Agatha.

"Our time will be better spent in prayer over this disheartening predicament. He will give us wisdom."

Mary was right, but Jocelyn's trust in God had faltered. And now, with the news she might be forced into an unwanted marriage, she wondered if God even cared about her plight. Perhaps a few extra prayers might reach His ears. "I suppose 'tis best to continue our work and prayer while plotting."

It took all she had within her to sink back to her knees and continue scrubbing the floor. Mary knelt beside her, and they worked again in silence, Mary no doubt praying while Jocelyn sought a way to freedom.

By the time Jocelyn finished the floor, helped serve the evening meal, and readied for bed, she knew what she needed to do. Two days hence she would leave under cover of darkness. That would give her enough time to gather a disguise and supplies, as well as learn the best way to travel home.

Once she reached Ramslea, she'd speak with Father and gain his aid to determine who wanted to keep her from home. Unless *he* instigated the plan to keep her away. Surely not. She'd believe it of Helen, but never of Father.

After nightfall and compline prayers, Jocelyn walked toward the dormitory with Mary and the other sisters. Their footsteps pattered an erratic beat in the silence of the dim hallway, rather like the unsteady pounding of her heart. After two days of preparation, tonight she would flee.

"Jocelyn, may I have a word?"

She jumped and turned toward the voice. The abbess walked toward her from the chapel. Had she found out her plan? Jocelyn twisted the edge of her sleeve. "Aye."

"I have found you a husband."

Jocelyn exhaled and squared her shoulders. "But I do not wish for a husband."

"You have been with us for four years now, educated in spiritual and earthly matters. It is time to make your vows to God or to a husband."

While she knew God was the great lover of her soul, she did not believe He had created her to be a quiet, demure wife of His church. That was the sole reason she had put off taking her vows. She wanted a family—to be the wife of a man who loved her as her father had loved her mother.

Not willing to risk her escape, Jocelyn let her gaze fall to the floor as she played her part. "May I ask the name of the groom you have found?"

"Sir Harry Wiltworth, a gentleman of modest estate a few miles west. 'Tis said he is—"

"I know of whom you speak." Jocelyn shuddered at the mention of the man three score years with a large gut said to match his fat purse. Gossip around the abbey told of his appetite for food and women. She lifted her head and looked at the abbess. "I shall let you know my decision after the morning prayers."

A hint of a smile flitted at the corner of the abbess's mouth. "Very good."

Jocelyn tipped her head, then continued to the dormitory. Thank God, tonight she'd be free.

She entered the dormitory and readied for bed. Mary lay in the bed next to hers, worry crinkling her brow. The other sisters settled in their beds, and Jocelyn crawled into hers, pulling the covers up to her chin. She lay still, her heart thrumming as she waited for the soft snores signaling the time to rise and don her disguise.

Finally, after what seemed to be hours, the sisters stilled. Their breaths deepened. Jocelyn slid out of bed, then crept across the cool floor. Mary would not be far behind.

Once in the hallway, Jocelyn hurried to the cellarium. She encountered no one and entered the dark storeroom. She couldn't risk a lamp or torch, so she felt her way around the edge of the windowless room lined with shelves of spices, baked goods, and other supplies.

Reaching the far corner, she knelt and reached behind a large crock on the bottom shelf, pulling on the bag she'd stored there.

The door creaked, and Jocelyn jumped, knocking the crock to its side so that it clattered against the stone floor. She grabbed the pot while her heart pounded like the hooves of a runaway horse.

"Jocelyn?"

The urge to laugh seized Jocelyn at Mary's soft whisper. "Faith, Mary. You scared me." Righting the crock, she stood with her bag in hand. "Stand guard while I change."

"Aye, but be quick."

Jocelyn disrobed, then bound her chest with strips of cloth. She pulled on the tunic and hosen, securing them with a rope belt. The oversized tunic should hide her feminine form. The old boots she had secured were a tad big, but they would suffice.

She pulled the knife out of her bag, then grabbed a handful of her long dark hair. She paused as she held the thick locks in her hand. 'Twas vanity to treasure one's appearance, but she held a special memory of Mother brushing the very hair Jocelyn intended to cut.

Remembering her quest for the truth, Jocelyn slid the knife into the wavy strands above her shoulder, sawing at her hair several times before the knife slid through. With each handful of hair, her resolve strengthened, releasing her courage. Without the extra weight, her waves sprang into curls. She pulled a piece of twine from her bag and tied her hair at the back of her neck.

All she had to do now was act the part. 'Twould take courage, but courage she had. No one would deter her from her plan to get home.

Gathering her habit, wimple, and shorn hair, she stuffed them behind the crock. She picked up her bag full of provisions, as well as a water bag.

Mary met her at the door. "Are you sure about this?"

"Aye, 'tis time."

Malcolm Castillon of Berkham sat atop his steed and watched his squire spew the contents of his stomach along the side of the dusty road. While sorry for the lad's sufferings, he cursed his own poor fortune at the start of his journey to Ramslea.

Malcolm tossed several coins to the ground beside his squire. "There's five shillings for you if you can make it to Ramslea without slowing us down."

"I shall be fine." John wiped his sleeve across his mouth. He walked to his horse and grabbed the reins with shaky hands. "'Twas something I ate."

"I'm not so sure." Indeed, John's white face looked like those in the villages where illness had rendered men useless for weeks. How many times would Malcolm need to stop before John's sickness ceased? "We shall proceed. We have but a few hours until nightfall and need to make it to the next village."

"Aye, 'tis but a sour stomach." John mounted his horse. "Let's be off."

Malcolm nodded, then urged his horse to a gallop. They alternated between galloping and walking, giving the horses, as well as John, respite from the quick pace.

After a few hours in the saddle, only stopping twice more for John to heave, they walked their mounts through a forested area. Shade from the trees provided a pleasant shelter against the blinding sun. Malcolm didn't want to tire the horses. Having won a purse of gold in France, he intended to win at the new tournament at Ramslea in the northern hills of England. He had only a se'ennight to arrive. An easy feat with rested horses and a healthy squire.

"Sir, should you win at Ramslea, will it be enough to approach the king for land?" John's soft voice broke.

Malcolm glanced at his squire. Once again, his face flushed. Not a good sign. "I *shall* be the victor."

"But will it be enough for land?"

"'Twill."

"And a title?"

"Wooing the king with my charm should help my cause. My father being a loyal baron should lend credence with him as well." Though 'twould never hold influence with Malcolm. While the king valued the fierce lords who served him, Malcolm had no love of his father's harsh treatment of his men and family.

"Sir, I fear I ..." John's head bobbed, then his body pitched to the side. He landed in a heap on the ground.

Malcolm cursed as he pulled his horse to a stop. Dismounting, he knelt beside John and rolled him over. Dirt clung to the boy's sweaty face as his body trembled. Malcolm put a hand to his forehead, confirming his suspicion.

They would travel to the next village and find a healer to give John herbs. Then he must leave his squire in the healer's care. He couldn't miss the tournament, not when he was so close to his goal.

Hauling John into his arms, Malcolm draped the lanky lad over his horse, securing him with rope from his saddlebag. Malcolm took the reins and tied them to his own saddle. Gaining his seat, he brought the horses to a trot.

As they traveled out of the forest onto hilly terrain, dusk settled around them as the sun set behind the western horizon. Above the rolling hills, light glimmered with the promise of a village up ahead. 'Twould be dark once they reached lodging.

Malcolm checked over his shoulder, making sure the boy was secure. Hopefully he would not contract the lad's sickness. He had worked hard to steer clear of those afflicted in France.

Darkness had indeed settled as Malcolm reached the village. Thatched huts lined the road. A taller building rose over the roofline, a cross at its peak. Was this place large enough to contain an inn? If not, 'twould be difficult to find housing, much less a healer. A few people walked along the road, but it seemed most had entered their abodes for the evening.

As he continued down the street, laughter and music reached Malcolm's ears. Possibly a tavern? Passing by stables and the smithy, he rounded a corner and spotted a thatched building double the size of the homes. Several men in various degrees of drunkenness littered the yard. One man sat on a chair playing a lute while a woman danced with several of the men, laughing as she weaved through them.

Malcolm stopped his horse in front of the group. An older man stooped with age drew near. "A traveler with a body." The man's gaze fell on John. "Is he dead?"

"Nay. Only ill." Malcolm dismounted and faced the man. "I'm Malcolm Castillon of Berkham, on my way to Ramslea. Is there an inn we might stay the night?"

"Name's Thomas, the brewer. We have no inn, but this is my home, and I have a few beds in the back I can hire out."

"And a healer?"

Thomas shrugged. "Bessie is not much to look at, but all we have to offer. She knows about healing herbs, though not as skilled when it comes to broken bones." He held out his arm and pulled up a sleeve, revealing a misshaped forearm.

Malcolm winced, thankful that John wasn't in need of such handling. "'Twill do well enough."

The man motioned for one of the less inebriated men. "Robert, fetch Bessie and be quick about it."

One of the men set down his ale and shuffled along the street.

Malcolm untied John and reeled at the stench. 'Twas the same odor that permeated the air of the French boat. The malodor of the sickness.

Malcolm fought the bile in his throat as he felt the lad's forehead. Cold. Too cold. He frowned and placed a hand on John's back, waiting for the rise and fall. None came. Malcolm stepped away from the body.

"Sir?" Thomas shuffled closer to Malcolm.

Malcolm shook his head. "My squire is dead."

Thomas crossed himself and stepped back. "Sir, you cannot stay here. I want no killing sickness in my home."

"Aye, 'tis sorry I am for bringing this upon you." Malcolm needed to bury John. "Could I purchase a plot in your chapel graveyard?"

"Nay, not with this sickness." Thomas crossed himself once more. "You must leave our village."

Malcolm pulled out several shillings and held out his hand. "For the trouble I've caused."

"Just leave the coins on the ground."

Malcolm nodded. After dropping the coins, he tied John in place and mounted his horse, heading north of town. He traveled a goodly distance until he found a small clearing next to a wooded area. The half-moon gave him enough light to gather wood for a fire. Though the night was cool, the fire was not for warmth. It was for John.

Malcolm laid the body on its deathbed. Using flint and steel, he started the fire, the slight breeze helping to fan the flames. Stepping back, he watched them engulf his squire.

He knew he should say a prayer of some sort, but he was not a praying man, at least not anymore. Still, he could speak for this young man.

"You were a good squire and friend. You were loyal and kind. From dust you came and to dust you shall return. Blessing upon you, John." 'Twas a fitting benediction.

Turning from the fire, Malcolm led the horses across the clearing toward a stand of trees. He unsaddled and tied them for the night. Retrieving his cloak from his saddlebag, he laid it beneath an oak tree.

He needed to get an early start in the morning. If he made good time, he'd arrive at Ramslea early enough to hire a replacement squire for the tournament. He wouldn't be able to find one such as John, though. He'd made sure Malcolm's chain mail gleamed, his shield shone, and his sword edge stayed sharp. Malcolm never worried about his clothes being clean or needing repairs. He never had to think about losing his equipment. John took care of everything before Malcolm could voice a need.

Aye, 'twould be difficult to find a good squire for the tournament, but victory would be Malcolm's and the reputation earned from winning would see him to his goal of land. His own land to govern and sustain. He had no need of a wife or family. After a life spent living under tyrants, dealing with deceitful women, and battling in tournaments, he longed for nothing more than peace and quiet.

A win at Ramslea would gain him that prize.

CHAPTER 2

The rusty lock would not budge.

Jocelyn blew a strand of unruly hair from her eyes and paused to still her racing heart. No matter how many times she'd practiced in the privacy of the garderobe, nothing had prepared her for the trembling of her fingers or the time wasted looking over her shoulder. Taking a deep breath, she pried the tip of her knife back into the lock, listening for the quiet catch of the spring.

"Jocelyn, make haste." Sister Mary stood guard several paces away.

Though the smaller postern gate at the back of the abbey was far from the dormitory, sometimes sisters were known to walk the nearby flower gardens for nightly prayer. Jocelyn prayed that none would be so inspired that night. "Do not fret. I shan't fail."

Her heart drummed in her ears. She fought down the panic welling inside as she wiggled the tip of the blade. The lock jolted open. Closing her eyes, she almost wept with relief. *Thank you, Lord.* She pushed against the heavy gate, wincing as it creaked, piercing the heavy mantle of silence.

Jocelyn turned to Mary who stood with her clasped hands pressed against her heart. She ran to her friend, hugging her tightly. "Pray for me. Pray for success in my quest."

Mary clutched Jocelyn to her. "The important thing is that you get to safety." She loosened her hold and smiled through her tears. "I will hold you close in my heart and pray for you constantly."

"And I you, my friend." Jocelyn grabbed her sack and ran.

Sweat trickled down Jocelyn's back as she struggled for breath. How long had she been traveling? It seemed morning should have come hours ago. She peered up through the trees. Instead of inky blackness, slivers of a dark-blue sky peeked through the leaves. What could be holding morning at bay? She pushed through the forest, keeping the road in view to maintain her course. But she paid a price for her stealth. Stones and roots bruised her feet. Branches clawed at her face. Thorny vines clung to her legs, slowing her progress.

She came upon an ancient tree with a massive, twisted trunk, one that would provide strength and security while she eased her tired body. Collapsing at its base, Jocelyn nestled as best she could within the arms of the roots. She closed her eyes, willing her mind, as well as her body, to rest. Yet only a short respite, for she must put more distance between herself and the abbess. Her body relaxed, and sleep claimed her.

The leaves rustled. Jocelyn sat up, tense. She crouched amid the thick roots around her, poised to run. Her gaze darted to a movement in a bush to her left. A rabbit poked its twitching nose through the leaves. She wilted, relief flooding through her.

With the road in her sights to her right, she began a slow run, wending her way through the towering trees. The birds twittered. Through the branches above, the sky boasted a deep lavender hue. 'Twould be good to have some light to see the ground before her. Stepping on stones and stumbling over branches made traveling difficult.

Her thighs burned at the continued strain. More strenuous work at the abbey would have better prepared her for this part of her journey, but as 'twas, hoeing the garden and scrubbing the floors had been the extent of her physical training.

Jocelyn pressed on until the sun shone brightly in the early morning sky. Gasping for breath, she halted, bent over with her hands on her knees, struggling to ease her aching lungs. Sweat dampened her hair and clothes. She wiped the sweat off her brow and took a drink from her water bag. The tepid water ran down her throat, quenching her thirst and reviving her resolve. Refreshed, she took a deep breath and reviewed her plan to return home.

She envisioned her father rejoicing at her return, but what if he was the one wanting her gone? Was Helen a part of the whole affair? Would returning home hold its appeal if they had betrayed her?

Jocelyn knew she would need to marry at some point but had hoped her father would find someone she could love as he had loved her mother. To marry someone like Sir Wiltworth turned her stomach. Needing to put more space between herself and that wretched man, she forced herself to run again. *Stay focused.*

The tunic and hose made traveling through the undergrowth easier than a long gown. She appreciated their simplicity and freedom, but the thick, scratchy hose slipped down her legs and bunched around her ankles.

Ignoring the discomfort, she pumped her legs harder. Aye, she would make it to her father's keep or die trying.

Birds trilled their morning songs as faint voices carried from up the road. Jocelyn stuttered to a stop and listened. The voices grew louder. She hurried deeper into the trees, crouching under the cover of the thick bushes. She tensed as she fought to slow her labored breathing.

The deep voices moved closer.

Jocelyn strained to see through the leaves. She could make out two men. A tall, thin man scuffled his feet in the dirt. The other man pumped his short legs to keep up with his companion. Dirt stained their clothes, mud caked their boots, and greasy hair clung to their heads.

"Just last night I managed to get 'er in my bed, I did."

"Did ye now? I imagine she was a good bedder, aye?"

"Of course she was, ye fool."

Their rowdy laughter revealed yellowed, broken teeth and spurred the birds around her into flight.

Jocelyn blushed. One of the men tromped through the brush toward her. Her heart thundered, and her mind willed him to change course, but he stopped mere handbreadths away. She held her breath.

The man made to undo his leggings.

Faith, he was going to relieve himself, and on her person! She couldn't creep away without him hearing her, so she sprang to her feet and ran.

The man cursed. "Obed, help me catch the lad! He may have coin on him!"

Running like a panicked hare, Jocelyn dodged through the forest, branches whipping her hair and face. She plunged blindly through a mass of vines and into an open field. Flying across the grass, pounding footsteps closed in from behind.

She looked over her shoulder as something hit her on the back, knocking her to the ground.

A body pressed her into the damp weeds, and she struggled for breath. She sent her elbow backward. The man grunted and fell to the side. Gasping, she twisted away, pulling herself out from under him.

She had to get free!

He caught her ankle, pulling her back. Grabbing her shoulder, he flipped her on her back and pinned her down once more. She slapped at him as he tried to grab her hands. Terror filled her as she screamed. No match against his strength, she still fought, pushing and clawing.

"Shut ye mouth, boy!" His hand cracked against her cheek.

She ceased fighting, shocked by the force of the man's hand. Her face stung. Tears filled her eyes, but boys did not weep. She must keep up her masquerade.

"Look 'ere, a wee boy who still screams like a gel." The man laughed.

"Aye, he's a feisty thing." The tall one leaned over, pushed off his friend, and hauled her to her feet. "Now then, laddie, what would you be doing scurrying around in the bushes scarin' poor souls such as ourselves?"

She looked at the ground. "Good sirs, I mean you no harm. I am a traveler such as yourselves journeying northward toward my kinsman's keep. I heard voices, so I hid—"

"An' scared me soul right to the grave, ye did." The burly one glowered and stepped toward her. "Ye shall pay. Hand over your coin."

She couldn't give up her precious coin. Turning to run, someone grabbed her by the arm and yanked her back. The tall one held her arms from behind as the short man approached. "I'll teach ye a lesson, I will. Then I will take ye coin."

His slaps stung like fire, prickling her skin. She bit back her scream, knowing it made her sound like a girl. The slaps grew harder, then a fist landed across her cheek, rattling her head. Another fist caught her temple, and stars speckled her vision.

The man grabbed her tunic. Should he discover she was a woman, she was doomed. She screamed, more fearful of exposure than death.

The man's laughter echoed in her ears. The pounding continued. Her eye throbbed and her stomach burned like fire. Her vision fading, she welcomed the coming darkness, hoping 'twould end the pain.

Someone shouted, and she fell, her head landing on the hard ground. Metal clashed against metal. Men bellowed vile curses. Then, all was silent but for the pounding of feet in the distance.

Strong arms lifted her, and Jocelyn succumbed to the darkness.

Malcolm laid the lad on the ground near his horse. Blood ran from a cut above the lad's eye, and his swollen cheek promised a colorful bruise. Sitting back on his heels, Malcolm cursed his chivalrous self. What was he to do with this dirty, bruised pile of skin and bones lying before him?

By the saints, he had neither the time nor the energy to care for a scrawny boy. He had a se'ennight before the tournament, and he was not about to miss it on account of a malodorous halfling. This journey proved one ache in the head after another.

The boy stirred, groaning.

Malcolm gathered water from his supply and poured some into the boy's mouth. Being chivalrous was not always convenient, but 'twas an oath he would not shirk.

The lad vaulted upright, sputtering as he whimpered. "Cease, please!" He rubbed his face, smearing dirt and blood across pale cheeks. As he looked up at his rescuer, his blue eyes grew wide.

Malcolm had to smile. Time spent in the lists honing his swordplay had made his shoulders broad and his arms well muscled. Boys stood in awe of him, men stood in fear of him, and women … well, women wanted him. He had long since been unaffected by the reactions his visage wrought.

"Little man, you are indeed fortunate I came when I did. Can you stand?"

Malcolm held out a hand, but the boy continued to gape. Malcolm grabbed the front of the boy's tunic and hauled him upright.

The boy gasped, pushing his hand away. "I do not need your aid." He teetered and fell on his backside. His bottom lip quivered, and his eyes glistened with tears.

"By the saints, I do not have time for this foolishness." Malcolm's shadow fell over the boy. "I have no need to be hindered by a filthy, ungrateful boy on this journey. I will gladly leave you be."

Malcolm turned and walked toward his horse, wrestling between his sense of honor and his desire to be free of the trouble he knew the boy would undoubtedly be. He clearly needed help, regardless of his protestations. Nay, Malcolm had to get to Ramslea and gain another win. Mounting his steed, he turned his horse to leave, glancing back as he did. The boy struggled to his feet, wobbling like a newborn colt.

Malcolm cursed under his breath. Whatever had possessed him

to take an oath of chivalry? While noble, at times chivalry interfered with well-laid plans. It was turning out to be a nuisance, to be sure. Steering his horse around, he pulled up in front of the lad.

"You may come with me or stay for the next pair of ruffians to accost you." Malcolm held out his hand. 'Twas a pity he'd sold John's horse earlier that morning, though he wondered if the lad before him could even ride. The boy clutched the neck of his tunic, eyes wide and jaw slack. By the saints, was the lad going to refuse him yet again? "Or perhaps you would prefer the company of a pack of wolves?"

The boy sucked in a deep breath, but he took Malcolm's hand. Grunting as he was lifted up, the boy settled behind Malcolm and grabbed hold of the back of his tunic.

"Put your arms around me, boy, lest you fall off and knock yourself senseless again." When the boy hesitated, Malcolm rolled his eyes. "You are a timid lad, for all your boasting."

The boy sighed as he slid his arms around Malcolm's middle, gripping tighter as Malcolm urged his horse to a gallop.

Most likely the child had not been trained in manly ways. Maybe he had only sisters, or maybe his sire was a weakling himself. Not everyone had the privilege of being raised among four brothers by a sire more fierce than a wild boar. At times too fierce, especially in the treatment of Malcolm's mother.

Memories haunted him as Malcolm tightened his grip on the reins. He would rather petition the king for a title and serve him than serve his heavy-handed father. Malcolm could serve another lord or even join the church, but he wanted his own land to rule as he saw fit. Peace to do as he wanted.

First, he must see the weakling behind him to the next village. A small hiccup and a sniffle affirmed his resolve.

By the saints, being a man of honor would be the death of him if he continued aiding poor souls like the one snotting the back of his tunic.

CHAPTER 3

Sunshine warmed Jocelyn's back, and she struggled to keep her eyes open. Though her face throbbed as she pressed against her rescuer's back, sleep summoned her. When the horse shifted beneath her, she tightened her hold around the man's waist. There was no doubt she'd fall off the monstrous beast if she fell asleep. What would Mary say if she saw Jocelyn now?

The welcomed gurgling of rushing water reached her ears. She licked her dry lips. They hadn't stopped for hours, and she had been too afraid to let go of her rescuer to grab her water bag.

The morning's unexpected events—not to mention the smacking she'd taken—made her head spin. If today was any indication, she could not make it home alone.

When she'd seen her rescuer kneeling over her, all thought flew from her mind. Faith, but he fair took her breath away. It was not that she had never seen such a specimen of manhood. Aye, she had memories of her father's guardsmen. She had watched them train in the lists from her perch on the parapet, so 'twas not the first time she had seen a man of such size.

This man, however, was as beautiful as he was strong. Her cheeks flamed as she held onto his waist, his muscles flexing under her fingers as he steered his horse toward the stream. A gust of wind blew his wavy hair about his head, and she admired the glints of red amid the deep brown. His strong jaw and crooked nose only enhanced his raw beauty.

Thankfully, he had not discovered her ruse. She shuddered to think what he might do should her gender be discovered. Who knew how far his chivalry extended? If only she could travel the rest of her journey as she was, safe and secure.

Her girlish reactions to her attack and rescue made her realize that clothing, clipped hair, and a dirty face were not enough to maintain her disguise. She must be more careful.

They stopped near the stream and dismounted.

"Do you have a name, boy?" The man knelt at the stream to drink.

"Aye." Jocelyn stretched her back and groaned, her muscles stiff and sore. "Jack. My name is Jack." She took the horse's reins and led it to water to drink. "And your name?"

"I go by Malcolm, but you may call me Sir. Now answer me this. Why are you out on your own?"

Jocelyn walked toward him, dropping her sack beside her when she stopped. "I am on my way to the Castle Ramslea."

Her rescuer choked. "Ramslea? As in Lord Ashburne's Ramslea?"

Jocelyn gasped. She struggled to remain calm at hearing her father's name. She lowered her voice. "You know him?"

Malcolm shook his head. "Nay, I do not know him, though Ramslea is my destination. I am to participate in the tournament there in a se'enight, supposing that I make it there in time. You, little man, are slowing me down." He came to his feet and wiped his hands on his tunic. "What have you need of at Ramslea?"

"I need to see my family." Jocelyn knelt for a long drink of water, mentally rehearsing the story she'd prepared. She sat back and looked at him. "I, um, I have been fostering with Lord Nichols of Pertrane. Being several years since I've been home, he thought my mother would enjoy seeing me and fattening me up with good food from her table."

Malcolm stared down at her from his impossible height and raised an eyebrow. "You were fostering with Lord Nichols? In truth, you do not look as if you could hoist a sword above your head."

Jocelyn had to admit the verity of what he said, but she had planned for such observations. "Truth be told, I am not as capable with the sword as I would like. Having only started my squiring duties, I've yet to acquire the strength needed."

Malcolm chuckled. "Just how old are you?"

For a moment, the stern warrior disappeared, replaced by ... by what, she couldn't say. Laugh lines creased the corner of his eyes, and a dimple marked his right cheek. Now what had he asked of her? Age?

She couldn't tell him the truth as she'd never pass for the score of years she was. "I am ten and five years. Even though I may not have my whiskers yet nor strengthened my arms, I am more than a match for anyone with a small blade."

Malcolm shook his head and quirked his lips into a crooked smile.

Encouraged by his smile, she stood and took a step toward him. "I know I'm not much to look at, but I can be of some aid. See me safely to Ramslea, and I will be your squire for the tournament."

"Humph." Malcolm reached into his saddlebag. He pulled out a piece of bread and took a bite.

As he remained silent, her anxiety increased. *Be bold like a man!* "Then you agree to take me to Ramslea?"

"I have not yet decided if I shall take you that far. You must prove yourself and your usefulness to me before I can guarantee your passage home." He paused and studied her, his eyes puzzled. "You say your family is at Ramslea and you also say you fostered with Lord Nichols. Ashburne of Ramslea had no son to foster off, so what sort of game are you playing?"

Jocelyn's mouth went dry as she tried to remember the details of her story. *Lord, help me.* "I, um, my family is at Ramslea, though my father is ... is but a guardsman for Lord Ashburne. I am like a son to Lord Ashburne, and as a favor to my father, who is the fourth son of a baron himself, Lord Ashburne fostered me off to Lord Nichols during my tenth year. While not of high noble birth, I managed to acquire the, um, the manly education due a lord."

She kept her eyes on Malcolm as she tried to gauge his reaction.

His brows drew together. He stepped in front of her, still chewing. She held her breath. His steely gray eyes bore into hers. Flecks of blue mingled in the gray near their black center.

He shook his head. "Do you have food?"

"Aye."

With a grunt, he turned away. "Eat something, wash your face, then relieve yourself if need be. We must continue on, and you best not cause me trouble."

Jocelyn expelled the breath she had been holding and nearly fell to her knees in relief. He would take her with him. Saints be praised!

Hurrying to the stream, she knelt and splashed water on her face. Rubbing her hands across her cheeks, she winced. A river of brown and red traversed her hands, and she splashed her face again. After she patted herself dry with her sleeve, she pulled the twine out of her hair to redo its binding. Pieces of dirt caked her hair, so she dunked her head in the cold stream, scrubbing her tresses clean. Once she squeezed out the excess water, she pulled the wet curls tight against her head and secured them with the twine.

Making sure Malcolm wasn't looking, she grabbed a handful of dirt and rubbed it onto her clean face. She must hide her smooth cheeks to stay disguised.

She also must convince him he needed her. She would be a companion, a helper, a confidant. Maybe not a confidant, for men didn't share the deep recesses of their souls like women did, but she would see to it he thought her indispensable. Her anxious heart unknotted. He was her best chance to make it safely home.

CHAPTER 4

After stopping at the stream, they traveled but a short distance before coming to a village. Malcolm pulled up at the stables.

"You need your own steed," he said, motioning her to dismount.

She slid off and walked over to the paddock to the right of the stables while Malcolm talked to the proprietor. Seven horses of various shapes and sizes milled about.

"I'm sure you can find one to your liking, sir." The owner opened the gate for Malcolm, then motioned for her to follow.

Malcolm walked through the horses, checking each one. A small black horse walked to Jocelyn and stopped. She stroked its forehead, and the horse took a step closer.

"I like this one." Jocelyn ran her hands over the shiny black coat, her fingers tangling in the long mane.

"'Tisn't a manly horse. I refuse to be the brunt of ridicule by riding through Ramslea's gate with a scrawny squire atop a dainty horse."

"I understand." Jocelyn cleared her throat. "I just thought this horse suited my small frame. I would look like a child on top a large horse."

"You make a good point." He pulled out his coin purse. Walking back to the owner, he gestured and grumbled until the poor merchant nodded.

Jocelyn grinned and whispered into her new horse's ear. "I think we shall do well together, you and I."

"Don't get too attached." Malcolm brushed past her, grabbed a saddle and bridle, and shoved them into her hands. "After the tournament, I'm selling the horse to pay for the trouble you're going to be."

Jocelyn frowned. She wasn't going to be trouble. She threw the saddle at her horse, not quite making it atop. Grunting, she pushed the leather up the horse's back.

"By the saints, you are weak as a maid." Malcolm adjusted the saddle with ease and then tightened the cinch, making sure 'twas secure. Without a glance at her, he turned and walked out of the paddock.

Frustration charged through her. How was she supposed to pass as a squire if she didn't have the strength needed to saddle her own horse? She prayed she would measure up and not cause him more hardship. The bridle in place, she led her horse out of the paddock to where Malcolm mounted his steed.

Her stomach fluttered. It had been years since she'd ridden, and she missed the freedom that flying across the countryside brought. She loved the feel of the wind whipping her hair and pulling at her clothes as if to rip away her troubles and to free her soul.

Eager to begin her journey home, Jocelyn put her foot in the stirrup and swung her other leg up, though not high enough. She fell backward, landing awkwardly on her foot. She glanced over at Malcolm, hoping he hadn't witnessed her fall.

Luck was not with her, for Malcolm sat atop his horse, his mouth open. "How can a squire not mount a horse?"

"I can mount." She glared at him as she gripped the pommel and a handful of mane. "Just not very well." She pulled herself up, slow and steady, determined not to fall. He'd leave her if he thought she couldn't ride. Indeed, what squire couldn't ride a horse? She slung her leg over the saddle and gripped the horse with both knees. Relief washed through her.

Finally balanced atop the horse, she nodded at Malcolm. "I am quite capable in the saddle. Have no fear."

Malcolm's brows rose, and he grunted. "Then let's be off."

Jocelyn nudged her horse with her heels. The horse sidestepped, throwing her off balance, turning her world turned upside down.

Her tailbone throbbed, and her arm tingled from her elbow to her fingers. She stared at the blue sky as she wheezed in an effort to gain breath.

Malcolm came into view and hauled her up. "Take deep breaths."

She sucked in a breath, gathering enough air to explain her fall in the face of his fierce frown.

"You cannot ride, can you?"

"I can." She breathed deep and coughed. "I was thrown off balance, 'tis all." She clasped Malcolm on the arm. "I'm unharmed, I assure you. Thank you for your assistance."

Malcolm strode away, muttering under his breath. Jocelyn wiped the sweat from her brow. Faith, she hadn't forgotten how to ride a horse, had she? If she couldn't ride, he would surely leave her behind. And take her horse with him.

They mounted once more. Jocelyn managed to stay upright though she bounced in the saddle, rattling her teeth. Malcolm laughed. Heat flooded her cheeks, but she continued on, settling into the rhythm of the horse. It wasn't long before she relaxed, melding with the saddle, able to keep up with Malcolm.

Finally, she could hold her own and not slow him down. Plus, she'd added humor to his ride. That must count as some benefit.

They rode hard all day, stopping only once to water the horses and eat. The sun sat low in the west by the time Malcolm finally veered off the road. Birch trees dotted the area, mingling with smaller blackthorn trees. A stream rushed over rocks, spilling into a small pool. Jocelyn yearned to ease her aching backside. Her cheek still hurt, and the gash on her head smarted, but she'd managed a good day's ride.

Sliding off the horse, she hobbled toward the pool. She knelt to drink, and a groan escaped her lips. Faith, after running most of the night and riding a horse all day, her legs ached. She drank her fill, then crawled to the carpet of soft, cool grass. She'd help Malcolm, but she needed to close her eyes for a mere moment.

A breeze caressed her face and played with the locks of hair that had escaped their bindings. Filling her lungs, she let out a slow breath. In the safety of Malcolm's nearness and the comfort of drawing nearer to home, her body relaxed as her mind drifted into happy oblivion.

Malcolm nudged her with his foot. Jocelyn jerked upright.

She blinked, noting the horses had been unsaddled and stood grazing nearby. "I'm so sorry I fell asleep. I didn't even help with the horses. I vow I shall do better next time."

He handed her a wedge of cheese and a portion of bread, then walked to a nearby tree and sat, stretching out his legs. "You managed to keep up with me today, and I figured you could use some rest after your ordeal this morning." He mumbled, his mouth full. Behind him, vines clung to a tree trunk, winding their way upward and through the overreaching tree limbs. 'Twas but another hour until nightfall, and the shadows stretched across the grass.

"I told you I could ride. I am but a wee bit out of practice." Her lungs filled to their fullest, and she smiled, satisfied she'd kept up and not once begged to stop for rest.

Malcolm huffed. "We shall see how you fare tomorrow. For a lad of your years, you are a mite small. I can imagine your foster father's despair at seeing to your training. If you were in my care, you would never leave the lists until you became a proper knight. I have a mind to take you in hand and see to the deed myself if only to see that you not shame me at Ramslea."

Jocelyn swallowed at the daunting notion of training with Malcolm. She tugged at a wayward curl. How could she train with such a mighty warrior? But what an excellent way of hiding from the abbess. Agatha would never think to look for Jocelyn in the lists. She snorted at the thought.

"What, pray tell, do you find so humorous?" Malcolm glowered in her direction. "I'll have you know I am one of the best knights in all of England. I haven't lost a tournament yet. You think to laugh, though you won't be laughing for long." He rose. "You'll need much instruction if you are to be my squire. I'll not be made a fool by one so lacking in skill. See if I don't fashion you into a proper man." He made his way into the surrounding brush before she could answer.

As he stomped around in the woods, she walked in the other direction to take care of her own needs. When she returned, he sat with two large sticks, curly bark shavings scattering across the ground as he smoothed the wood with his dagger.

Faith, he meant what he said about training her.

He glanced up as she approached. "You are fortunate, for I have found the perfect tools to train you. We have a bit of daylight left, so we shall use it to your advantage."

"How fortunate." She nodded, hiding her fear behind a straight face. She could barely walk. How could he think of training at swords? She thought to say nay but remembered her goal. He was the only safe way to get to Ramslea.

"Take your weapon, little man." Malcolm stood holding both sticks.

Jocelyn took one and gripped it with both hands, hoping to survive the schooling. She had no illusions of impressing him but hoped not to overly frustrate him.

"I know you've already been trained, but I shall teach you my way. Mirror my movements and keep the pace. This will teach you the proper positions for holding your sword and how to move your body when wielding your weapon."

Malcolm moved the stick up and down. He lunged left and right. He held the stick two-handed, then one-handed.

Jocelyn glanced at his face as she mirrored his steps. My, but he was so serious with his lips pursed and a line between his brows. His face twisted into a scowl, and a laugh escaped from her lips. She clamped a hand over her mouth.

Faith! Boys do not giggle.

Malcolm poked his stick in the ground and placed his hand on his hip. "By all that is good, you are such a maid! You stand like one, you look like one, and now you snicker like one!"

"I cannot help it if my voice has not finished deepening. And as for my laughter ... well, I find you humorous."

"Humorous?"

"In truth, your face was so serious, what with your brows furrowed over those fierce eyes." She turned down her lips and drew her brows together, imitating his intense expression.

He took up his stick and swung at her.

Jocelyn yelped, though she'd deflected his blow. The contact rattled her bones. The next stroke landed on her forearm. "Ouch! That hurt!"

"Of course it hurt. You must to learn to anticipate. It could save your life."

Taking a deep breath, she lifted her stick, gathering her strength and continuing without complaint. She tried to anticipate where Malcolm would strike next, but she took many blows to the arms and legs. She'd be covered in bruises on the morrow.

"Enough." Malcolm dropped his stick.

Jocelyn swiped her brow with her sleeve and collapsed against a nearby tree. Her bound chest fought for breath as she looked to the darkening sky through the treetops. Insects buzzed around her as an owl hooted in the distance. She breathed in the pungent, earthy scent of the woods and knew she would rest well.

"We need wood for a fire." Malcolm walked toward the trees.

Jocelyn struggled to her feet. "I can help." She searched the ground around her. Exhausted though she was, she would make herself useful.

After filling her arms, she returned to camp, where Malcolm had started a small fire. She sighed in anticipation. The fire would give them warmth against the brisk breeze. She dumped her wood on top of Malcolm's, then went to her sack and pulled out her cloak. "Do you have a cloak in your bag, sir?

"Aye."

She found his cloak and brought it to him. He sat several feet from the fire but stood to spread his cloak before sitting once more.

She spread her cloak on the opposite side of the fire and laid on her side facing the flames.

"You did well, little man." The side of Malcolm's mouth quirked. "You have more stamina and determination than I gave you credit for. With that kind of persistence, you'll manage not to disgrace me."

Jocelyn thanked the dancing flames for concealing her blush. She gave Malcolm a weary smile through eyes half closed. "Thank you. I hope to not shame you."

Frogs croaked around the pond as the rustling leaves provided a lullaby ripe for sleep. Malcolm whittled on a stick with his dagger, the blade sweeping over the chunk of wood.

"What are you making?"

"I don't know yet."

"What do you usually carve?"

Malcolm paused and put his hands down. "Animals, I suppose."

"You should carve your horse. Does he have a name?"

"Horse." Malcolm picked up his stick and ran his hand over the rough wood.

Jocelyn chuckled. "Horse is the name of your horse?"

Malcolm shrugged and smiled. "Aye."

"I will call mine Black. 'Tis a nicer name than Horse, to be sure."

Twigs snapped behind her, and she bolted up, twisting to peer into the darkness. Her pulse thundered as she listened. Was it an animal foraging for food? She glanced at Malcolm, whose hands worked at his carving.

Would he notice her skittishness? She couldn't help but be nervous. Malcolm might think her a coward, but she must be on her guard. Though he could handle whatever came their way, she would keep her knife at the ready as she learned what he had to teach her, for there would come a time when he would no longer be by her side.

What a troublesome thought.

CHAPTER 5

Jocelyn sat up before the sun crested the horizon. Pushing aside her cloak, she winced. She wouldn't groan. Not today. Today she would impress Malcolm no matter how much she ached. She watched as he shook out his cloak and put it away. He moved with ease, and she'd wager he didn't entertain any sore limbs.

Stiff and sore, she rose and stuffed her cloak into her bag. She heaped dirt onto the glowing embers of their fire, then saddled Black. At least she attempted to saddle him. Try as she might, she could not lift the seat onto her horse. Her arms trembled from the night's swordplay. She looked for a stump to stand on.

"Go fill our water bags, and I will saddle your horse."

Jocelyn startled and glanced at Malcolm, afraid to see the disgust on his face. But his face held no expression except for the hint of a frown. "Thank you, sir." She moved out of his way and hastened to fill their water bags. Strange how he didn't grumble or complain about her lack of strength. She hoped that wasn't a bad omen.

After putting the waterskins into their bags, she walked over to Black. She checked the stirrup, cringing at the thought of getting atop her horse. 'Twould hurt, but she would not ask for help.

And she refused to groan.

Arms shaking and legs trembling, she gritted her teeth and pulled on the pommel, swinging her leg over Black's back without so much as a whimper. First victory of the day.

They rode hard, pushing the horses for long stretches. By late morning, her legs and backside had worked out their soreness though every other part of her screamed with each movement, all due to Malcolm's tutelage. Jocelyn would not complain, though. The prize of getting home would make the pain worth it.

The sun shone high overhead by the time the spires and roofs of a fair-sized village appeared in the distance.

"We'll stop for provisions up ahead!" Malcolm yelled over the pounding of the horses' hooves.

Jocelyn nodded, ready to stand on her own two legs.

Slowing their horses to a walk, they wove through the village in search of food. Jocelyn smiled as they passed a group of laughing children playing with a litter of yelping pups. The sharp, rhythmic clang of metal against metal drew her gaze toward an open-fronted shed where a blacksmith worked at his anvil, spraying sparks like fiery water droplets as he pounded out a piece of glowing iron. Just past the smithy's shed, a group of older boys with axes chopped dried boles into cordwood, stacking the split logs onto a cart.

Jocelyn breathed deeply, and the scent of yeasty bread caused her stomach to clench in hunger. She had eaten nothing but stale bread, cheese, and berries for two days and was ready for more hearty fare. Set before her a beefy steak or a leg of mutton and she would show Malcolm she could down enough food to satisfy even his idea of a manly appetite.

Not that what he thought mattered to her.

Along the street, women followed Malcolm with their eyes. Faith, but some were nigh unto fainting—even a couple of matrons old enough to be the man's mother.

Jocelyn snorted.

Malcolm's face and form may be worth swooning over, but he wasn't perfect. He snored like a mad bull and muttered when annoyed. She shouldn't count that as a fault since she enjoyed the play of emotions on his beautiful face when he did so.

She snuck a glance at his profile and had to admit he was indeed lovely to look upon. She couldn't fault the women for appreciating him.

"Let us eat here before we purchase supplies." Malcolm stopped in front of a building in sad disrepair. The door hung loose, and pieces of thatch hung in disarray from the roof.

Grateful to stop anywhere, Jocelyn slid from her horse, put her hand on her back, and stretched. She followed Malcolm into the hovel. Stepping through the low doorway, she blinked against the smoky haze that engulfed her.

Raucous laughter filled her ears as numerous men sat at tables scattered around the room. Layers of dirt clung to most of the men and, judging by the odor, possibly something worse. Though she suspected she was every bit as filthy, Jocelyn hoped she smelled a mite better.

Serving maids milled about handing out drinks, kisses, or whatever the men wanted. Jocelyn had never seen so many women with low-cut dresses, their bosoms spilling over the top of tight bodices. Her cheeks burned at the sight. A man reached out and pinched one wench's bottom. The woman only laughed and sidled away, serving more drinks.

How did these women manage their work with men pawing them? Jocelyn would have spent most of her time striking the men rather than serving them.

"Jack."

Jocelyn turned as Malcolm offered her a mug of ale. Surprised he'd procured drink so quickly, she took the mug. "Thank you, sir."

Malcolm motioned for her to follow him to a table in the corner. Jocelyn waited for him to sit, then sat on the bench opposite him. Parched, she took a large swig from her drink, spewing the amber liquid on Malcolm.

Malcolm grimaced as he wiped his face with his sleeve. "Can you not stand strong drink, boy?"

Jocelyn coughed. "Aye, but Lord Nichols' cellar was full of watered-down swill. I was unprepared for the strength of this good brew."

"This is stronger than I prefer, though it's cool and wet." Malcolm leaned against the wall. His eyes traced around the room.

Jocelyn followed his gaze toward the door.

Three men stooped through the doorway and paused. Well-muscled and broad-shouldered, hands resting on the swords strapped to their waists, they regarded the room. The hair on Jocelyn's neck stood on end as one of them looked her way.

"Malcolm ... sir," Jocelyn said, her voice quiet. "I think 'tis best we be on our way. We need to make good progress on our journey today."

"Nay, not yet." His focus never left the men. "I must see to some pressing business."

Malcolm rose and approached one of the more comely serving maids. As he spoke to the woman, he put a hand on her shoulder and let his fingers drag down the length of her bare arm. The woman smiled at him, stepping closer.

Jocelyn tore her gaze away. She didn't want to waste time watching Malcolm pursue a woman. Pushing aside the bitter ale, she stood, skirting the room while giving the three men a wide berth.

Once outside, she sat on a bench along the wall of the tavern, thankful to be out of sight of the three suspicious-looking strangers.

Jocelyn shook her head as her mind replayed the vision of Malcolm and the serving girl. She understood that some men favored women who were free with their kisses and other intimacies. Truth be told, 'twasn't only the men who played the game. She had seen maids willingly give their kisses, and she knew those kisses often led to more intimate behaviors. Still, she held to the conviction one's body should be reserved for marriage. The way God intended.

Aye, the convent taught about purity, and Jocelyn had witnessed a faithful love at home. The kind of love she hoped to have one day.

She sighed. What did she care if Malcolm desired a woman? He was nothing to her but a safe passage home.

'Twasn't as if she was jealous, to be sure.

Malcolm ambled out of the tavern and Jocelyn jumped to her

feet, coming alongside him. "Your business with the wench was not overlong." Jocelyn looked away, her cheeks growing hot.

"Nay, she was but a ploy to get close to those men who came in at the last. One had the look of a competitor who owes me coin. The wench allowed me to get close enough to hear some of their conversation." Malcolm grinned at her and lifted an eyebrow. "The ladies always seem to fancy my charming self."

How would a lad respond to such a comment? Jocelyn smiled. "'Twould seem so." Curious about his past, she had to ask. "But have you ever wooed a woman? In a serious manner?"

"Nay, I've no need of a wife."

"But surely you want to carry on your family name."

Malcolm shrugged. "My father has many sons to carry on the name. It matters not to me."

"But—"

"What about you, little man?" A sly grin crept across his face. "I would surmise that, with your lack of whiskers, the maids don't yet even bring a blush to your smooth cheeks." He laughed and mounted Horse.

Jocelyn refused to react to Malcolm's teasing. He seemed to enjoy riling her, and she could admit she enjoyed the playfulness.

She mounted her horse and pulled up beside Malcolm as they rode down the street. "What did you learn of the men you saw? Were you able to gain information?"

"Aye. They are seeking a daft woman from a convent who has wandered away. The convent is trying to find her. Nothing of importance."

Jocelyn's chest constricted. The abbess had indeed sent searchers, and brutes at that. Their broad frames boasted leather sashes loaded with daggers slung over their shoulders. Swords hung by their sides and one had a crossbow strapped to his back. Jocelyn shuddered. She couldn't return to the abbey, not when she was so close to home. She must discover the reason for her father's silence, as well as who was trying to force her into marriage.

Glancing over her shoulder, she pressed her horse to a trot, pulling ahead of Malcolm.

"Jack, slow down, boy. We have need of food for our journey, especially as we failed to eat at the inn. Follow me. We shall not be long." Malcolm led them down the street, weaving their horses through the villagers along the way. The street opened to a large area filled with merchants selling their wares, carts filled will fresh vegetables, wagons loaded with kegs of ale, and tables stacked with cloth, yarn, and thread. Voices rose as sellers and buyers haggled over prices. Malcolm moved toward a bakery stand and dismounted.

Jocelyn slid off Black and reached for the coin purse tied beneath her tunic.

"Nay, put your coin away. As long as you are with me, I shall see to your food."

"I thank you, sir." Jocelyn put back her purse, grateful for his generosity. She silently pledged to work hard for her keep.

Jocelyn stayed close to Malcolm but continued to check behind her. Was her disguise strong enough to outwit the searchers? If only she had procured a hat to cover her hair and shield her face. Her one solace being they were seeking a woman, not a boy. Even Malcolm had not yet realized the truth, and they had ridden together.

After what seemed an eternity, Malcolm purchased bread, cheese, and various dried fruits. They packed their bags and mounted. Jocelyn followed Malcolm out of the village, the incessant chattering of its people fading away. She breathed easier, the tension leaving her body with the steady cadence of Black's canter.

They rode past several farms into a heavily wooded area. A scream cut through the pounding of hooves. Malcolm spurred his horse to a gallop and Jocelyn followed, her heart drumming. She had no desire to run into danger.

As they rounded a curve in the road, the trees thinned, opening up to farmland. On the side of the road, a young woman held a rope tied to a milk cow as she struggled in the grasp of the very men the abbess had sent for Jocelyn.

She slowed her pace, stopping a good thirty paces behind Malcolm, not far from the men's horses. The binding around her chest threatened to choke the air from her lungs, and she squirmed on her saddle.

"It seems the lady has no wish to be bothered." Malcolm sat atop Horse, hands resting on the pommel of the saddle.

"'Tis none of your concern." The largest of the three stepped forward. "Mind yer own affairs and be off with ye."

"Miss, do you live nearby?" Malcolm nodded at the woman, held by the other two men, one on either side.

Her wide eyes focused on Malcolm. "Aye, good sir. I live just down the road." She pulled her arms, but the two men gripped tighter. The lass winced, sucking in a breath. "These men asked questions of me, then began to … to bother me."

"Were your questions answered?" Malcolm turned his focus to the large man.

"If ye had any sense, ye would leave us be. Yer outnumbered, even with the wee lad you have with ye." The man glanced at Jocelyn. She looked at Black's mane, fear coursing through her body.

"I have no wish for combat, though you *will* leave this woman undisturbed."

Malcolm dismounted, and Jocelyn looked up. He stood tall before the men.

One man pulled his sword and swung at Malcolm's head.

She gasped. "Sir!"

Malcolm, sword already in hand, deflected the blow with ease. The man sliced his blade across, but Malcolm jumped back. Stepping forward, Malcolm's cutting edge repeatedly slashed at the man.

Jocelyn's blood pulsed like the heavy march of a warrior army, her palms slippery with sweat. Malcolm parried his opponent's clumsy blows, driving him back toward the brush.

The other men pulled out their swords and circled Malcolm. With shaking hands, Jocelyn closed her hand on her knife. Could she use it if need be? One of the men lifted his sword.

"Malcolm, behind you!"

He turned, deflected the blow, and, with a quick thrust, ran the man through.

The third man ran toward her, his sword raised. *Dear Lord, help me!* She drew back her arm, hesitating but a moment before hurling her knife with all her strength. The blade sank into the man's chest. Relief and horror swirled within her as his dying eyes fixed on her. He dropped his sword, clutching at the knife, his face twisting into a grimace. He fell to the ground, dust scattering around him.

Jocelyn's breath caught as the man jerked, then went still. What had she done? The world spun around her, and she gripped the saddle pommel, praying she wouldn't faint.

She'd killed a man. One of God's creations. In truth, 'twas to save herself, yet she grieved for the life she had cut short.

Tearing her eyes away from the body, she looked up in time to see Malcolm press his sword against his assailant's throat. "Do you want to live?"

On his knees, the man glared at Malcolm. "Aye, but I will not beg for my life."

Malcolm lowered his sword. "Then I suggest you leave and look for your daft nun elsewhere."

The man rose, then walked to the man Malcolm had slain. Marking a cross over his chest, he picked up the body, securing the dead man over one of the horses before mounting another.

"You are only taking one?" Malcolm pointed to the other dead man.

"This one is my brother." The man nudged his horse toward Malcolm. "Ye may be thinking yer a chivalrous man, helping a lass and sparing my life, but ye'll regret yer interference. Watch yer back." The man kicked his horse and rode away.

Icy fear traveled through Jocelyn's veins. Would he return to the abbess and report his failure, or would he keep searching for Jocelyn? Either way, she wished he'd met his death at the tip of Malcolm's sword. Lord forgive her for such a wicked thought.

Her body trembling, Jocelyn looked around for the young maid. She must have run away. 'Twas what Jocelyn would have done in the same situation. She slid off her horse to help Malcolm deal with the dead body.

Malcolm walked toward her, sheathing his sword. "By the saints, you actually killed the man."

Jocelyn cleared her throat, remembering anew that her actions had taken a life. "Aye, I did." She sucked in a ragged breath. "He was coming for me. I had to defend myself."

"You defeated him thusly?" His brow rose. "With one throw?"

Jocelyn nodded. "Aye. I told you I was skilled with a knife, though I confess I have never killed anyone before. I pray I never have to do it again. 'Twas most unpleasant."

Malcolm clapped a hand on her shoulder. "You speak like a maid, yet you have the courage to defend yourself. Now, let us clear the road of this rubbish."

Jocelyn pulled the knife out of the man she had slain, and her stomach heaved. *Lord, forgive me.* She walked to the side of the road, wiped her blade on the grass, and then retched, emptying the contents of her stomach. Her eyes blurred with tears. She must push past the remorse. Be strong, like a capable squire. She swiped at her tears, removing the evidence of her womanly heart.

Gentle hands took her by the shoulders, helping her stand. Malcolm turned her toward him. Jocelyn's heart stuttered at the compassion in his eyes and his small, crooked smile.

"I got sick with my first kill. Heaved all over my brother's new boots." Malcolm shook his head, his mouth twisting. "I soon forgot my sickness in the scuffle that ensued."

Jocelyn sniffed. "Having older brothers kept you in line, I'm sure."

"They made me strong in their own unique way." Malcolm pounded her on the back. "We shall toughen you up, have no fear."

She put a hand to her chest, hoping to toughen in haste. If the past two days were any indication, Malcolm would be plunging into heroic deeds at every turn.

They worked together, hauling the body to the side of the road, where they covered it with brush. While Jocelyn wanted a proper burial for the man, they had no tools to dig a grave. Malcolm lit a fire in the brush to burn the body instead. Once the fire burned well, they mounted their horses.

"We need to move fast to make up for lost time." Malcolm quirked a brow. "Can you keep up?"

"I shall do my very best." She would not disappoint him.

"Then let us be off." He kicked his horse's flanks and sped off at a gallop.

Jocelyn did the same, leaning low over Black, loving the wind on her face that seemed to blow away her mind's clutter. They raced past vast farmlands, some ready to be harvested while some sat fallow at the start of the cooler season.

Jocelyn charged faster as if to escape the demons at her heels. Her hair escaped its bounds, but she didn't care. She was filthy and unkempt, but free. Free from the abbess and free to go home.

They rode hard for what seemed an eternity, then alternated between walking and galloping to give the horses a break during the arduous journey. When they slowed, the worries Jocelyn had thought to outrun returned to haunt her. Would that Malcolm had dispatched all three of her pursuers. The man he had released would surely return to tell the abbess. Her only consolation was that by the time Agatha learned that Jocelyn was still at large, she would be at Ramslea, safe and free.

Yet unanswered questions festered at the thought of Ramslea. Did her father know of her refusal to take her vows? His silence disturbed her. He could be ill or injured. Or worse, he might want to forget about her. But the abbess had called the blackmailer *she*. That couldn't be her father.

Frustration burned in Jocelyn's belly. She longed to return home and see her father, to be surrounded by familiar faces and resting comfortably at home. Hopefully, once there, her father would welcome her and help her to solve the puzzle causing havoc in her life.

God, show me the way and help me to uncover the truth.

CHAPTER 6

Over the treetops, the sun settled low in the western sky. Malcolm glanced at Jack slouching in his saddle, no doubt tired from their long day's journey. Despite rescuing a maid and dispatching the harassing men, they had travelled a fair distance.

To the east, a clearing came into view, and Malcolm veered off the road to make camp for the night. A stream ran through the clearing and into a densely wooded area. The sky's yellow-gold rays peeked through wispy clouds in the west, though enough light remained to test Jack's skills with the knife. He'd been impressed with the boy's kill earlier but needed to see if his skill matched his claim of proficiency.

Malcolm suspected Jack's killing had been plain good fortune. Perhaps the boy had some skill, but Malcolm would wager precious little on it.

After they set up camp, he found a fallen tree in the forest. The rotten wood broke apart with ease, so he took a fair-sized chunk to use as a target, setting it upon a large boulder not far from the water.

"Jack, I would see your famed throwing skills." Malcolm rubbed the wood chips off his hands. "Bring your knife and let's see what you can do."

A grin fanned across the boy's face as he walked to where Malcolm stood roughly twenty paces from the target. "No swordplay this eve? Finally, something I am adept at."

'Twas good the unimpressive boy had something to boast of. Malcolm laughed. "Ah, even you can admit you are sadly lacking in the other skills befitting a squire."

Jack shrugged. "'Tis true." He faced the target, steadied his hand, and—with a quick flick of the wrist—loosed the blade. It flew fast and straight into the center of the wood, splinters flying into the air.

Malcolm's brows lifted in surprise. "Well done, little man." Pulling the knife from the target, he returned it to Jack. "Let's see if you can hit it farther out." He grabbed the lad by the arm and pulled him back ten paces. "Now."

Jack took the knife and, with but a moment's pause, threw it into the mark. He turned to Malcolm and smiled. "I believe I can go farther out if you want me to try."

"Truly? I'd like to see that." Malcolm retrieved the knife. He dragged Jack back another fifteen paces and then handed him the knife. "Again."

Jack turned toward the target. He steadied his hand and closed one eye, his long lashes fanning his smooth cheek. Saints, the lad could pass as a girl given the right clothing. A pretty lass, at that. Malcolm cleared his throat.

Jack dropped his hands, his brow crinkling. "'Tisn't fair to make noise whilst I throw."

"If you are as good as you say, then you should be able to focus regardless of distractions."

Jack drew in a deep breath and threw the blade. It sailed into the target. It hit off center, though it hit nonetheless.

Slapping Jack on the back, Malcolm smiled. "You are indeed a surprise. I never would have dreamed you had any skills worth mentioning. Well done."

"Thank you, sir. Would you care for a friendly game? Though, of course, you might not care to be bested by a wee lad such as myself."

Malcolm doubted he could best Jack with the knife, but admit it to the lad? Not for half the king's gold. The last thing the boy needed was fodder to boast. "You are skilled, I give you that." He gripped Jack on the shoulder. "But 'tis with a sword that you need expertise. 'Twill build your strength and stamina. Now, let us get to the training of you."

Jack's posture wilted, and Malcolm laughed. The boy had pride, weakling that he was.

By the time dusk clouded his vision, Malcolm was spent. The lad barely had the strength to stand and quickly fell asleep by the fire, his soft breathing filling the quiet stillness. Malcolm settled himself on the opposite side of the flames and pulled out his dagger. A heavy stick flattened the grass nearby, so he scooped it up, plying the steel along the side of wood.

The uneven wood took shape beneath his knife strokes, shavings showering the ground below. In no time a wildcat emerged, its sleek form smooth in his hands. He'd learned the skill as a child and had developed an aptitude for forging life forms out of nothing. Many times he'd gifted his mother with his creations—one of the few things that brought a smile to her lips.

Across the fire, Jack curled up on his side with his cloak wrapped tightly around him. Malcolm had begun to enjoy his company. True, he was not much of a squire, but he was willing to work and willing to train, even asking questions about battle techniques and weaponry. He showed stamina and determination, both qualities Malcolm valued. Having Jack around was akin to having family—a younger brother whom he could tease and teach.

Malcolm sighed, pleased with how the trip had turned around. After losing John and the upheaval of saving Jack, the journey now progressed as it should. He put away his knife and lay down. The quiet snapping of the fire, along with the leaves rustling in the wind, provided a relaxing lullaby for his soul. His mouth curled into a smile as he drifted into nothingness.

Jocelyn's eyes flew open. Leaves crunched behind the crop of trees. She fumbled for her knife, her ears attuned to the sounds in the night air. Frogs croaked. An owl hooted.

Her eyes adjusted to the dull light of the dying fire just as Malcolm jumped to his feet. Metal clashed against metal. Malcolm ducked under a blow as a large man stepped into the light.

"Ye shall die for murdering my brother!"

Heart hammering in her chest, Jocelyn scrambled backward. 'Twas the man Malcolm had spared! "Oh God, help him."

The man pushed Malcolm toward the fire, the flash of blades glowing in its faint light. They grunted and swung.

How could she help Malcolm? The cool hilt of her dagger spurred her into motion. She leapt to her feet and looked for an opportunity to aid him.

"Sir! I—"

"Nay, boy! Do not even think of—"

Malcolm pushed his attacker back, opening space between the two. Jocelyn whipped her knife through the air. Malcolm cried out. She gasped. He stumbled but continued to fight.

Jocelyn ran around them, trying to see where her knife had landed.

Searching the ground, the moonlight gleamed off the blade, right in the pathway of the battling swords. She couldn't easily grab it, but what if Malcolm needed help? Or worse, what if he fell to the attacker's blade and she must defend herself? She watched the duel, her body humming with fear. Would she be quick enough? When Malcolm and his attacker moved a few feet, she lunged for the blade.

"Jack, nay!"

As her hand closed around her knife, Jocelyn looked up. A sword bore down upon her. Even as she rolled to the side, pain seared her skin and stole the breath from her lungs. Her vision blurred as she blinked. She struggled to crawl away from the fight, her arms and legs moving as though through cold honey.

Malcolm's shouts faded into a distant rumble. She clawed across the ground until she collapsed, her body refusing to go farther. How could she have been so daft? She put her hand to her side and grimaced at the warm stickiness. Her vision darkened. Her body trembled. Faith, she was going to faint again.

Strong hands gripped her arms as the blackness swam across her eyes. She struggled to focus as Malcolm called out her name.

"Jack … Jack!"

What would it be like to hear her real name uttered from those lips? Preposterous. He could never find out she was a woman.

CHAPTER 7

Malcolm picked up Jack, limp and bleeding, and laid him close to the fire. He threw pieces of wood on the flames, then stripped Jack of his tunic. Malcolm's hands stilled at the sight of the bindings around Jack's chest. Had Jack been wounded before?

Malcolm drew out his knife and cut through the fabric. The cloth broke free. He froze. By the saints!

He tore his eyes away. Malcolm sat back on his heels and wiped the sweat from his brow. What was he to do with a lass? An injured one at that?

Think, man. Think.

First, he must stop the bleeding. He would deal with Jack and his—rather her—secret later.

Spreading his cloak on the ground, Malcolm laid Jack, or whatever her name was, face down on the rough material. He needed no distraction while tending her wound which, thankfully, was not too deep. The cut stretched a good four inches from her side toward her back. While not a mortal wound, it needed to be closed.

Malcolm took his blade and stuck it into the fire, regretting the lack of needle and thread. He cleaned the wound with water from his waterskin and then pulled the knife out of the red-hot coals. The blade glowed crimson, and Malcolm sucked in a breath. He had endured similar ministrations and, while he chafed at admitting it, had passed out from the pain. Though she remained unconscious, searing her wound shut would be painful.

With a quick hand, he pressed the knife to her skin, the soft flesh sizzling against the red-hot steel. The girl cried out but remained unconscious, a blessing for them both. He pulled the knife away and inspected the wound, noting that it still bled at one end.

Plunging his knife back into the fire, he took a deep breath. Bile rose in his throat at the heavy stench of her burnt flesh. Her face, pale against his cloak, stirred his mind with questions. Who was she? What was she running from?

More questions tumbled as he pulled the knife from the fire and finished the task. Though the nights had begun to cool, the healing herbs he needed to keep the wound from festering would still be in season. He covered the lass with her cloak before grabbing a stick out of the fire.

Using the branch as a torch, he threaded his way into the woods. He rummaged through the brush, not finding anything he could use. Hurrying his pace, he searched near the edge of the forest until he found a few yarrow plants. That would do. He snapped off the tops of the plants and headed back to camp.

Malcolm returned to the imposter and dressed the wound, using bandages he cut from the bottom of his cloak. Though he kept her chest covered as he worked, 'twas impossible to not be aware of Jack's form. She must have been most uncomfortable with binding tight enough to conceal such a womanly figure.

With swift hands, he wrapped the strips of cloth around her and then clothed her in her bloodied tunic. He cushioned her head, covered her with a cloak, and hoped she would rest well throughout the night.

Wanting nothing more than to lay his head down and sleep, Malcolm sighed. First, he must deal with the body of his attacker. Bone-weary, he trudged to the man and searched through his clothing. A dagger was hidden in one of the boots, and a small coin purse hung around the man's neck. The purse weighed heavy in his hand, most likely a week's wage in coin.

Revenge was a destructive force, but Malcolm understood the need of the man to avenge his brother's death. He would have felt the same were the situation reversed. Then again, he wouldn't have started a fight in the first place. Fighting was for defending, for taking care of one's own. Murder was the way of cowards, not the way of honor.

Malcolm grabbed the man by the feet and dragged him into a dense area of the forest. Then he trudged back to camp, sat by the fire, and winced at the pain in his leg. Foolish girl. Trying to knife someone in the dark—what was she thinking?

After cleaning his wound, he treated his thigh with the leftover herbs. Checking one last time on Jack, Malcolm lay down by the dying fire, stiff and sore.

By the saints, it had been a long day.

Everything made perfect sense as he thought back on the past two days. He was a fool not to realize the truth. So much of Jack's behavior spoke of her true gender.

How had Malcolm ever believed those eyes belonged to a lad?

He'd bet his horse that most of what Jack had told him were lies. Fostering with Nichols, indeed. Malcolm would strangle her pretty little neck.

Used to simpering maids fawning over him, he admired her courage. Traveling in disguise, attempting to squire, and submitting to sword training couldn't have been easy. Cursing, Malcolm ran a hand over his face. The bruises she must have received from his own hand during swordplay. Aye, she was a courageous one.

And daft as they came. Had he not saved her that first day, if those men had found out her secret … he could scarce bring himself to consider the consequences.

Yet the more he reflected on the event, the more his blood boiled. She didn't speak like a peasant, which meant she might well be a noble's daughter. If that were true, he was in a mound of trouble. Not only was her reputation in jeopardy, but his as well. 'Twas twice now he'd been deceived by a woman, and he didn't cater to a forced marriage with a lying wench. All he wanted was peace and quiet on a bit of land to call his own. If anyone were to find out about her true nature, his peace would be forfeit.

He must determine a way to leave her behind. Jack would not like it, though it must be done.

Jocelyn moaned at the burning pain in her side. She tried to catch her breath as she forced her eyes open. Her lids fluttered against the light of the early morning sun.

Malcolm stood over her, brows furrowed, his eyes piercing her with their pale hue. She moved to sit up, but pain shot through her side. Last night's events flashed before her, and she gasped. Feeling the bandage on her wound, she moved her hand to her chest. Heat flooded her face. She peered up at Malcolm.

He knew.

He knew and was not pleased.

Jocelyn sat up and sucked in air, searching for words to make him understand. "I … I …" She couldn't look him in the eye. "I … am not a boy."

"'Twas most obvious last night when I tended to your wound." He ran his hand through his hair. "What were you thinking, traipsing about as a lad?" He knelt in front of her, his face set. "I would have the truth, and it best be good enough to settle this to my satisfaction."

Jocelyn gulped. She hated lying, but there was nothing else to be done. Remaining anonymous would give her the freedom to investigate who wanted to keep her from Ramslea. "I am running away from home."

"I thought Ramslea was your home." One of Malcolm's eyebrows rose.

"Nay. I told an untruth. My home is a four-day journey south. My father was forcing me to wed a man three times my age, and I couldn't bear it."

"Why do you go to Ramslea?"

"I had heard Ramslea was a grand place where one could find work. I thought to seek work as a kitchen maid and then, when

Lord Ashburne's daughter returns, possibly her maid."

"Ramslea may be the place to find honest work, though becoming Jocelyn Ashburne's maid will not be one of them. She perished from a plague more than a year ago."

Jocelyn blinked. Did she hear him aright? "In truth, she is dead?"

"Aye, 'twas a terrible plague, if memory serves. Ashburne could not retrieve her body from the convent because they had to burn it along with all her possessions. Many perished and no one was allowed in or out. 'Twas for the protection of all."

Everyone thought her dead? Did her father know that she was alive? If so, to what purpose? She had to get to Ramslea and learn the truth for herself. He may have grown indifferent toward Jocelyn, but he had never been cruel.

"Surely you could find work nearby, maybe in one of the villages."

"Nay." Jocelyn shook her head. "I must get far away from my home so they cannot find me, and they will never find me at Ramslea. I've heard 'tis a grand castle with a large village in which to hide."

Malcolm rose and squared his shoulders. "I cannot travel with a woman. 'Tis too dangerous."

"Dangerous for whom? It seems I am the one who has received most of the beatings and wounds. What have you to fear of me?" Jocelyn stood, grimacing at the stabbing pain in her side.

Malcolm's eyes narrowed. "'Tis I who received a knife wound in my leg, and by your hand I might add. If it became known that I travelled with a woman, we would be forced into marriage and I, for one, refuse to be married to a daft wench running around the countryside in hose."

Jocelyn gasped. How dare he? "Daft? My father refused to listen to my pleas for a different husband. I couldn't stomach marrying an old man known for beating his previous wives. If that makes me daft, then so be it."

Her chest heaved in anger, paining her side though she stood tall and pushed her shoulders back. She would not be left behind. "We will continue on as we have, with me as your squire. No one will know the difference. If we are found out, so be it. I can steal away once more. You shall be free of me regardless of the outcome." In truth, if they were discovered, she didn't know if she could run away. If she had to marry, Malcolm would not be an altogether unpleasant husband. 'Twould be better than scrubbing floors as a servant.

Malcolm stepped in front of her. "What is your real name?"

Jocelyn hesitated, regretting the need for yet another lie. "Jacqueline."

Malcolm's gaze bore into hers, but she resisted the urge to glance away. He stepped closer and folded his arms across his broad chest. "I don't like it, Jack. Who is your sire? He might be hours away, ready to throw me in his dungeon."

Her heart skipped at his nearness. She must spin a tale to ease his mind. "My sire is but a small landowner of no significance. He is an indolent fool and wouldn't have the gumption to search for me. He'd rather sit in a drunken stupor than exert any effort on my behalf, so have no fear that he will come for me."

"If you arrive at Ramslea as my squire, you cannot find work as a maid. Have you thought ahead?"

Jocelyn paused, for she had not considered such a thing. "Nay, I haven't thought that far. Only take me as far as Ramslea for now."

Malcolm ran his hands over his face. "You had better heal quickly if we are going to pull this off by the time we get there. Now see to your needs before we leave camp." He walked away, muttering.

Jocelyn closed her eyes, relieved. Until the news he delivered repeated in her mind. Her father thought her dead. How was it possible?

No wonder she stopped receiving missives from Ramslea. Ice cold fear trickled down Jocelyn's spine. Whoever orchestrated such deceit wanted Jocelyn gone for good. Was she up to the task of ferreting out the truth? She needed strength for such a task. Aye, she had endured much thus far but, given the cunning of her adversary, more danger was sure to come.

Malcolm watched Jacqueline walk away, her gait stiff. While part of him wanted to foist her off at the nearest village, his sense of honor compelled him to take her to safety, far from her family home. Doubt crowded his thoughts. She hadn't been honest with him before, so he struggled with believing her story. But what if it were true? Though 'twas a foolish thing to do, he admired her bravery at escaping in disguise. And to insist that he take her further? Women never stood up to him, and it fair stole the wits from his sorry head. The strong-willed wench. Were she in a foul mood, she'd be ferocious, indeed.

He grunted as he bent to retrieve his leather bag and their gear. What was taking Jack so long? Had she become lost? Or passed out from pain?

He stepped toward the woods, but a rustle in the brush halted him. Jack emerged from the trees, her walk slow and measured. A good sign considering the wound she had received and the treatment administered.

Malcolm had saddled the horses before Jack awoke and they now grazed near the trees. He brought Jack's horse to her. "Let me help you today."

"A real squire would be able to mount on his own, even with a wound."

"But you are not a real squire anymore."

Jack pursed her lips and nodded, then turned her back to him and reached for the pommel.

Malcolm placed his hands on Jaqueline's hips, easily lifting her onto the saddle. Heat crept up his neck at the swell of her flesh. By the saints, he hadn't blushed since a lad of ten and two. He kept a hand on her back as she settled on Black, thinking she might need the support. 'Twasn't because he liked her warmth.

After making sure she had her seat, he mounted Horse. "I will have my way in this, Jack. If you are of a mind to get to Ramslea with me, then you must obey."

Jack held his gaze, then nodded. "Aye. I will do your bidding." A dimple marked her cheek as she grinned. Spurring her horse past him, she yelled over her shoulder. "But I don't have to like it!"

Malcolm choked on a laugh. By the saints, Jacqueline was feistier than his little man Jack. 'Twould be a most interesting journey.

CHAPTER 8

Jocelyn's gaze drooped with weariness and her side burned. For two long days Malcolm had pushed the horses—and their riders—to their limits as they raced to reach Ramslea. Nearing her breaking point, she prayed he would soon give them respite. Her bottom ached, and she wished for a soft patch of grass on which to lay her head.

The once-flat terrain rose beneath them before descending again. She remembered these hills from her youth. They were getting close.

Water roared in the distance. Malcolm pointed to the right and veered off the road. They followed the sound of the rapids, wending their way through the scattered trees until they found a large pool nestled by precipitously craggy cliffs. Water poured from the top of a cliff, sending ripples across the surface. Under the shade of the tall, leafy trees, the cool breeze felt like heaven against her sweaty face. Without waiting for Malcolm's command, she dismounted and prepared their camp near the pool.

Her wound pained her but was healing faster than expected. She thanked God she had not succumbed to a fever and knew she should thank Malcolm as well. Though he had been relentless in gaining ground on their journey, he had insisted they stop to gather more herbs. She applied them to the wound and changed her own bandages. Malcolm had offered his aid, but she assured him she was up to the task by herself, even if the wound was difficult to reach.

After unsaddling Black, she led him to drink, then let him graze while she gathered wood for a fire.

"You rest." Malcolm took the sticks from her arms. "I will gather the firewood."

"I am capable of finding wood. My soreness doesn't render me useless." She wasn't a weakling, woman or not.

"Aye, it has been two days, but you must take care of yourself." He motioned to the horses. "If you insist on helping, retrieve our provisions. I will start a fire."

"Then I will find sticks for practice." She appreciated his care but had missed his teaching the past two days. It could be she missed his conversation more than the exhausting play of blades, as he'd kept to himself since learning she was a woman.

She headed for the trees. Before she had taken two steps, he grabbed her by the arm.

"You will do no such thing." He dropped his hand, clenching then releasing his fist. "I ..."

"You do not teach the wounded?" She cocked her head to the side. "Or you don't teach women?"

Malcolm folded his arms across his chest, his brows coming together as he frowned. "What would a woman need of swordplay?"

Jocelyn choked back a laugh. "Do you jest? It is acceptable for me to throw a knife but not to wield a sword?" She shook her head. "Surely you would want your woman to defend herself if need be? You—"

"You are not my woman," he said, his voice low and firm.

Indeed, she was not, though for a moment she wondered what 'twould be like to be his. "Aye, 'tis true. However, someday you will have a wife, and she may desire to defend herself should you be away doing whatever lords do."

Malcolm grunted. "Should I marry, my wife will have guardsmen to protect her." He knelt and picked up the wood. "If she still desired to learn how to use a dagger, I would send her to you." The corner of his mouth lifted into a half smile. "I'm starving. Go ready our meal instead."

Jocelyn snorted. 'Twould seem her knight had a sense of humor.

She went to his horse and pulled out provisions. Her stomach rumbled in anticipation of their meager fare.

Malcolm dumped the wood in a pile, then built a fire, adding logs once the flames flickered to life. He rolled a chunk of a fallen tree from the edge of the woods to their camp, then sat back against it and took the bread she offered. She settled against the trunk and bit into the hard bread. Dusk settled and the air grew cooler. Birds gathered in the trees, preparing to roost.

Malcolm chewed his food and swallowed. "We need to bathe before we arrive at Ramslea tomorrow. I will not appear looking poor and dirty."

"You may bathe, though I most certainly will not." While she longed for a bath, she wouldn't disrobe with Malcolm nearby. She reached into their bag of provisions for some nuts.

"Aye, I think you shall." He set down his food.

Jocelyn froze at the look in his eyes. Ripples of warning crossed her skin. "You mean now?"

"Aye."

She jumped up and ran for the trees, but he caught her by the hand and swung her up in his arms, keeping a careful grip away from her wound.

Though no match against Malcolm's strength, she pushed against his hard body. "Let me go!"

He laughed as he tossed her into the pool.

Cold water sluiced over her. Kicking wildly, she broke the surface, gasping. Pushing the hair from her eyes, she growled in frustration, helpless against his actions. "You beast!"

Malcolm stood on the bank, his arms folded and hip slack. He gave her a small smile. "I told you to obey me on this journey. I'll not be crossed. I suggest you wash yourself and your clothes, so I don't have to finish the job for you." He tossed her a cake of soap.

Jocelyn gasped. "You wouldn't dare." She slapped the water, trying to douse him.

Malcolm stepped back. "I shall gather more wood for the fire while you bathe, so you best hurry." He grabbed her cloak and laid it by the bank. "Cover yourself in this while your clothes dry." Before she could protest, he added, "You know you cannot keep your bandages wet."

Jocelyn sank until the water touched her chin and watched Malcolm disappear into the surrounding woods. Was it poor form to pray he received a sudden onset of blindness while she bathed?

The thought of Malcolm making good his threat spurred her into action. She stripped off her clothes, grabbed the soap and washed them, then threw them on a rock when she finished. Soap still in hand, she scrubbed herself all over, taking special care with her tangled hair. She groaned with pleasure as her fingers dug into her scalp, working the soap into her mass of curls.

The longer she scrubbed in the cold water, the more she shivered, her teeth knocking together. Making sure Malcolm was not nearby, she scrambled out of the pool and donned her cloak. She hurried to their gear and found Malcolm's bag with its herbs and clean bandages. After packing her wound, she retied the binding. She paused to listen for Malcolm's return. Only the coo of birds and the rush of the waterfall sounded in the night air.

She wrung out her leggings and tunic, then stood by the fire and combed her fingers through her hair. Leaves crunched behind her.

"Are you bathed and presentable?" Malcolm's deep, smooth voice cut through the darkness, sending a different type of shiver through her limbs.

"Aye." She gathered the cloak securely about her, suddenly awkward as he came into view.

His gaze caught hers and he stopped midstride. Fire threaded through Jocelyn's veins down to her toes at his perusal. She pulled the cloak tighter as he set the gathered wood by the fire and came to stand before her.

Jocelyn couldn't form words out of her jumbled thoughts. Her mouth went dry as Malcolm stood in silence, his gray eyes searching hers. Her heart stood still as he reached out a finger and caught a droplet of water from the tip of one of her curls.

"By the saints, how could I have mistaken you for a lad?" he murmured. His gaze moved over her face and lingered on her lips. Heat bloomed on her cheeks, and her breath hitched as he moved closer.

How would his lips feel against hers? The thought surprised her. Yet, he had been kind and chivalrous. Brave and protective. And he was so very pleasing to the eye. She knew she should push him away, but her eyes closed of their own accord.

Malcolm sucked in a breath, jostling her back to reality. She opened her eyes as Malcolm shook his head, backing away. A mixture of regret and relief washed over her. She squared her shoulders, offering him a faint smile.

He crossed his arms over his broad chest and lifted the corner of his mouth. "You clean up fairly well for a lady fugitive. 'Tis possible you won't shame me, *little man*."

Insufferable wretch. He'd been about to kiss her, but instead, he jested. She took a step toward him, wanting to push his miserable hide into the pond but, realizing she was still wrapped in the cloak and unlikely to summon the strength to move him, stayed her ground.

"'Tis my turn. Don't wander far." Malcolm pulled off his tunic, revealing a torso chiseled by years of training in the lists.

Jocelyn's eyes widened. She stepped backward but tripped on the long folds of fabric clutched around her. She lost her footing and landed with a jolt on her backside.

Malcolm stepped toward her.

"Don't you come near me, you big oaf!" She pulled on the bottom of the cloak to free her tangled feet.

He halted, hands raised in surrender, and backed away, laughing. "My *lady*, were you flustered by my fine form? I meant no harm, I assure you."

"If you think to shock me, you are mistaken. I spent a fair

amount of time watching guardsmen in the lists back home and have seen males without their tunics. You, I might add, pale in comparison." Holding the cloak tight, she stood, drawing herself up to her full height. "Now, I suggest you build up the dying fire." As soon as she issued her command, she knew it had been a poor choice. 'Twas her job as squire to help *him*.

Malcolm's face clouded and his eyes narrowed. "I am the one in charge here, as you might have forgotten. I have no desire to be saddled with an ailing, whining brat of a girl who has turned out to be nothing but a pain in my backside. You succumbing to a fever would rid me of much trouble." He pointed to the pile of wood by the fire. "Put more wood on the fire yourself."

Jocelyn glared at him but knew he spoke truth. Lifting her chin, she turned on her heel and went to the wood pile.

My, but that man could be infuriating! It was a struggle to control her emotions around him. In the convent, there were no tantrums or frustrations among the sisters, so there were few wayward feelings. While she had learned to control her outward actions, her heart was not so easily conquered.

How did one master the affairs of the heart? At the convent, thinking on pleasant things or doing a chore focused her mind on the good instead of the bad, but it 'twas hard to think of a distraction when dealing with Malcolm for, in truth, he *was* the distraction. He set her mind to turmoil. He made her angry. He made her nervous.

He made her heart stop with a glance.

She did not need such distractions.

She had a father to reunite with and a mystery to solve. Aye, she needed nothing to confuse her already addled mind. There was enough to deal with without adding a handsome knight to the list.

Jocelyn had known from the beginning of her escape that her life would be in danger. She had not thought her heart might be as well.

CHAPTER 9

Malcolm dove into the pool and swam deep through the cool water. Dusk had turned into a sable sky, and his vision blurred in the inky darkness. He broke through the surface and rubbed his hands over his face.

What was wrong with his sorry self? He must stay focused on his goal but, as a woman, Jack provided a serious distraction. And a feisty one that. He pitied the poor family who had the taming of her.

All sense had left him when he saw her after her bath. With her face freshly scrubbed and free of dirt, he once again wondered how he could have thought her to be anything but the lovely woman she was.

She stood wrapped in naught but a cloak, her eyes shining bluer and clearer against the creamy skin of her face. Her lashes longer and darker. Her lips fuller and redder. What would those lips taste like?

By the saints, he would have to make her dirty again if he were to pass her off as his squire. Otherwise, they would never succeed with their ruse.

Malcolm finished his bath and washed his clothes. After wringing them out, he put them on. He'd dry soon enough by the fire. Stalking across the camp, he sat near Jack, leaned against the trunk, and took the food she offered.

He murmured thanks and bit into the cheese, relishing its sharp bite. They ate in the quiet of the evening, watching the smoke drift and listening to the crackle of the fire. Silence bore down like heavy armor.

He stole a glance at her. His gaze traversed her face. It was difficult to find any trace of the boy Jack. Much to Malcolm's dismay, a beauty had replaced the dirty lad.

"What are your plans after the tournament?"

"Winning at Ramslea should earn a good enough reputation to be granted land from the king."

Malcolm cleared his throat. "I have heard Ramslea to be a grand place. 'Tis said the land is rich with green, rolling hills, and many streams nearby to water crops. The castle is also one of the largest in northern England. It is nestled against the peaks bordering Scotland."

"I look forward to seeing it." Jack offered him the last of her bread. "Where is your home?"

Malcolm took the bread, the touch of her fingers soft. Stuffing the piece in his mouth, he concentrated on his dirty boots. He should clean them.

"Malcolm?"

He raised his eyes to Jack's and quickly swallowed. "Aye?"

A slow smile crept across her face. "I asked where you are from."

"My family's holdings are near Lomkirk Abbey."

"Is it a substantial piece of land?"

"My father is titled, though not wealthy. We lived well enough, but with five brothers I needed to seek out my own fortune." He wiped his mouth with the back of his sleeve. "I know about your father, but what of your mother? Surely she is frantic over your disappearance." Malcolm watched her eyes grow dim.

"My mother is dead. Theirs was a great love, and my father never recovered from the loss." Jack paused and stared into the fire. "She fell ill of a fever and became delirious. My father held her as she thrashed about, trying to keep her from hurting herself. When her fever finally broke after a se'ennight, her body was weakened. She never regained consciousness." Jack closed her eyes. "I remember him holding her for hours after she died, weeping and rocking. I believe 'twas because of his deep love for her that he pushed me away. I remind him of her."

Malcolm reached out and put a hand on her shoulder. She looked at him, her eyes glistening with unshed tears.

"You are most fortunate to have witnessed a great love." Withdrawing his hand, he poked a stick into the fire. "My sire had little use for my mother, other than to beget a brood of sons. 'Twas difficult to watch my mother try to please him, even after he heaped upon her a mountain of insults. 'Twould have been a most blessed day to have seen my father holding my mother as your father had done."

"I imagine 'twas difficult to leave her to become a knight." Her gentle voice moved him, reminding him of his mother.

His voice grew thick with emotion as the hurt welled up. "I didn't leave her. She left me. She wasted away to nothing but bones. When I was thirteen, well past the age to foster elsewhere as a squire, I finally stood up to my father when he mistreated her, receiving more lashes than I can count. When she died a year later, I packed my belongings, earned my spurs, and began to tourney."

Malcolm sensed Jack's gaze upon him, but he was not ready to lift his misty eyes. Saints, he hadn't shared his life with a soul. What was there about Jack that pulled one's hidden emotions out of the dark corners of one's heart? After gaining a semblance of control, he turned and was nearly undone.

Her wet face glistened in the light of the fire. He reached out to catch a tear making its path down her cheek.

"Your eyes are leaking," he whispered.

"Aye," she said, wiping her other cheek with the edge of the cloak. "I hurt for us both I suppose."

Her hair had dried into large, loose curls about her shoulders as her eyes shimmered with tears. Her chin quivered. The firelight danced about her face.

His heart wanted to speak but could not find the words. It took action instead.

Leaning toward her, he threaded his hand through her curls.

Thick and soft, just as he knew they would be. He cupped the back of her head and pulled her close.

Her eyes fluttered closed as his lips drew close. His heart thundered, and he pressed his lips to hers. Ah, but what sweet lips they were. Soft and yielding. Inexperienced. The tasting of her made him want more. He groaned, deepening his kiss.

She pulled away and slapped him, pain slicing his face. He blinked, confused. Had she not responded to his kiss?

Jack scrambled backward, clutching her cloak about to her. "Nay." She sucked in a breath. "I beg you, never do that again."

Malcolm shook his head, clearing his jumbled thoughts. Jack's white knuckles gripped the cloak tight around her, her eyes wide. By the saints, what had he done? He scrambled to his knees, and she inched away from him.

"Jack, nay. I meant no harm." Malcolm tried to think of his reason for the kiss. He could hardly speak the truth since he wasn't sure what the truth was, other than he ached to hold her, to kiss her. "It was merely a kiss of comfort." He closed his eyes, frustrated at the inane answer. "Aye, a kiss of comfort." He opened his eyes to Jocelyn's fierce frown.

"You kissed me because I looked sad? Do you always kiss sad women thusly? A special custom, perhaps?"

Malcolm cringed. He didn't know how to explain, so he would have to do what he did best. Infuriate her. "In truth, my only thought was to cease your tears and prevent a deluge of more sad tidings. I couldn't bear another spewing of such womanly tales." He watched Jack rise, her chin lifting. Her eyes seemed to draw fire from the flames at her feet.

My, but she was magnificent.

"Might I remind you, you were the one who asked about my mother. 'Twould have been rude not to answer." She grabbed her clothes from the large rock nearby. "As for using a kiss to stop my compassion, you can rest assured that 'twill never happen again."

As she stomped into the woods, she heaped upon his sorry

head what amounted to at least a day's worth of insults. He knew he deserved the words. At least some of them.

Malcolm gathered their provisions and put them in his saddlebag. Taking his cloak, he spread it near the fire and laid down. How inane he must have sounded. A kiss of comfort, indeed.

When she returned, she made her bed on the opposite side of the fire, still muttering. He hoped they both could sleep.

Instead, he watched Jack toss and turn. Was she reliving their kiss as he was? In all his days, his heart had never leapt as it had when his mouth hovered over hers.

A rare occurrence, indeed.

CHAPTER 10

Try as she might, Jocelyn couldn't control Black. He had a mind to follow close behind Malcolm, which made it impossible to avoid the thick mud flung back by Horse's pounding hooves. It pelted her freshly-scrubbed self and fueled a certain satisfaction at undoing Malcolm's demand for cleanliness.

Overbearing man, yet such a sweet temptation. She shivered remembering the warmth of his breath upon her face. His lips teasing hers. Shame coursed through her that she had allowed the intimacy, mortified that she enjoyed his closeness and warmth. Such liberties were for those bound in marriage.

Thank the Lord her wits had resurfaced, and she gave him what he deserved.

Though she knew the kiss was inappropriate, it hurt to think he had not been affected by it as she had. How could he not? Perhaps he had kissed so many maids he was immune to such feelings. A handsome warrior such as Malcolm was sure to receive kisses from any maid who allowed such privileges.

She would not be such a maid. Not again, anyway.

Jocelyn breathed in the crisp, afternoon air. The land rolled like lush green waves before them. Tall, stately trees speckled the earth, and soaring blue-gray mountains dotted the horizon. They would ride into Ramslea before the sun set. Her stomach fluttered.

Black finally responding to her, she surged past Malcolm, happy to be free from the shower of clods. She chased the wind, ready to see her father.

Their horses churned the ground. As the sun touched the western horizon, Ramslea came into view. Jocelyn's breath caught at the sight, memories of home nearly overwhelming her.

Situated high atop a hill, stately peaks surrounded Ramslea to the north and west, and a river wound near the east side toward the forest beyond. 'Twould be difficult to penetrate such a structure with its walls between one- and two-score feet tall. Four towers rose above the walls, each waving a flag bearing her family's coat of arms. Her heart swelled with pride at its magnificence.

Jocelyn pulled up Black to take in the sight as Malcolm stopped beside her. She glanced at him and smiled. "What think you?"

Malcolm's gaze roamed over the castle. "'Tis a most impressive view. 'Twould be a privilege to own such land as this."

"Aye, 'twould be a grand place to live, to be sure."

Malcolm smirked. "'Tis a good thing you are muddied up once again. I was about to suggest we coat you with dirt to hide your smooth face, though it seems you managed on your own."

She rubbed her hands over herself, knocking the larger clumps off but leaving what was most assuredly a thick layer of filth. He spoke truth. She must keep her disguise, for she had information to gather.

Nudging Horse forward, Malcolm's smile grew wide. "Let us go meet with our futures. Me with my win and you with a new life."

They rode at a swift pace, only slowing as they neared the gate. Guards stood atop the parapet above and at the barbican beneath.

One of the guards stepped forward, raising his hand in greeting. "State your name and business."

"Malcolm Castillon of Berkham, here to enter the tournament."

"Check in at the guardhouse, and you will be shown to the stable." The guard stepped aside to let them pass. "Through the barbican and to your right."

"My thanks." Malcolm nodded to Jocelyn, and they moved past the guards.

They walked their horses through the bailey, Jocelyn's gaze taking in the view of home. The structure remained mostly unchanged, yet the blacksmith's forge had grown and the stable boasted of stone feeders instead of wood. The improvements pleased her.

After they checked in, they left their horses in the stables to be cared for by Ramslea's hands. They had arrived too late for a tent to be readied, so they left their gear in the storehouse until the morrow. As they made their way to the great hall at the keep, Jocelyn marveled at the number of people milling about. Knights boasted of their skills with the sword, lords compared the size of their garrisons, and the ladies twittered about their gowns and shoes. Dresses of every hue, decorated with ribbon, beads, and even bells surrounded her. She'd never seen such finery in all her life.

Jocelyn stepped into the great hall behind Malcolm and paused. Freshly spiced rushes covered the clean floors and fires blazed in the fireplaces set into the walls on either end. Improvements had been made, for she could now see across the entire hall without smoke stinging or watering her eyes. Her throat tightened, remembering the many meals eaten with her mother and father. Such happy times.

Aye, 'twas good to be home.

Knights and ladies filled long tables scattered about the hall, talking, eating, and drinking. A servant passed by with a trencher full of roasted meat, its aroma filling Jocelyn's nose. Her stomach rumbled.

"Bring more wine and ale."

Jocelyn turned toward the voice and forgot her hunger. Lady Helen sat in the middle of the main table, tall and regal as if holding court. The blue headdress atop the plaited golden hair matched her azure eyes and embroidered gown. Jocelyn watched her, waiting to be recognized.

Malcolm wended his way through the crowded tables as Jocelyn moved toward the wall to the side of the main doors. He walked to Helen and bowed.

"I am Lady Helen Ashburne of Ramslea, your tournament

hostess. From whence do you come?" She tilted her head and smiled, her gaze travelling up and down Malcolm.

Jocelyn's stomach soured.

"My lady." Malcolm took Helen's hand and kissed the back of her fingers. "Sir Malcolm Castillon of Berkham. I have traveled from France, though my home is in the southernmost part of England. I am most eager to win your esteemed tournament and take the prize. Might a kiss from the beautiful Lady Ashburne be included with the winnings?"

Jocelyn rolled her eyes as Helen's lips curled into a smile.

"That is arranged easily enough." She lifted her brows. "You are the famed Castillon who has been the talk of all England with your many tourney wins in France, are you not? You've made quite a name for yourself with your sword arm, Sir Malcolm, and I am sure your presence will make this tournament most interesting."

"I confess I've won a good many tournaments in France but will enjoy the challenge that awaits me here, my lady." Releasing her fingers, Malcolm rested a hand on the pommel of his sword.

"Well said. You shall have fierce competition on the morrow, for Sir Rolland Fallon of Sheltmore is here." She turned to the man seated on her left and placed her hand on his arm. "He is favored to win."

Sir Rolland smiled at Helen and placed a hand on hers. She smiled back. Uneasiness settled in the pit of Jocelyn's stomach. Where was her father? Shouldn't he be acting as host? She wished Malcolm would ask about him.

Helen raised her hand. A servant rushed to her. "See to Sir Malcolm's needs."

Taking his cue, Malcolm bowed and turned to seek a seat at a nearby table. Laying eyes upon Jocelyn, he nodded, summoning her.

She made her way through the hall to where Malcolm sat at a less crowded table with only a few knights. A servant brought a trencher piled high with delicious-looking food, and her stomach clenched in hunger. She started to hook a leg over the bench but remembered almost too late—she was a squire. She quickly backed up behind Malcolm, heat suffusing her face.

A bear of a man with a scruffy beard snorted. "I see you have a forgetful squire." Half-chewed food spilled out of the man's mouth and onto his beard.

Jocelyn gagged and ducked her head, nausea threatening to spew the meager contents of her stomach.

"Aye, that I have." Malcolm sipped from his cup. "I trust his manners will return once he has filled his belly."

The man laughed and shoved a piece of meat into his mouth. "I've found that a good lashing will bring obedience quicker than anything else."

"True enough, though I need his aid during this tournament and don't need him whining about the whipping he so thoroughly deserves." Malcolm glanced back at her and cocked a half-grin. She raised a brow, then bowed in deference. Playing the part, though she really wanted to slap him upside the head.

As Malcolm ate, Jocelyn watched the other squires to see how she should behave. Following their examples, she refilled Malcolm's cup and trencher until he required no more. Then, she brought water for him to rinse his hands and a towel to dry them. When her stomach rumbled, Malcolm waved a hand. "Go eat before you faint."

Trembling with hunger, she glanced at the table for squires. Rowdy lads joked and laughed while eating their fill. 'Twas best to avoid such a crowd in her disguise. She headed for the kitchens through the door at the back of the great hall. She prayed the staff would be forthcoming regarding information about her father.

While she enjoyed being near Malcolm, squire duties did not come easy. She grew weary of being bound to service. First to the convent, and now to Malcolm.

CHAPTER 11

Tension filled the air as servants jostled each other in a frantic pace to prepare meals for those at the tournament. The smell of savory spices wafted through the air, tickling Jocelyn's nose. She breathed deeply, taking in the tantalizing aroma of hot bread fresh from the oven.

Not wanting to be in the way, she stepped to the side of the kitchen and waited for an opportune time to filch some food. Or at least ask for some.

"May I—"

"Out of my way. I've more to feed." A middle-aged woman pushed by Jocelyn, an empty tray in her hands.

Jocelyn pressed herself against the wall. A young girl moved toward her. "Miss, may I have—"

"Sorry, but this is for the Lady Helen." The girl hurried past and out the door.

Jocelyn edged along the wall, her eye on a pile of roasted pig. She'd have to get her own food. If only she could reach the platter before 'twas sent out to the knights.

A wide body appeared before her, and Jocelyn gulped. Her gaze traveled up the triple-layered neck and into the wrinkled face of Nelda, the castle cook. Jocelyn had feared Nelda as a child, for Nelda was a good six feet tall with a temper that sent Ramslea's guardsmen running.

Jocelyn ducked her head and looked at the floor. What if Nelda recognized her?

"What, may I ask, is a filthy wee lad doin' in me kitchen?"

"My lord and I have only just arrived, and I am near fainting with hunger." She glanced up to judge Nelda's reaction. A frown. At least she wasn't yelling. That must be a good sign.

"Yer a squire?" Nelda put a hand on an ample hip. "'Tis scrawny, you are."

Jocelyn returned her gaze to her toes. "Aye, I'm small for my age. Maybe your cooking will fatten me up. Might I have some food, good woman?"

Nelda snorted. "Good lady, indeed." She walked away. Jocelyn looked up as Nelda motioned for her to follow. "The squire's food is on this back table." She gathered pieces of chicken, two roasted potatoes, and several pieces of sweet cakes. Wrapping them in a cloth, she handed them to Jocelyn.

She reached for the food, surprised at how much she'd been given.

Nelda did not release the food, however. "Heavens, I have not seen eyes of that hue since the sweet lady of the house left to be with the good Lord above. Such a bonny lass, she was." She cocked her head to the side, searching Jocelyn's face. After a moment, she reached out and patted Jocelyn's cheek. "Och, I have too much to do to be standing here taking care of a scruffy lad. Off with ye now."

Jocelyn clutched the bundle of food to her chest and bowed. "Thank you." She rushed out of the kitchen, relieved Nelda had not seen her as anything other than what she pretended to be.

Walking out to the bailey, Jocelyn devoured the food as she strategized. How best could she obtain news of her father? She could hardly explore the keep, as she had to assist Malcolm after his dinner. Nay, she must find someone to give her the information she needed. A maid, perhaps. Females gossiped more than males. Aye, that was a good plan.

Jocelyn savored the honey cakes, licking crumbs from her fingers as she proceeded back toward the kitchen to find a maid with a loose tongue.

Stars shone in the dark sky as people dressed in colorful

garments milled about the bailey. Torches set in the walls cast soft light about. Faith, how her life had changed. Four years ago, she wore beautiful gowns and designed embroidered tapestries. Now, she wore men's clothes and gathered wood. What did God have in store for her next?

Someone grabbed her from behind and whirled her about. Jocelyn drew back a fist, then punched her assailant in the face.

"Jack!" Malcolm grasped his nose.

"Malcolm, I—"

"By the saints, can you at least attempt to not bring all eyes to yourself whilst we are here?" He grimaced, pinching the bridge his nose.

Jocelyn glanced around, marking the stares from those passing by. "I'm sorry, but you were the one who came up behind and seized me. After what I have been through on our journey so far, I … I overreacted."

Malcolm frowned, then motioned for her to follow him around the side of the smithy a few paces away. Once out of sight, he stopped and faced her "You never came back from the kitchens, and I grew worried. Coming to know you as I have, I thought perhaps you had gotten yourself into trouble."

Jocelyn sighed. He was right in that she had indeed needed his help to get to Ramslea. But now that she was here, she needed no protector. Only he couldn't know that. At least not yet. "Thank you for your concern but, as you can see, I am fine." She rubbed the sore knuckles on her hand and smiled. "Except for my hand."

Malcolm took her hand in his, inspecting the skin. "Possibly a bruise, but not enough to hinder your tasks. Remember, you are my *squire* at this tournament and need to stay close," he said, his voice low. "No running around the castle grounds alone. I have no wish to be caught in a scandal whilst half of England is hereabouts." Malcolm's brows pressed low over his eyes, his lips forming a thin line.

My, but he was fierce.

"I will try to be a better squire." She scrunched up her nose. "I had forgotten how squires are little more than slaves to their knights."

Giving her a half grin, he shrugged. "You were the one who wanted to aid me in return for safe passage here."

"True. Though if I had remembered all that was involved, I would have given it more thought, to be sure."

Malcolm threw his head back and laughed. "You would have more likely stolen my horse and made your way here by yourself had you known all that would be required." He wiggled his brow. "I heard baths are being provided each eve for all the knights. Aided by their squires, of course. I shall certainly be looking forward to mine."

Jocelyn gasped.

"By the saints, you are much too easy to rile." He searched her eyes in the dim light of the torches. "'Tis a temptation I cannot seem to keep at bay, for I dearly love to see your eyes dance with ire."

Jocelyn could scarce breathe, let alone speak. His gaze roamed her face. His hand still held hers, his thumb caressing the inside of her wrist. She trembled with awareness.

Malcolm dropped her hand and stepped back, the warmth of his closeness draining away. He cleared his throat. "Don't let it happen again, boy, for I will not be as merciful the next time."

Voices carried from around the corner. Jocelyn swallowed, realizing Malcolm had saved them from discovery.

"Aye, sir." She bowed her head.

"Very good, then. Let us be about getting ourselves a decent night's rest."

Malcolm strode away, so Jocelyn followed behind, rushing to walk beside him.

He rubbed his hands together. "I have good and bad news. It seems the king sent his chief justiciar to act on his behalf. Lord Hugh Talbot, Earl of Pembury is his name. He shall preside over the tournament, set to begin at midday tomorrow."

"I saw no sign of the justiciar."

"He has already retired for the night, worn out from his journey no doubt."

"There are ill tidings as well?"

"'Tis good and bad at the same time. It seems that Lord Ashburne had been sick for some time and died not a se'ennight ago."

Jocelyn's knees buckled.

"Jack, what is wrong?" Malcolm stopped and grasped her arms. "Why should you care so for Ashburne? Did you know him?"

Nay, it could not be! It never occurred to her that he might be ill, much less dead. It couldn't be. "I must... I must ..." Tears filled her eyes.

She must get a hold of herself. Jocelyn squared her shoulders. "Nay, 'tis a sad affair, is all." She cleared her throat. "First the daughter, then the father. I wonder how Lady Ashburne is faring." Jocelyn had seen no sign of her stepmother's grieving. On the contrary, Helen seemed in good spirits. What was going on?

"There is more. Lord Talbot has granted a petition by Lady Ashburne, and the winner of the tournament will become Lord of Ramslea with her as wife."

Jocelyn's body shook. Her father dead, and Helen would still be Ramslea's lady.

All the things Jocelyn had discovered the past week muddled her head. The abbess blackmailed. Her own supposed death. Then her father's. And now the petition by Helen to marry the tournament victor. Was there a connection between them?

This was not how she had envisioned her homecoming.

Malcolm's voice broke through her thought, and she rushed to catch up with him, focusing on his face. What did he say?

"To be lord of Ramslea." He ran a hand through his hair. "'Tis a magnificent piece of land. Beautiful, prosperous—"

"Ramslea comes with a wife." Jocelyn's voice sounded hollow, even to her own ears.

"Aye, there is that. Though Ramslea looks worth taking on a wife. In truth, she is lovely."

But what manner of wife would he acquire? Helen could possibly be the instigator of Jocelyn's troubles.

Malcolm reached a hand toward her, then pulled back. He pointed to her head. "Your hair is escaping."

She put her hands to her head and cringed. Many curls had escaped. Pulling her hair tight, she retied the locks. "'Tis better?"

"Aye." His eyes crinkled at the corners. "Come, we shall bed down in the hall until they set up a tent for us."

Jocelyn took a step, then froze. "The great hall? But 'twill be packed with men. I cannot bed there."

"Aye, you must." Malcolm graced her with a frown. "'Tis the best way for me to keep my eye on you."

Jocelyn did not want to sleep there, but she followed Malcolm into the room where a wave of foul air assailed her from the sea of bodies now covering the rushes. They made their way to the far side of the room, not too far from the fireplace.

"Lie down by the wall." Malcolm pointed to a vacant spot on the floor.

Jocelyn inspected the ground, making sure there weren't any insects scurrying around, then laid down. The rushes provided little padding. Malcolm unbelted his scabbard, then laid beside her, setting his sword on his other side. He tucked an arm beneath his head and closed his eyes.

Men's snores echoed each other throughout the room. How could they sleep through such ruckus? Though she had learned that Malcolm snored, she'd grown accustomed to his rumble, and it didn't disturb her slumber.

Jocelyn closed her eyes, her thoughts turning to her father. Tears came, and she let them fall into her hair, allowing her grief to run free. How she wished she had been there to nurse him in his sickness, to be there when he drew his final breath.

As she silently mourned her father, her thoughts continued to turn. Though he had died, she most certainly had not. She needed to learn why she had been declared dead, and to what purpose. Tomorrow, when she was not aiding Malcolm, she would make discreet inquiries. Surely someone had information.

Malcolm shifted beside her. His arm pressed against hers, his warmth a welcome distraction. Could he hear the thrumming of her heart? It rivaled the cacophony of snores. Malcolm's breath grew deep, and she marveled at his ability to fall asleep in such a short time. 'Twasn't fair, to be sure. As his breathing slowed, her body relaxed.

Though her body clamored for sleep, her mind whirled, keeping slumber at bay. She was an orphan now. If she revealed her parentage—

Jocelyn gasped as her eyes snapped open. She would be forced to marry the victor of the tournament. After running from one forced marriage, she didn't want to walk into another.

But there was Malcolm to consider. While a stern teacher, he'd been patient with her when she struggled with swordplay. He'd been considerate—even thoughtful—after her injury, making sure she didn't tire overmuch. Marriage to him would be better than marrying someone she hadn't met. Or worse, Sir Wiltworth. She had rather enjoyed Malcolm's kiss and wouldn't mind continuing the practice.

As the rightful heir of Ramslea, what options did she have? Could she stay in disguise and watch her stepmother become mistress of her home? Nay, never! She could run away and live the life of a servant in another village, but that left her open to the possibility of a cruel master. Life with Malcolm would be preferable to that. The only other option for someone like her was to join the church, living in quiet reflection the rest of her days.

The memory of Malcolm's hand upon hers quickened her breathing. Marrying Malcolm would suit her better than taking vows.

Still, Jocelyn needed more information before making a decision. What better way to sneak around the castle than masquerading as a squire? And under the cover of darkness was a perfect time.

Sitting up, she glanced around the hall. Should she slip through the maze of men and investigate tonight? Nay, she would trip and end up with a knife in her belly. She would wait for the morrow.

Jocelyn lay back. There wasn't much room, but she managed to settle on her side with her back against the wall. In the fading torchlight, she could faintly discern Malcolm's profile.

This fierce warrior should frighten her, though something about him drew her. She felt safe when he was near. 'Twas comforting to know he cared about her welfare.

Of course, there was also his fine form and visage. Aye, that drew her as well. Not many men measured up against Malcolm. Though powerfully built and beautiful, she rather liked his eyes best. Steely gray framed in dark lashes, laugh lines marking the corners.

Jocelyn sighed. She'd never get to sleep thinking about Malcolm. But considering her future kept sleep at bay too. If only she'd prayed over her journey, she would feel more secure in her path. She still could not fathom what God wanted of her.

Forgive me, Lord, for neglecting You.

Jocelyn would neglect Him no longer.

Please, align my path in an obvious way. If not, grant me the wisdom to make the right decision.

And the strength to live with the consequences.

CHAPTER 12

Malcolm woke with Jack's face pressed against his arm. Her dark lashes fanned across dirt-smudged cheeks. She looked lovelier than ever. He fought the urge to taste her lips once again.

Bodies stirred around him, so he sat up, rubbing his face to clear his head of such daft thoughts. He mustn't let his feelings rule his mind. Growling with frustration, he jostled Jack awake.

She moaned and opened her eyes. "'Tisn't even light outside." She sat up and rolled her head around, stretching her neck.

Malcolm wished he could let her sleep, but he needed time in the lists. "Get up, little man. We have much to do before the tourney begins." He grinned. "You may want to do something with that riotous hair of yours."

She gathered her mass of curls, tying it at the nape of her neck. Dark circles rimmed her eyes. Had she been able to sleep? Being raised with brothers, he had learned to sleep anywhere he laid his head. 'Twas a most useful skill but not one everyone possessed.

His stomach rumbled. He stood, grabbing his sword and belting it around his waist. He glanced about the hall. Torches gave light to the few men still asleep on the floor and to those now eating at the tables. "Come and we'll break our fast. We need strength for the day ahead." He held out his hand, and she took it, standing with a loud yawn.

"Squire work is the worst kind of work." She tripped over the foot of one of the still-sleeping men as they made their way to the tables where sleepy-eyed men ate. The scent of bread permeated the room. Malcolm's mouth watered for a taste.

Sitting at a table near the fireplace, he glanced behind him and smiled. Jack stood with her hands behind her back, her eyes scanning the room and her brow furrowed. He could only imagine what musings churned in her curly topped head.

A servant brought out trenchers filled with bread, meats, and porridge. Malcolm tasted the thick stew and nodded. 'Twas much better than the fare served at his family home. Ramslea's cook knew how to prepare food. After eating his fill, he pushed back from the table.

Jack yelped.

"Are you injured or did I wake you?" Malcolm stood.

"Neither, sir. I … I … oh, aye." Her shoulders slumped. "I was almost asleep." She rubbed her eyes, still looking as if she needed a half-day's slumber.

"Go, fill your belly, then come to me in the lists."

Jack nodded before heading to the kitchens. Malcolm's gaze followed her hips swaying under her tunic. They would need a miracle to escape being caught if she kept forgetting to walk like a lad.

Turning on his heel, Malcolm made for the lists. Having had only Jack to spar with, he needed real swordplay to strengthen his arms. 'Twas a good time to practice, as Lord Talbot had not made an appearance at breakfast. Was he still abed like the women?

Noble blood did not better a man, at least not that Malcolm had seen. The men he most admired were those who worked hard to make something of themselves. While he respected some of the nobility he knew, he hadn't experienced it overmuch.

The bailey buzzed with activity in the early dawn light. The smithy teemed with knights. The stable lads pulled horses out of their stalls. Servants hauled split wood for the many fireplaces in the keep.

The clang of steel against steel met him as he entered the lists, and he studied the men at work. Men paired up, testing their swordplay skills. He flexed his muscles, ready to engage. Ready to win.

Grasping the hilt of his sword, he slid it out of its scabbard. Swinging it in an arc, he smiled at the whisper of steel cutting air.

Three men stopped before him, their faces grim and their bearings fierce. The tall one folded his arms across his chest. Malcolm's grip tightened around his weapon.

A smile broke out on the tall man's face. "I am Ian McGowan of the clan McGowan."

Malcolm relaxed a notch and nodded.

Ian glanced at the men flanking him. "My friends here say you've never lost a tournament, though I know that can't be true. Surely you aren't invincible?"

"Nay, I've lost once before." Malcolm shrugged. "Only because I was competing against my oldest brother."

"Then you might be the next lord of Ramslea." Ian pulled out his sword. "I would test my future lord's sword arm."

"You're a guardsman here? Not entering the tournament?"

"I am captain of my Lord Ashburne's guard, though 'tis early to say if I will remain so. It depends on who wins the tournament." Ian held up his sword. "As for the tournament, I did enter. I shall go far with my sword, but the joust … it seems I'm not suited for long sticks on a horse."

Malcolm laughed and touched his sword tip to Ian's. "Then let's see what you have to offer."

Malcolm stepped forward, striking several times while pushing Ian back. Ian deflected Malcolm's thrusts, striking harder and faster, but Malcolm stood his ground, parrying each blow.

They fought for several minutes until Malcolm discovered Ian's weakness—his backhand. Swinging toward the guard's knees, Ian swept his sword in a low backhand. Malcolm twisted his sword against Ian's weak grip and whipped the weapon out of his hands.

Malcolm picked up the sword and handed it to the guard. "You do your lord credit, Ian. Any man would consider it an honor to have you among their guard. Whether I am that one remains to be seen."

Ian took his sword and smiled. "You are gracious. I like that in a lord. My hope is that you send Rolland scurrying like a dog with his tail tucked between his legs."

"You do not care for Rolland?" 'Twas the first Malcolm had heard of anything untoward regarding the knight.

"He is not a compassionate soul. 'Tis not one I wish to serve." Ian sheathed his sword and dipped his head. "May God be with you." He turned and walked toward the water buckets, his companions trailing after him.

Across the lists, Rolland partnered with another man. A crowd surrounded them, so Malcolm pushed his way through to see the action.

Quick and ruthless, Rolland's powerful arm pushed his opponent back to the stone wall. His partner staggered beneath the blows. Rolland would indeed be a challenge. Malcolm best continue to hone his skills.

He approached a knight who stood alone along the wall. "Do you need a partner?"

The man studied Malcolm from head to toe, then unsheathed his sword. "Aye."

Once they found a clear area, they began their exercise. Within minutes, Malcolm knocked the sword from his partner's hand. Another knight waited nearby, ready to test his skills. 'Twas a longer duel, with equal thrusts and parries, both standing their ground, but the man tired and Malcolm's quickness brought him to his knees. Malcolm tapped his sword to his competitor's chest.

After an hour of sparring, Malcolm called cease, needing to rest before the tournament began. He turned from his opponent as Jack walked toward him with a cup of water. 'Twas what Malcolm needed. Blue eyes to drink in and cool water to quench his thirst.

"You've become quite useful, little man." Malcolm smiled.

"I owe you two days of service, which I will try to do with as little complaint as possible." She sighed, a small smile lifting the corners of her mouth.

Malcolm chuckled. "I would expect nothing less."

With the lists still full of knights practicing, the noise made it difficult to hear. A man cried out and voices raised in protest. Malcolm twisted around to view the commotion. Rolland backed away from his fallen partner, a thin smile on his face. The man clutched his side. Blood seeped between his fingers.

Malcolm handed Jack his cup, then moved toward Rolland. "'Tis a bit harsh to wound a man right before a tournament." Malcolm stopped beside the ruthless knave.

"No loss with that one. He wouldn't have gotten far in the games anyway." Rolland didn't bother to look up as he cleaned his blade. "'Twill only make my win come sooner."

"I would not be so quick to declare a winner. You know the saying, 'Pride goeth before destruction, and a haughty spirit before a fall.'" Malcolm stalked back to Jack, surprised at what he had just uttered. It had been years since the words of God had come forth in his mind. His mother's influence, to be sure.

"You had better watch yourself, Castillon. You are no match for my skills. I will enjoy watching you lose."

Malcolm glanced over his shoulder, noting Rolland's smirk. He'd enjoy wiping the smile off that knight's face. Malcolm nodded for Jack to follow. They retrieved their gear from the storehouse, then approached the table near the gate to sign in. "Malcolm Castillon of Berkham. Is my tent prepared?"

"Aye, let me find you a lad to show you the way." The man whistled, and a young lad ran to him, rubbing the back of his hand across his nose. "Show Sir Malcolm to the tent put up this morn."

The boy bowed to Malcolm. "Follow me, sir."

Malcolm and Jack followed the boy as he threaded his way through the crowded bailey, through the barbican, then through the gate. Cutting across the grass to the left of the road, he led them to the many tents set in rows near the tournament field.

The boy stopped in front of a tent situated in the last row, farthest from the castle. "'Tis your tent, sir."

"Thank you." Malcolm lifted the flap and entered, Jack following close behind. Inside, bedding had been laid out for their comfort, and new clothing lay upon their beds. Malcolm grinned when Jack rushed to gather up the rich blue tunic he had chosen for her.

She turned to him, her eyes sparkling. "These are wonderful! How did you ever get them?"

"'Tisn't too difficult in a place as grand as Ramslea. The seamstresses here had clothing of all sizes stored away for needy people such as ourselves."

"It must have cost you a good many coin for clothing of this quality." She rubbed it against her cheek, inhaling the scent of new cloth. "'Tis so soft."

"By the saints, Jack." Malcolm took the tunic from her hands. "You must cease with your womanly manners. You can't be seen caressing a piece of cloth like a maid."

"But no one can see us." Jocelyn took the tunic from him and sat on the makeshift bed, stroking the fabric.

Malcolm didn't know whether to throttle her or kiss her senseless. Seeing her love on that bit of clothing made him wonder if she would ever appreciate him as much, but he had no time for that. He had a tournament to win and land to claim.

"Change your clothes, while I wait outside." Malcolm threw back the flap and stepped outside. Walking between the rows of tents, he spotted a barrel of water nearby. He strode over to it and dunked his head. The cold liquid cooled his face, clearing his thoughts.

Malcolm stood, running his hands over his face. He must remain focused. This land could be his. Here, he could find satisfaction in owning something of worth and beauty. Of course, it came with Lady Helen. While beautiful, he knew nothing about her. He hoped she wouldn't hinder the peace he desired.

Jocelyn savored the softness of her new clothes. She had worn nothing of color since she entered the convent, and the beautiful depth of the cobalt tunic made her feel less of a boy. How would she look in a gown of this hue? Would she look the part of a grand lady? Would Malcolm notice? She snorted. Malcolm noticed nothing beyond the tournament. Not that she cared what he noticed. At least, she shouldn't.

She stepped out of the tent. A squealing pig ran past a moment before a girl bumped into Jocelyn, knocking her to the ground.

"I'm sorry!" The girl waved but didn't stop her pursuit.

Scrambling to her feet, Jocelyn joined in the chase, passing the girl and catching the pig on her third try. She handed the small wiggling animal to the girl.

"Thank you, sir. With so many people about, 'twas difficult to catch him." The pig squealed in her arms. The arms of a young maid. While Jocelyn needed to attend Malcolm, she seized her opportunity—this girl might have some information.

"I'm Jack, Sir Malcolm Castillon's squire. Do you work in the keep?"

"Aye. I help in the kitchen most days. My brother tends the pigs, and several got out of the pen while we were talking. I went after this one." She smiled. "I'm Lisbet."

"Do you know the Lady Ashburne?"

"I don't know her, but I see her some."

"Who is her maid?" Jocelyn glanced around, scouting for Malcolm. She must hurry.

"Why do you want to know?"

Faith, she should be more subtle. Jocelyn focused her attention on Lisbet. "I … I thought to inquire what Lady Helen's favorite flower is. My lord seeks to please the lady."

The pig squealed and squirmed in Lisbet's arms. "I need to return it to my brother before I lose it again."

"Of course." But Jocelyn wanted to dig deeper, even if Lisbet had no contact with Helen. "May I see you later?"

"After supper, when the kitchen is cleaned, we can meet by the pig pen."

Lisbet's upturned lips pricked Jocelyn's conscience. She hated this masquerade with all its lies—she hated using the girl for her own gain—yet she needed information. "Very well. Until then." Jocelyn gave a small bow before continuing her search for Malcolm.

Was meeting Lisbet God's leading or Jocelyn's own willfulness coming to the forefront? *Lord, please help me learn the truth.*

Hurrying through the bailey, she searched for Malcolm. She neared the paddock teeming with stable hands saddling horses and dressing them for the melee. Jocelyn glimpsed Helen slipping out through the stable door, glancing around as she headed toward the keep. Odd. What had she been doing? Meeting Rolland? Or possibly Malcolm? Jocelyn veered toward the stables, pausing at the doorway. No Malcolm. Not even Rolland. Jocelyn frowned. What business did Helen have there?

Shaking off her concern, Jocelyn left the stable. She must find Malcolm. She checked the hall, the kitchen, the lists, everywhere she thought he might be. He had only stepped out to allow her to change clothes. Maybe she'd missed him, and he was back at the tent. If so, he would think she was off getting into mischief. She broke into a run.

Jocelyn pushed through the tent flap and stopped in front of Malcolm, now dressed in a new burgundy tunic that accentuated his gray eyes. New boots and a belt completed his attire. Only a furrowed brow marred his handsome face.

"Where have you been?" He pulled the chain mail over his head, letting it fall to his waist. "You must stay close during the tournament, for I shall have need of you."

"I was looking for you." Jocelyn picked up the arm guards laying on his bed. "Then I got distracted."

"Distracted by what?" Malcolm took the guards from her and pulled them on. "Cinch these tight while you tell your tale."

Jocelyn tightened the laces. "I helped someone chase a pig."

Malcolm looked up from her handiwork and then laughed. "Jack, you and your exploits. Please don't say this someone was a maid."

"Aye, 'twas. I am a lad to all here and expected to be chivalrous to a lady in need."

He shook his head. "Jack, you are *not* a lad. The more you are seen roaming the grounds, the greater the chance you will be discovered."

She didn't want to tell him she was meeting the girl again, for he would forbid it, so she took a breath and nodded. "Aye, you are right. 'Twon't happen again." She wouldn't chase a pig again—that, she could promise.

Malcolm raised one brow but said nothing. Jocelyn picked up the leg chausses.

"I will manage those myself, as the ties are in a location lasses should not be."

Jocelyn's cheeks grew hot, and she dropped the armor onto the bed, looking for something else to do. "What do you need next?"

"Let me finish dressing, then you can carry my equipment."

Relieved, Jocelyn opened the tent flap.

"Don't wander off."

She stepped back into the sunshine, letting the flap fall behind her. Unsure of what else to do, she stood at the entrance of the tent and crossed her arms. *Humph.* He wanted her help. He didn't want her help. He wanted her to leave. He wanted her close. She could be gleaning clues at the castle, yet she must stand guard. Rolling her shoulders, she blew out a breath. Squiring for Malcolm was impeding her progress and testing her patience.

"Jack!"

She shuffled back into the tent. Clothed in chain mail and a cobalt surcoat, Malcolm seemed larger … imposing. Faith, he must be a fearsome sight on the battlefield.

He grabbed his sword. "Carry my shield and hood. We must pick up Horse."

Hefting the heavy equipment, Jocelyn followed Malcolm to the stables, thick with activity. A stable boy led them to Horse, already saddled and decorated with a trapper matching Malcolm's surcoat. Horse tossed his head as they approached.

Shifting the items in her arms, Jocelyn took the reins and led Horse behind Malcolm to the tournament field. She had only witnessed one tournament before, and that had been eight years ago, just before her mother passed away. She'd forgotten how festive they could be. Crimson banners lined the tournament field like a ring of fire whipping in the wind. A rainbow of colorfully dressed people filled the stands.

Lord Talbot, decked in a navy surcoat, sat on a raised platform under a crimson canopy in the middle of the crowd. His gray hair and beard gave him a distinguished air. To his right sat Helen in a gown of deep purple. Many of the king's court surrounded him. Jewels sparkled from their necks, their ears, their fingers, even their gowns. Lower ranking folk filled the rest of the stands while Ramslea's serfs lined the field railing.

Once Malcolm reached the field, he took the reins from Jocelyn, then mounted Horse. She handed him his hood, then his shield. He didn't even glance at her as he donned his hood. "Stay to the side of the field by the fence with the other squires."

Jocelyn bowed her head, then looked up with a smile. "I shall ever be obedient, sir."

His solemn face relaxed, and he laughed. "Jack, your humor slays me at times."

A trumpet blasted signaling the start of the tournament. Malcolm spurred his horse to one of the lines forming at the field entrance for the melee. Lots had divided the competitors into two teams. Malcolm's team wore blue, the other team red. As both lines filed onto the field, a herald announced each participant. Sixty men in all. The crowd roared.

Jocelyn found a place to the left of the stands at the end of the field. Many squires joined her, so she moved to the railing to better view the event.

The two lines faced each other across the field, awaiting the signal. Jocelyn glanced at Lord Talbot in his chair, holding a black flag in the air. He brought the flag down, and trumpets blared. Horses whinnied as knights spurred them into action. The lines charged toward one another, the knights holding their swords high.

Jocelyn held her breath as Malcolm rushed toward the opposing team. As the lines clashed, Malcolm's team stayed in formation, swords slashing at their opponents. 'Twas chaos. Was this how real battles were fought?

Ducking beneath a swinging blade, Malcolm stripped his opponent of his sword, raising it high with a victorious yell. The defeated man trotted to the side of the field. Malcolm continued his fight, claiming victory over six more opponents. Pride swelled within her at Malcolm's bravado. He held no fear, easily stripping each man of his blade.

The field cleared, one by one, until only a handful of men remained. Malcolm battled a young knight whose strong strokes pushed Malcolm back several paces. Horse stutter-stepped and Malcolm grabbed the pommel of the saddle.

Jocelyn hadn't seen Malcolm falter before. Was Horse injured? Malcolm shifted in the saddle, leaning to the right. What was going on?

The opponent pressed forward with quick strokes. Malcolm struggled to deflect each blow as he gripped the pommel. He leaned toward the right as the saddle slid the opposite direction. Faith, the saddle was loose!

Swinging his blade with all his might, Malcolm halted his opponent's advance, giving him enough time to slide off Horse. Jocelyn swallowed. How could he defeat the knight on foot?

The knight seized the opportunity, raining heavy blows upon Malcolm. Gripping his sword with both hands, Malcolm blocked each stroke. Holding his sword aloft against the assault, Malcolm lunged forward. He grabbed his opponent's ankle and pulled.

Thrown off balance, the knight ceased his attack, grabbing onto the saddle.

Malcolm dropped his sword and grabbed the man's foot with both hands. Jocelyn sucked in a breath. Was he daft? Even she knew a competitor never dropped his sword in battle.

The knight struggled to remain atop his horse, so Malcolm pulled harder, bringing the man to the ground. As soon as he toppled, Malcolm let go of the man and grabbed his sword. His opponent rolled, coming to his feet. Malcolm advanced, slashing at the knight with renewed vigor. Without the advantage of height from atop the horse, the man couldn't regain the offensive. He stumbled, and Malcolm pushed him to the ground.

"Yield!" The knight dropped his sword, holding up his hands. Jocelyn loosened her grip on the railing, thankful Malcolm's plan worked.

Malcolm lowered his sword. "Well done." He helped the man to his feet, then glanced around the field. Only Rolland and one knight left. They battled, but Rolland finally knocked the sword from his opponent's hands. Rolland drove his opponent to his knees.

Guiding his horse around, Rolland spotted Malcolm. He slid off his horse and strode toward Malcolm, slashing his sword through the air.

The men faced each other, both of them glistening with sweat and panting heavily. Rolland flexed his arms and bellowed, his voice penetrating through the roar of the crowd. Dread cracked Jocelyn's confidence in Malcolm. The men circled one another, swords raised, their movements slow.

"Fight!"

"Get on with it!"

"Take him down!"

The crowd yelled, chanting for their favorite players.

Rolland lunged forward, swinging his sword and driving Malcolm back. Jocelyn clenched the fence railing. Her ears buzzed with the roar of the crowd.

With a clash of steel, the warriors met nose to nose. Snarling, Rolland pushed Malcolm and lunged, thrusting his sword toward Malcolm's chest. Malcolm deflected. He swung his sword in quick succession, driving Rolland back several feet. They fought with a fierceness Jocelyn had never seen. How could Malcolm keep his strength at that pace?

Raining vicious blows upon Rolland, Malcolm pressed forward. Rolland roared. He lunged again, flipping Malcolm's sword out of his hand. The crowd gasped, quietening for but a moment. Cheers and boos ensued as the crowd came to their feet.

Malcolm dove for his sword, losing his shield as he hit the ground. Rolland's blade swung downward as Malcolm twisted. He cried out.

Nay! Jocelyn jumped the fence and ran toward Malcolm, only to be grabbed by the arm and pulled back.

"Nay, squire. Your job is to cheer on your lord." Ian, Ramslea's chief guardsman, maintained a firm grasp.

"He may injure himself further." Jocelyn yanked her arm to no avail.

Malcolm grappled for his sword.

"Your lord would off your head if you interrupt his play. Now come with me." Ian hauled her to the side of the field where many of the ransomed knights stood closer to the fight. There he released her and pounded her on the back. "Watch your lord and be proud."

Malcolm now stood. Sword in one hand, he clutched his side with the other. Rolland inflicted blows in quick succession. Malcolm staggered back but managed to deflect the attack.

Lord, help him!

With his eyes on Malcolm, Rolland stumbled over a glove on the ground. Malcolm took advantage. Releasing his side and grabbing his sword with both hands, he drove Rolland to his knees with powerful strokes. Twisting his sword, Malcolm sent Rolland's blade flying, then pressed the tip of his blade at Rolland's neck.

The crowd grew quiet.

Jocelyn's breath stilled in her throat.

"Do you yield?" Malcolm's ragged voice carried across the arena.

"'Tis obvious you are the victor." Rolland raised his chin.

"Aye, that I am." Malcolm took a step closer, his sword still pressed to Rolland's neck. "I want to hear you concede."

Rolland's lips thinned. "I concede. But you will never have Helen as long as I have breath in my body." His voice dropped low, but Jocelyn heard every word.

Malcolm's jaw clenched, but he lowered his sword and backed away from Rolland. He turned to the stands and lifted his sword above his head, sending the crowd into another swell of cheers.

Sheathing his sword, Malcolm searched the arena until he found Jocelyn. Her heart stuttered as the corner of his mouth lifted into a slow smile. She might serve as his squire for the rest of her life if she could be the recipient of that smile each day. My, he was beautiful when he smiled.

Malcolm walked toward the canopy. He pressed a hand over his chest as he knelt before Lord Talbot.

"Impressive, Sir Malcolm." Lord Talbot stood and walked to the railing. He motioned toward the people in the stands. "You've stirred the crowd with that performance. Congratulations."

"Thank you, my lord."

"You do your liege proud. The team of blue has won the melee, and each man on the winning team shall receive five shillings from the king's treasury." The blue knights cheered. "As for the individuals defeated, you shall pay your captor three shillings as ransom."

The knights around Jocelyn cheered. Ian clapped her on the back. "This is a cheap ransom. A year past, the ransom was your horse."

"That seems harsh."

"'Twas much walking for the poorer knights. Most of us have

more than one steed."

Lord Talbot raised both hands. "And now for a special prize." He reached out to Lady Helen. She rose, placing her hand in his. "I believe a kiss for the victor is in order. What think you, Lady Helen?"

"As you wish, my lord."

Lord Talbot nodded to Malcolm. "You may come claim your prize, Sir Malcolm."

Malcolm walked up the wooden steps to the platform, knelt before Helen, and lifted his face. Jocelyn's chest tightened.

The crowd cheered when Helen smiled, then bent low to bestow Malcolm's winnings. She took his face in her hands, bringing her lips to his forehead, but Malcolm leaned up and caught her lips with his own.

Jocelyn gasped. The crowd cheered. Helen broke away and stepped back. Putting her hand to her mouth, her gaze darted to Rolland, his face solemn.

Malcolm rose and faced the crowd, his hands raised in victory.

The smile on his face fell, as did his arms. Malcolm stumbled down the steps. What was happening? Jocelyn ran to him. Once his feet touched the ground, he fell to his knees, pitching forward.

"Malcolm!" Jocelyn dropped to her knees beside him. She tried to roll him over, but she could not move him. Curse his heavy armor!

"I'll see to him." Ian stooped and rolled Malcolm over.

Jocelyn inspected his body, finding a gash in the chain mail along his side. Blood soaked the left side of his hose and through his chausses.

"He's losing blood." She looked at the knights gathered around them. "Help me take him to the healer."

Ian pointed to the three closest men. "You, take hold of his arms and legs. I've got his head."

They picked up Malcolm and carried him past the tents and through the barbican to the thatch-covered healer's hut. The knights stooped when they entered the short wooden doorway. Jars and baskets lined shelves along the walls and a small fire burned in the fireplace near the back of the room. Dried plants hung from the ceiling, bumping against their heads.

Jocelyn rushed around them and approached an old woman grinding herbs near the hearth. "Sir Malcolm needs you."

"It seems he does." Stooped with age, the healer's voice crackled as she spoke. She hobbled to the table where Malcolm had been laid. "You may leave him with me."

"I will stay." Jocelyn would not leave Malcolm. He had tended to her when she was wounded. She would do the same.

"Very well. You shall help me if you remain."

Jocelyn nodded.

"Help me undress him." The healer took off Malcolm's hood and dropped it on the floor. Jocelyn helped her remove the chain mail, then the tunic, revealing Malcolm's chiseled torso marred by several scars. The battle wounds of a warrior.

The woman gathered cloth and a bowl of water, then handed them to Jocelyn. "Clean the wound while I gather bindings and herbs."

Jocelyn set the items beside Malcolm, then dipped the cloth in the water and squeezed out the excess, cleaning the wound as best she could. Blood flowed freely, making the task difficult. The cut was a hand's breadth in length, running from the left side of his chest and across his ribs. It wasn't as deep as she had feared, but he had lost much blood.

"Press this on the wound." The healer handed Jocelyn another cloth. "I am almost ready." She went back to her baskets, pulling out various herbs.

Jocelyn pressed the cloth onto the wound, leaning against it to arrest the bleeding. Malcolm's hand closed over hers, and she looked to his face. A small smile spread across his pale skin.

"You didn't realize your duties would include tending my wounds."

"Nay, 'twas not on the list of requirements." His warm hand still covered hers. "Are you in pain?"

"'Tis but a scratch."

Jocelyn snorted. "'Tis more than a scratch, I assure you."

"I've had worse." Malcolm pulled his hand from hers and tried to sit up.

"Och, dearie, you must stay still while I tend you." The healer hobbled over to Malcolm, pushing him back. "It must be stitched."

"I've no time for stitches. Sear it shut and be done."

The healer nodded. "As you will." She went to a small chest in the corner of the room and drew out two large daggers. She thrust them into the fire before preparing a poultice to aid the healing.

Jocelyn glanced at Malcolm. He watched her. Heat crept up her neck at his perusal.

The healer grabbed a knife out of the fire, and Jocelyn pulled her attention to the task at hand. The woman poised the knife above the gash. Jocelyn's stomach churned. She looked at the wall as the healer pressed the blade against the torn skin. Malcolm grunted as his skin sizzled. Jocelyn looked at him in time to see his eyes rolled back in his head. Faith! He had fainted.

"'Tis fortunate he is not awake, for I must do one more pass." The healer took the second knife out of the fire.

The scent of burnt flesh turned Jocelyn's stomach as the healer finished her work. Malcolm moaned but did not awaken. *Thank you, Lord, for easing his suffering.*

The healer's unhurried movements soothed Jocelyn's ragged nerves. "Your young knight shall be fine, dearie." She offered a toothless smile. "You need not fear. He is strong of body and, I daresay, strong of will. He shall awaken in short order."

Jocelyn sighed, taking a seat by the table. "I thank you for your healing touch. He is also stubborn and will no doubt be most unpleasant when he awakens."

The old woman chuckled and focused on Jocelyn. "We are all at our worst when our deepest desires are threatened."

Jocelyn grew uncomfortable under the knowing eyes of the healer. "Aye, his dream of land depended on winning this tournament." She glanced at Malcolm and wrinkled her nose. "He'll be in a most foul humor with his dream destroyed." He wouldn't easily assent to recuperating abed.

"But often the plans we make are not the plans that fate has decreed for us. We might win our prize, though often not by playing the game we have chosen for ourselves."

Jocelyn frowned, not pleased with the turn of conversation. She rose from her chair and went to Malcolm's side. "May he be moved?"

"Aye, though not too far. There is an extra room in the back."

Jocelyn nodded. Stepping outside, she stopped two of Ramslea's knights as they walked by. "Could you help me? Sir Malcolm needs your aid."

"Certainly," said one of the knights. They followed Jocelyn into the hut and moved Malcolm from the main room to the back bed.

"Thank you, sirs." Jocelyn nodded. "I shall tell Sir Malcolm of your kindness."

As they left, she examined the room. A small fireplace filled the far wall. A large animal skin covered the stone floor, and a pile of blankets stood in the corner.

The healer entered and covered Malcolm with woolen blankets before starting a fire. "Come. Your knight will rest while we eat a bite of stew."

Jocelyn's mouth watered at the mention of food, so she followed the healer to the main room where a black pot sat among the coals. The healer ladled stew into a bowl and handed it to Jocelyn. She breathed in the spicy aroma of the hearty broth, hoping the mixture was free of toad livers or lizard hearts. She'd heard many healers used unusual substances in their potions and didn't want to think what creepy crawlies might be entering her mouth.

Bugs aside, the stew was delicious, and Jocelyn ate her fill. She gazed out the window to where the afternoon sun shone brightly across the bailey. What an interesting God she served who led her back home as a squire and to the healer's hut instead of feasting with her father in the keep.

What is the path you have for me, Lord?

CHAPTER 13

After checking on Malcolm and finding him still asleep, Jocelyn left the healer's hut to gather clean clothes and check on Horse. Few people walked the bailey this afternoon, a welcome change from earlier.

She went to their tent and gathered braes, a tunic, and hose. Bundling them, she went to the paddock and found Horse. He came to her when she reached the fence. Stroking his head, she enjoyed the feel of his slick hide.

How was she to gather information with Malcolm wounded and out of the tournament? While he might remain at Ramslea to recuperate, she doubted he'd rest long, forcing her to continue their charade. She must hurry to unravel the secrets hiding within the castle or risk never knowing who sought her demise.

Lord, give me wisdom.

"I've been looking for you." Ian joined her at the fence. "Something's amiss."

"What do you mean?"

"Did you check Sir Malcolm's saddle before he rode today?"

Apprehension needled through Jocelyn. "Nay, why?"

"I thought it strange that Sir Malcolm's saddle came undone. Saddles wear out, but with such a grand prize at this tournament, I doubt he let his saddle deteriorate into such a poor condition."

"True. He prides himself in the quality of his gear."

"I inspected the saddle, and it looks as though someone cut through part of the cinch."

Jocelyn's jaw slackened. Someone deliberately sabotaged Malcolm's chance in the melee? Helen's visit to the paddock flashed through Jocelyn's mind. Bumps pebbled her skin.

"There is no way to know who the culprit is, as every contestant here could want Sir Malcolm out of the way." Ian pushed back from the fence. "I only share this with you so you can be diligent in protecting your lord. I will do what I can to help."

Jocelyn gulped. "I will do my best. Thank you." How was she supposed to protect Malcolm? He was *her* protector.

Ian marched toward the guardhouse, leaving her alone. Jocelyn stepped away from the paddock, her gaze traveling around the bailey. Any one of the knights or squires could have damaged the saddle. Or Helen.

Jocelyn replayed the scene with Helen over and over in her mind. Could she be responsible? Jocelyn needed to continue her investigation.

She headed for the kitchens, hoping to snatch one of Nelda's sweet cakes as well as catch a glimpse of Lisbet.

Though the sun shone brightly in the afternoon sky, the breeze sent a shiver through Jocelyn as she rounded the corner of the castle near the kitchens. She slowed, to her left were several servants gathering produce from the garden. Lisbet worked among them, rising with a basket of green vegetables.

Now was a good time to see what information the girl might have. Jocelyn entered the gate, walking toward her. "Hello, Lisbet."

The girl jumped, gripping the basket tighter. "Oh, you startled me."

"I'm sorry. The games have finished for the day. When I saw you working, I thought I'd say hello."

Lisbet shot a look at the castle. "I must gather more food for the evening meal." She knelt and pulled on a head of cabbage.

Jocelyn stooped down to help. "How long have you lived at Ramslea?"

"The whole of my life. My mother is a handmaiden to Lady Ashburne."

"That is quite an honor." Jocelyn placed a cabbage in the basket.

"Is the Lady Ashburne a kind mistress?"

Lisbet glanced at the workers nearby. "Nay," she whispered. "She is dreadfully harsh. Though 'tis an honor to be a handmaiden, and my mother is grateful for the work."

"'Tis a shame Lord Ashburne had to die right before the tournament. I heard many honorable things about him." Jocelyn prayed Lisbet would offer news of her father. Any piece of information would ease her searching heart.

"Aye." The girl smiled. "He was a good man. Harsh in some ways, but a good man. My mum said he was never the same after his wife passed away. 'Twas rumored the new Lady Ashburne pressured him into sending the daughter away, never intending for her to return."

"I heard the daughter died."

"Aye, she did, and Lord Ashburne never recovered, truth be told. Said he should not have sent her away. My mum said after her death he refused to take the lady to any festivals or tournaments. He spent his time alone in his chambers most days and then, a few months ago, he turned sickly and died."

Lisbet glanced over her shoulder. "The lady has been happier since his passing. In truth, she has been happiest these past months, entertaining Rolland a good portion of the time."

"Lizzy! Quit dawdling and get in here with the food." A woman stood at the kitchen door drying her hands on her apron.

Lisbet rose. "I must go. Can we talk later this eve by the stables?"

"Aye, tonight after we sup."

The girl's smile returned and hurried to the kitchen, the basket pressed against her hip.

Mulling over what Lisbet had shared, Jocelyn walked back through the bailey. Her father regretted sending her off to the convent. In truth, it gladdened her heart to know he cared, even if the knowledge came too late.

Hopefully, she could glean more information after supper. Of course, Malcolm might be too weak to attend the festivities. He'd chafe against staying abed for any length of time. What if he'd already awakened? Jocelyn hurried back to the healer's hut and knocked. After a moment, the old woman opened the door.

"I've come to attend Sir Malcolm."

The healer stepped back and opened the door wide. "Come in, dearie. He is still asleep." She poured some warmed mead into a cup and handed it to Jocelyn.

"Thank you." Jocelyn took the cup, then went to the back room where Malcolm lay. She sat on the floor beside the bed, not wanting to disturb him. A fire crackled in the fireplace, and she watched the light play across his face.

His lashes lay dark against his pale skin. Her heart squeezed at the thought of him withdrawing from the competition, but he wouldn't have the strength to endure tomorrow's joust. He wouldn't be able to win Ramslea. Or Helen.

If he were assured victory in the tournament, Jocelyn would gladly reveal herself as heir and claim him as her husband—even if he loved her not. But now that he was injured, Rolland would most likely be the victor and …

She closed her eyes against the selfishness in her heart. While devastating for Malcolm, the turn of events might be her answer—she could leave Ramslea with him. Perhaps she could convince him to continue as they were, with her as his squire.

Jocelyn knew what his answer would be, and it tore her heart asunder. How could she part from Malcolm? She pushed a fallen curl behind her ear and froze. Was this what love felt like? An awful ache at the thought of separation? Surely 'twas more than that. Jocelyn considered Malcolm's noble heart and sense of honor, his protectiveness and his fierceness. She smiled at the thought of his teasing—even his growl. He was everything she wanted in a man.

Aye, she loved him.

She glanced at Malcolm. So peaceful. So beautiful. She rose and sat on the side of the bed, brushing the hair from his brow. Her fingers skimmed the side of his face, and she marveled at how

God could fashion a man with such masculine beauty.

Heat swirled through her as she remembered his kiss upon her lips. How she ached for more. She glanced over her shoulder, checking the doorway, then leaned over Malcolm and slowly pressed her lips to his. Eyes closed, she savored the warmth of his touch. What would it be like to have his lips to savor at will? This kiss would be for her memories, to cherish once they parted.

Malcolm stirred beneath her. She pulled back, eyes wide. To her horror, his eyes were open and his gaze fastened upon hers. His eyes flickered before his lids slid shut once again.

Jocelyn's face burned. What had she been thinking?

She slumped to the floor and laid her head on the bed. When had life become so complicated? With the dream of reuniting with family now dead, all she could hope for was to love and be loved. If she could gain Malcolm's love, she'd give up Ramslea and its familiar beauty. Being loved by him would be a prize indeed. But how did one make someone else fall in love?

Love, as I have loved you.

How did the Lord love? Sacrificially, giving of one's self. A type of love that did not come naturally to Jocelyn. *Lord, show me how to love as You love.*

CHAPTER 14

Malcolm blinked against the light streaming through a small window across the unfamiliar chamber. Where was he?

He tried to sit up. Pain shot through his side. He fell back, gasping for breath.

Jack pushed up from the floor and grabbed his hand. "Malcolm, are you hurting?"

He must have woken her, for her tousled hair bounced about her shoulders. "'Tis nothing."

"Thank the Lord you woke. I feared you might succumb to a fever." She squeezed his hand.

"'Twill take more than a flesh wound to hasten my end, little man." Malcolm grimaced, trying to sit once more.

"Nay, you must stay abed." Jack pushed him back. "'Tis too soon."

Malcolm snorted. "I am well, I tell you." He swung his legs over the side of the bed and stood. The room spun. He swayed, bringing Jack to his side.

Heat radiated through him at the feel of Jack's arm around his bare waist. Odd, since he had felt those arms around him before. "Hand me my tunic."

Jack left his side and picked up clean clothes from the end of the bed. "Malcolm, you need to be in bed."

"Step outside the room while I change." Malcolm undid his braies and made to push them down. Jocelyn gasped and ran out of the room, as he hoped. With shaky hands, he donned his clothes. By the saints, he was as weak as a maid.

"Sir, are you all right?"

Malcolm would not acknowledge that question. He needed no aid. But when he didn't respond, Jack rushed into the room, coming to his side.

"I am in fine form." He cleared his throat and sucked in a shaky breath. "All I need is a hearty meal." He took a few steps before stopping. "What day is it? I didn't sleep through the tournament, did I?"

"Nay, the melee was earlier today. 'Tis late afternoon." Jack's brows rose. "Malcolm, you cannot think to compete on the morrow."

"Aye, I will finish this tournament and secure my land. I have fought too long for this, and here Ramslea lies, waiting to be won. I can win."

"But Malcolm—"

"But nothing, Jack!" Malcolm clenched his fists. "I will fight, and no one shall say me nay."

He stormed out of the room, his gait stiff, with Jack close behind him. No doubt she expected him to fall on his backside. Entering a larger room, an old woman rose from a chair beside a fire. He opened his mouth to thank her, but Jack rushed in between them.

"Tell him he cannot fight in the joust. He is too weak and will harm himself further. Tell him!"

Malcolm frowned at Jack, then looked to the healer. "Good woman, you are to be commended, for your ministrations have worked miracles. Aye, I am sore, yet am capable of knowing my own limitations." He glowered at Jack. "I will fight."

The healer gave a toothless smile and nodded. "'Tis the hardest passage that brings us to our heart's true home." She turned and hobbled out of the room.

He shook his head, not understanding her words. Mayhap the blood loss had addled his brain.

"Malcolm—"

"I shan't have any more arguments, Jack." He lifted his sword off the table and strapped it to his side. "I shall fight. I will win."

He ducked through the door and stepped into the bailey. The air had cooled, reviving his spirit as it soothed his skin.

As he walked toward the hall, he glanced behind him. Jack followed, a frown marring her face. Was it concern for him that made her angry? 'Twas a nice thought, though she should know by now he could manage well on his own.

They entered the hall where knights and ladies awaited their food. A servant rushed to Malcolm, bowing before him.

"M'lord, I was instructed to seat you when you arrived. If you will, follow me to the head table."

Malcolm glanced at Jack, who nodded and went to a table reserved for the squires of those at the head table. Then he followed the servant up the dais. Several men sat to Lord Talbot's left while Helen sat to his right with Rolland by her side. An empty space sat between Lord Talbot and Helen. Possibly for him, as victor of the melee? Rolland talked with Talbot and laughed, more relaxed than Malcolm had ever seen him.

Applause and cheers erupted as Malcolm walked across the room. Rolland spotted him and his smile slid into a frown. Malcolm grunted in satisfaction.

The servant reached Lord Talbot and bowed low. "My lord, Sir Malcolm Castillon of Berkham."

"Sir Malcolm, come and eat." Lord Talbot gestured to the empty chair beside him.

Malcolm bowed. "Thank you, my lord." He walked around the table and slid onto the chair. "I have a most hearty appetite."

"Eat your fill. You have earned a full belly."

A servant placed a trencher piled with roasted venison, various vegetables, and bread in front of him. Another poured ale into a goblet. Malcolm took a drink.

"You were badly wounded this morn. By my hand as I recall."

Malcolm looked around Helen to Rolland, whose dark eyes glowered. "'Twas but a flesh wound. I hope I did not disappoint you with my quick recovery."

Rolland's face reddened. "I confess at being surprised by your presence, though you know that I am a master at the joust and will best you. 'Twould be most unfortunate were you to reinjure yourself and not be able to claim the prize."

Malcolm smiled. "That would be unfortunate, yet have no fear, Sir Rolland. I am equal to the task and shall give you a fight you shall not soon forget."

Rolland cursed.

Malcolm looked at Helen, who had been silent since he sat down. "Lady Helen, forgive us this unpleasant talk. You look lovely this eve." He took her hand and kissed the back of it.

"You are a flatterer, Sir Castillon." She gave a coy smile. The light-blue gown brought out the blue in her eyes.

"Nay, my lady, I speak only the truth."

"How can I be sure? I know nothing but of your fierce reputation with the sword."

"I am the last of five sons born to my sire, Lord Phillip Castillon of Berkham. I earned my spurs early and have toured the French tournament circuit. 'Tis not an interesting tale." Malcolm picked a piece of venison from his trencher, relishing the smoky flavor.

"Five brothers and no sisters? If you were to win this tournament—and win me—I wonder if you would know how to treat a lady."

A slow smile stretched across Malcolm's face. "I assure you, my lady, I know well how to please a woman."

Rolland muttered.

Lady Helen laid a hand on his arm.

Rolland shrugged it off as he glared at Malcolm. "You go too far, Castillon. You will cease with your flattery and your empty promises."

"I speak the truth, Fallon. Only the truth."

Lady Ashburne whispered something to Rolland, who grunted and reached for his drink.

They ate the rest of the meal in silence as Lord Talbot told stories about court and past battles. Malcolm didn't mind the lack of conversation, as the tension about the table made his head pound.

While they ate, minstrels played in the corner of the hall. As people finished their meals, servants pushed back the tables to allow the company to dance to the merry music.

Malcolm took in the scene, musing on the possibility of this hall being his to lord over. It boasted plenty of space for dancing. Large tapestries hung on the walls, giving the castle a sense of home. Wine and ale flowed freely, and laughter and good humors ensued. 'Twould be a grand honor to win this castle.

Malcolm sipped his ale. He looked for Jack, but she had gone from the table. Glancing across the hall, he spied her exiting through the door leading to the kitchens. Snitching more food from under the cook's nose, no doubt.

Rolland rose from the table and escorted Helen to the middle of the hall where a new dance began. Malcolm watched them move through the steps. Helen smiled up at Rolland, her face radiant. When they came together, clasping hands after circling another couple, Rolland pulled her close and whispered in her ear. 'Twas clear Helen favored him.

After the dance ended, Rolland led Helen to the fireplace on the opposite side of the room. Heads together, they talked until Rolland pulled away and crossed his arms, his forehead furrowed. Helen glanced over her shoulder at Malcolm, then leaned toward Rolland, putting a hand on his arm. Were they discussing him?

Drinking the last of his ale, Malcolm rose and wended his way through the guests toward them. He bowed before Helen, ignoring Rolland. "My lady, would you favor me with a dance? I would be honored to partner such a graceful lady."

"Of course." She placed a hand on Malcolm's proffered arm, and he led her onto the floor.

As they moved through the steps, she said not a word. When they came together in the turns, she would not look him in the eye.

"You care not for my company," said Malcolm. 'Twas obvious to him, though he wondered if she would admit to the truth.

Her gaze lifted to his. Small lines formed between her brows. "I find you arrogant and much too sure of yourself."

Malcolm's mouth quirked to the side. "Ah, surely you would prefer a man that knows his strengths and how to use them. You seem to be a woman who knows what she wants." He cast a glance at Rolland, who watched them with arms still crossed. The man glowered as Malcolm led Helen by the hand.

"I do, indeed, know what I want. And you are not it."

Malcolm shrugged. "'Twill prove to be a most difficult marriage between us if you persist in this poor attitude." Truly, life with this woman could be hazardous to not only his peace of mind but his ability to sire an heir. Jack would be a more preferable bride than Helen.

"You, sir, have not yet won this competition." Her eyes narrowed, and her lips thinned, turning downward. He had the strongest urge to pull away from her. Life with her would only prove difficult. Of that he was certain.

The dance finally ended, and he led her back to Rolland, pleased to be rid of her. Then he searched the room for Jack, but she had not yet returned from the kitchen. He'd best check on her.

Malcolm walked down the congested hallway to the kitchen and stepped through the door. The hot, crowded room bustled with servants carrying dirty trenchers and goblets, some holding trays of sweet bread and some scrubbing pots. But no Jack. Where had she gone now?

"M'lord, pray, have you need of more food?" A large woman wiped her hands on a towel as she drew near. "I shall give a scolding to the servants who have neglected their duties."

"Nay, I ate plenty of good food. Thank you. I seek only my squire."

"Small lad? Dark curls pulled tight?"

"Aye, that is the one."

"He went out to the bailey through the back door." The woman pointed to the far end of the kitchen.

"Thank you." Malcolm walked across the kitchen, through the door, and into the bailey. He blew out a frustrated breath and ran a hand through his hair. He cared not for the feelings that washed over him at the thought of Jack traipsing around alone at night.

The gardens sat to the right of the kitchens, the washroom to the left, and the vast bailey beyond. "Jack!" No answer. Malcolm continued through the bailey. Still no squire. Once found, he'd give his foolhardy *little man* a scolding she wouldn't soon forget.

Jocelyn rubbed her arms in an effort to ward off the chill in the air. Though the clear sky invited a brisk wind, she was thankful for the full moon that aided her walk to the stables. She doubted the intelligence of meeting Lisbet this late at night, but, with Malcolm occupied in the great hall, it provided the perfect opportunity to gather more information about Helen and her father.

Jocelyn unlatched the paddock gate and made her way to the back entrance of the stable. Once inside, she let her eyes adjust to the thick darkness. Keeping her hand against the rough wood railing of the stalls, she moved down the aisle.

"Jack."

Jocelyn jumped at the loud whisper. Lisbet pulled her into an empty stall, but Jocelyn backed away, not wanting the maid to think anything untoward. "You startled me."

"I am sorry. I saw you and didn't think." The girl's lips curved into a coquettish grin.

"Let's talk." Jocelyn sat in the hay and motioned for Lisbet to do so.

"Talk?" A frown puckered Lisbet's forehead.

"Do you not want to talk?"

"Aye." She sat close beside Jocelyn. "Indeed, I do."

Jocelyn scooted away. Lisbet moved closer. This was not

turning out as Jocelyn had planned. She rose, not sure she wanted to continue her investigation.

"What is going on here?"

She froze. With a sinking heart, she turned to face a furious Malcolm.

His glare traveled from her to Lisbet, then back to her. "Both of you get to your beds immediately. You will not see each other again, nor shall you speak of this to anyone."

Lisbet gathered up her skirts and fled out the stable door.

Pulling her shoulders back, Jocelyn walked past Malcolm only to be grabbed by the arm and swung around.

"You are daft, woman!" He hissed. "Should your secret be discovered, I could be stripped of my spurs, and you labeled a whore."

Jocelyn wrenched her arm from his grasp. "You needn't worry. Men's grievances are overlooked, so I doubt you would lose your knighthood." She turned on her heel and began the long trek back to the tent.

She expected Malcolm's heavy footsteps behind her, but none came. With a quick glance backward, she saw he walked in the other direction. Good. She needed to gather her thoughts before facing him again. Truth be told, he was right. She was foolish for meeting Lisbet, but her desire for information compelled her.

The lack of clues disheartened her. What if she never discovered the truth? Could Jocelyn live with that?

CHAPTER 15

Malcolm rose before dawn, but Jocelyn kept her eyes closed, unwilling to face him after the previous night's ordeal. He'd come to the tent in the middle of the night, not bothering to be quiet as he prepared for bed.

Where had he gone? And with whom? She wished it did not matter to her.

It wasn't long before the early morning sun brightened the tent and Jocelyn slipped from the covering, grateful she'd slept in her clothes. It was too cool to dress. Donning her shoes, she stepped outside. A light fog blanketed the field, clouding her view like the mantle of mystery that lay upon her life. Perhaps the sun would break through the low-lying clouds and burn away the murky air in time for the joust.

Jocelyn hoped Malcolm was correct in his estimation of his jousting ability. Perhaps if he were whole, he would do well, but with his wound, she questioned his stamina.

She heaved a sigh yet smiled. She shouldn't worry, for Malcolm's determination made him nigh invincible. At least ... she hoped 'twould.

He was seated at the high table as she entered the hall, but he did not acknowledge her entrance. He was too busy bestowing his smile upon the ladies nearby. A part of her rejoiced that he hadn't berated her more regarding her meeting with Lisbet, and yet his disregard hurt in a manner she couldn't explain.

Jocelyn approached a table ringed by pages and squires filling their bellies with bread, fruit, and various meats. She sat at the end and ate her meal in silence, listening to her companions.

"I have a lass at home who is awaiting my return." A thin squire smiled, then stuffed his mouth with a piece of bread.

Another lad wiggled his eyebrows. "I have a lass at home too but found a girl last night who praised my kissing expertise."

Jocelyn snorted. They all turned their gaze upon her.

"I meant nothing." She coughed and hit her chest with her fist. "I choked, 'tis all." Head down, she continued her meal.

"'Twouldn't do to make enemies here," said one of the squires.

Jocelyn looked at the wooing braggart. The other boys nodded as they continued to stuff food into their mouths. Not wanting to create more trouble, she bobbed her head in deference.

Eating the rest of her meal in peace, she kept an eye on Malcolm. He never looked her way but smiled and laughed with those at his table. Neither Rolland nor Helen had made an appearance. Maybe 'twas the reason for Malcolm's good humor. At one point he winced and stilled, but never ceased conversing. He should not be fighting today if his wound pained him so. Would that Jocelyn could talk sense into his stubborn head.

When Malcolm stood and left the room, Jocelyn gulped down the last of her drink and followed him out to the bailey. Catching up with him, her heart sank when he did not even glance her way. "Are you going to ignore me thusly the rest of the tournament?"

He grunted.

Jocelyn wasn't sure how to respond. She could not explain her reason for meeting with Lisbet without revealing herself. Nay, she couldn't reveal her subterfuge.

"I accept your anger and am sorry. Truly, I … I only wanted female companionship." While not entirely true, Jocelyn realized she did miss Mary and their easy conversations.

Malcolm stopped and faced her. "While you are my squire, you need to keep your head down and do your job. You can find female companionship after the tournament." He continued on to their tent, running his hands through his dark waves.

She followed close behind, searching for words that would ease his frustration. There were none. At least none that would appease him. Best to change the topic of conversation. "Are you sure you are up to fighting today? I know your wound pains you."

"I am fit enough."

"But—"

"Not another word."

Jocelyn swallowed another argument. The stubbornness which made him a fierce warrior made him the worst patient in England. Lord, help them all.

Inside their tent, Malcolm slid the padded chausses over his hose while Jack gathered the rest of the equipment. He attached the mail chausses, then waited as Jack helped him into the padded hauberk and mail. He bit back a groan as the armor pressed against his wound. 'Twas most uncomfortable. 'Twould be difficult to make it through the day, much less as victor. Difficult, though not impossible.

What was impossible was Jack. Aye, Malcolm feared the damage her exposure could bring to him, yet he feared for her as well. He didn't want any harm to befall her, but once she left Ramslea, his responsibility for her would cease. He wasn't sure he cared for the idea. He'd miss their conversation. Her questions. Her ire.

He'd miss *her*.

"Jack."

She laced up the arm guards, yanking the leather ties tight.

"Jacqueline," he whispered.

Hands still, she looked up, her face pale and her eyes full of dread. By the saints, she must truly fear for his life. The thought gave him pause. No one had worried over him since his mother passed. 'Twas comforting to know someone cared enough to fret over his actions.

Placing a hand on her shoulder, he smiled. "I will come out alive. Methinks you are beginning to care about me, Jack."

A flush suffused her cheeks and she ducked her head. "Aye, I care." She jerked the laces tighter. "I care to the extent I do not want to deal with burying your broken body."

He threw his head back and laughed. "Ah, Jack, you are such an encouraging lass."

She rolled her eyes. "You have an odd sense of humor if my insults bring you joy." She finished with his leg guards and straightened.

"You can protest all you want, Jack, yet I know you care." He raised an eyebrow. "Your kiss yesterday spoke of your feelings."

Jack gasped, her hands cupping cheeks that were now a delightful pink. "You"—she closed her eyes and groaned—"you were awake."

Her shoulders slumped, and he wished he had said nothing. He pulled her hands away from her face, but she stared at the ground.

"I'm sorry I spoke of it." He lifted her chin. "Jack, please do not fear."

The dark lashes against her dirty cheeks lifted, and her chin trembled. She was so lovely, so vulnerable. His gaze travelled from her large blue eyes to her full pink lips. He bent his head to hers, his fingers skimming her chin to cup her cheek. Her lips, soft and yielding, moved under his and his heart tumbled. By the saints, she moved him like no other.

His other hand slid around her waist and clutched her to him, hating the chain armor that kept her soft body from his. Her hands traveled around his neck, threading through his hair, and he groaned, deepening the kiss. Sweet saints, she tasted of heaven.

A trumpet sounded in the distance. Reluctantly, he pulled away. Her cheeks flushed under her dirty disguise, and she put a hand to her lips.

Guilt tugged at his soul. Her innocence needed his protection. He shouldn't trifle with her, knowing he would soon marry Helen. Instead, he forced himself to step back. "You should get to the field."

Jocelyn gathered his helmet, shield, and sword. When she faced him, she gave him a faint smile. "Here. Go win your land." She handed him the equipment. "I shall check on Horse and meet you at the field." With that, she stepped outside.

Malcolm closed his eyes. Why was it so difficult to keep his distance from her? Nothing could come of it, so why indulge the temptation? Another trumpet sounded, and he shook off the oppressive thoughts. He had a horse to mount and competitors to unseat.

After strapping on his sword, he stepped outside, gripping his shield in one hand and helmet in the other. A brisk wind blew, but the sun shone brightly and would warm the air as it rose in the sky. He hoped to compete later in the morning, for his body responded better when not stiffened by the cold.

Malcolm joined the group of knights at the edge of the field. A low fence ran down the middle of the field, decorated with banners on each side. Highborn and commoners alike gathered in the stands and along the outskirts of the field, adding excitement to the air.

Lord Talbot strode in and sat with Lady Helen. Lovely in a deep-green gown, she fiddled with her hair as she searched the field. She smiled as Rolland walked toward her and graced her with a low bow. They shared a lingering look. When Lady Helen looked Malcolm's way, he bowed. She nodded, giving him a small smile.

What a tangled web. Would he be the one to keep Helen and Rolland apart? And what about himself? He tried to picture life with Helen, though the only face he could conjure was Jack's.

Nay. He pushed the thought aside. 'Twould take more years of tourneying to earn land such as Ramslea. It was too grand of a place to set aside for a woman. Even for a woman who crept into his thoughts and, truth be told, his heart.

Trumpets blared, and the justiciar stood with his hands raised. "Let the jousts begin!" The crowd erupted in cheers. Malcolm returned to the edge of the field to await his round. He took time to observe the other knights in case he came up against them. With his physical strength impaired, he needed cunning to win.

Jack came to stand by his side with Horse in tow. She chewed on her fingernail as she watched the proceedings. It still amazed him others saw her as a lad when he could plainly see her feminine nature. Of course, the dirty face hid her loveliness, as did the occasional scowl she'd been wearing the past few days.

"Sir Malcolm Castillon of Berkham to compete against Sir Geoffrey Melbourne of Aldmore."

Malcolm jolted out of his reverie and took the reins from Jack, her lips pressed together in a thin line. "'Twill be alright, Jack. Melbourne lacks experience."

"I shall pray for you, Malcolm."

Malcolm half expected Jack to cross herself, but she patted Horse on the rump, then turned to retrieve his lance. Between her prayers and his determination, he would be victorious. He hoped.

He rode to the starting post, the crowd's cheers eliciting anticipation. His body hummed with it. Malcolm bit back a smile as Jack struggled to carry the lance to him. Several squires rushed to her aid, and he soon had the weapon in hand.

Facing his opponent across the field, Malcolm took a slow, deep breath and waited for the flag. The crowd thundered. Horse pranced, ready to run. Malcolm gripped the reins tightly, holding his shield close to his chest.

A tournament official waved the starting flag. Malcolm spurred Horse into action. Lance lowered, he raced across the field. He took careful aim as Melbourne's lance came straight at him. The lance glanced off Malcolm's shield, rattling his teeth. His own lance hit Melbourne square on, knocking him flat on his back.

The crowd cheered.

Malcolm's side burned as he returned to the mounting block. Nothing wet seeped under his armor, and he sighed. His wound remained closed. For that he was thankful.

Trying to catch his breath, he spied Jack running to him. "I am unhurt." Though as he spoke, his armor chafed his wound.

"I am sure you are, though I would like to reassure myself." Jack tried to take the reins from him.

"Nay, Jack." Malcolm pulled away from her grasping hands. "My next round will be soon and I must stay close at hand. I am well, I tell you."

He led Horse to the watering trough. He did not want her fawning over him. He needed to remain focused.

He cared for his own needs, endured his own pain. He did not need her sympathy or her protectiveness, though he had to admit the liking of it.

CHAPTER 16

Jocelyn stood at the end of the field, her arms folded on the top fence railing as she watched the jousting. She had performed her duties for each of Malcolm's jousts, keeping silent throughout the day. He managed to defeat each opponent and qualified for the final.

She knew he was in pain by the winces and grimaces that passed across his face, but he did not complain. How would he have the strength needed for the final joust?

While Malcolm struggled, Rolland unseated each opponent with just one pass. He need only secure this round in order to fight Malcolm, and he was favored to win. Waiting for the starting flag, Rolland glanced around the stands and smiled at Helen as if success was in his grasp.

The crowd chanted Rolland's name, calling for his opponent's demise. Jocelyn shuddered at their lust for bloodshed. While she greatly appreciated the skills required for these games, she hated the crowd's cries for violence.

The starting flag raised, and the spectators grew quiet. The flag dropped. Rolland and his opponent charged, their horses thundering across the field. The top of his lance pounded his rival's shield, knocking him to the ground. The crowd cheered.

"Rolland is the superior jouster."

"Malcolm takes risks that make him unpredictable."

"Malcolm may be the supposed loser, but he has a good seat and will give Rolland a fair fight."

All around her, knights and squires speculated. Jocelyn prayed 'twould be a good fight. One which Malcolm survived unscathed.

Leaving her spot at the fence, Jocelyn went to Malcolm where he paced near the starting post, leading Horse behind him. She checked the laces on his arm guards and helped him strap his helmet on. He didn't speak, so she prayed for him, for his safety, and for his heart, should he lose. Without a word, Malcolm mounted Horse and rode to his starting point.

Waiting atop his steed, he sat tall, holding his lance steady with one hand while reining in Horse with the other. He looked ready to fight. Ready to win. Ready to be lord. Was he ready for a wife as well?

Jocelyn's chest constricted.

The trumpet blasted. She stepped away and stood by the extra lances should he need another. Rolland guided his mount to the opposite starting post. Both men readied their lances. The crowd grew quiet, amplifying the creaking of the saddles and the clanking of armor as the warriors settled into place.

Jocelyn held her breath. *Lord, protect him from harm.*

The official raised the flag. The crowd jumped to their feet. Jocelyn lifted her hand against the sun that now shone high in the afternoon sky. Horses pawed the ground, billowing the dust. Would the flag ever fall?

The official whipped his hand down, the flag crackling with the motion. The horses flew across the field, hooves thundering. Jocelyn's heart stood still as Malcolm's lance slid over Rolland's shield. It caught him in the shoulder, splintering. Rolland yelled.

The force of Rolland's lance thrust Malcolm back in his saddle. Leaning against Horse, he twisted forward, managing to pull himself aright. He leaned over Horse as he directed the steed back to his post. Jocelyn ran to him.

"Are you badly hurt?" Her voice cracked over the words, fear tightening her throat. He didn't answer. "Malcolm! Speak to me!"

"Aye." His voice rasped.

"Forfeit, Malcolm. Please, do not go further. 'Tis madness."

"Nay, I will not yield." He breathed in deeply, closing his eyes.

"I will win this." With a groan, he pulled himself upright in the saddle.

"The hit has addled your brain." Blinking back tears, she retrieved another lance for the stubborn fool. A trumpet sounded. Jocelyn struggled with the pole, dragging one end of it on the ground.

"Let me assist." Ian took it from her with a smirk. "Once Malcolm is lord, I will work to build your strength, little squire."

"If Malcolm isn't speared to death first." She muttered, trotting to keep up with him.

Ian hefted the lance to Malcolm, helping him position it under his arm. "Are you sure you are well enough to face Sir Rolland, my lord?"

Malcolm raised a brow. "I am not your lord yet, but when I am, you shall pay for that question."

"A word of advice, if I may. Aim high. Mayhap the fear of you hitting his shoulder will cause Rolland to be careless." Ian stepped away and patted Horse on his rear.

Malcolm nodded at Ian and then looked at Jocelyn. He quirked a brow and gave her a weak smile. "I will be in need of a bath when this is over."

Jocelyn gasped as he turned Horse around and made his way to his starting post. How could he jest so when he had so little strength to spare?

The crowd roared as Malcolm and Rolland faced each other again. Malcolm sat straight in his saddle, looking every bit the lord he would one day become.

The judge's flag rose, paused another eternity, and then dropped. Both men spurred into action, racing across the field. Malcolm's lance dipped low. The crowd gasped.

Jocelyn glanced at Rolland whose lance aimed true. Malcolm could not take another hard hit. With growing horror, she watched them draw close, Malcolm's lance swaying every which way.

Jocelyn fought the panic rising within. *Please, Lord, do not let him perish!*

Malcolm's lance tipped. Then, as Rolland drew close, he raised the weapon high. Both lances met their targets. Rolland flew off his horse, clutching his shoulder.

Jocelyn's mouth dropped opened.

Malcolm hung over Horse, listing to the side while the crowd exploded.

Jocelyn stifled a sob. Malcolm lived! The winner of the tournament. The new Lord of Ramslea. She fought the tears as she ran to Malcolm.

"Malcolm!" She took hold of Horse's reins as Malcolm swayed in the saddle. "Malcolm!" He didn't respond. She yelled over her shoulder, "Ian, help me!"

Ian ran to her side. "Let's get him down."

As they reached for him, his eyelids fluttered. Jocelyn breathed a prayer of thanksgiving. "Can you sit upright? Do you require aid?"

He grimaced as they pushed him to a sitting position. "I can manage." He sat for a moment, his gaze wandering over the cheering crowd. His lips lifted into a weak smile. Finally sliding off his horse, his knees buckled as his feet hit the ground. Ian stepped forward and helped him stand.

"Where is Rolland?" Malcolm glanced around, sweat rolling down his face despite the cool air.

Jocelyn pointed to the middle of the field. "There, in much pain." Sir Rolland's moans traveled with the breeze as his squire and several others attended him.

Ian, along with a few of Ramslea's guardsmen, escorted Malcolm to Lord Talbot. As always, Jocelyn followed close behind. The crowds cheered as he stiffly bowed before the justiciar. Turning toward the people, Lord Talbot motioned for their silence.

"Sir Malcolm," he said in a loud voice for all to hear. "You have won the melee and now the joust. You have proven yourself worthy, and I declare you the winner of the tournament."

The crowd erupted. Malcolm raised his arm.

Lord Talbot held up his hands, and the crowd grew quiet. "As winner of this competition, you have shown yourself to be a man of strength. By the authority of the king, I hereby bestow upon you a new name. Malcolm Castillon, Lord of Ramslea."

The people cheered as Malcolm bowed once again. "Thank you, my lord. You are most generous."

"Also as a reward, I hereby give the Lady Helen Ashburne of Ramslea to you as your wife and your lady. The wedding will take place on the morrow. I shall stand as witness."

Malcolm walked over to Helen and knelt before her. He took her hand and kissed it. Lady Helen smiled at Malcolm and cupped his cheek with her other hand. She did not once glance over to Rolland, lying wounded across the field.

Jocelyn's heart shattered. Was now the time to step forward and declare herself the heir of Ramslea? She had learned nothing about the deceptions or Helen's ties to them, yet she could not stand by and let Malcolm marry her stepmother. Not when she loved him and could have him for herself. But when to reveal the truth?

'Twas too chaotic and rowdy for such a declaration. She'd do it that night at the feast. Perhaps she might glean some more information before then.

Jocelyn squared her shoulders and took a deep breath. Malcolm turned to the crowd, raising his arms. He swayed, then crashed to the ground.

Jocelyn cried out and ran to him, fear choking her. Ian had already rolled him over by the time she reached him. Blood pooled beneath him, soaking into the ground. "Quickly! Get him to the healer!"

'Twas though she trudged through mud as she followed the men carrying Malcolm. She prayed 'twas only his wound that reopened, nothing more.

They burst through the healer's door. The old woman sat sewing by the fire. The large table in the center of the small room stood empty, so they laid Malcolm upon it.

As the room cleared, Jocelyn helped the healer rid Malcolm of his armor, leaving him bare and bloody. His wound had indeed reopened. Jocelyn breathed a sigh of relief.

"Press on the wound, dearie."

Jocelyn took a cloth and pressed on the wound while the healer stuck her knives back in the fire.

This time Jocelyn was prepared for the stench as the healer pressed the red-hot knife to Malcolm's flesh. They worked quickly, Jocelyn handing the healer paste and bandages in quick succession.

Once they finished, Jocelyn stuck her head out the door and called for help to move Malcolm to the back room. He remained unconscious while they moved him.

Once the men had left, she sat on the edge of the bed and took Malcolm's hand. Here she was, yet again, watching over his damaged body. She cared not for it.

"Dearie, you needn't worry overmuch," the healer said, placing her gnarled fingers on Jocelyn's head. "He will return to his own self sooner than you think. He might be weak, but his life is not threatened."

Jocelyn sighed, her throat thickening at the good news. "Thank you for taking such good care of him."

"Now that he is resting, I must see to an old soul who has need of one of my special potions." The healer cackled as she left the room.

Wanting to be useful, Jocelyn went back to the main room and retrieved cloth and a bucket of water. Returning to Malcolm, she wet the cloth, then bathed his forehead. Her fingers trailed the lines by his eyes that crinkled when he smiled. A scar gleamed white near the hairline by his ear. How had she not noticed it before?

What a rough life he'd led.

Malcolm stirred and opened his eyes. "Saints, 'tis nice to waken to your face," he whispered.

Her heart squeezed, and she smiled. "'Tis good to see you open your eyes. I feared you might never have the opportunity." She stood and placed the cloth on a wooden chest on the other side of the room. In that short time, Malcolm swung his legs over the side of the bed, a grimace marring his face.

Jocelyn rushed to him. "Malcolm, you will not remove yourself from this bed." Taking his feet, she put them back under the covers.

Malcolm fell over with a grunt, panting for breath. "By the saints, Jack. Have a care."

Guilt stabbed her. "I am truly sorry, but to heal you must keep abed. You are not as strong as you think."

Malcolm scowled. "I am strong and will attend the feast this eve. I have had more serious wounds than this." He pushed himself back up to a sitting position. "'Tis nothing but a trifling flesh wound."

Jocelyn snorted. "That took you to your knees in front of all present."

A sheepish grin stole across his face. "Aye, it did at that. Most embarrassing."

Jocelyn chuckled at his admission. He looked at her, cocking his head to the side, his eyes intense.

She sobered immediately. "I was not mocking you."

"You haven't laughed overmuch since I found out you were a maid." Malcolm lifted the corner of his mouth into a smile. "I would hear it more often."

Jocelyn's heart pounded. She needed to tell him the truth. "Now that you are lord of Ramslea, I have something to tell you."

A series of emotions washed over Malcolm's face. "I am lord of Ramslea," he whispered. "This land is truly mine."

"Aye." She sat on the edge of the bed. "'Tis."

Malcolm sighed. "'Tis all I've ever wanted."

Jocelyn eyes misted. With his victory came the fulfillment of her dream to marry for love. Even though he might not love her yet, she hoped her love for him would soften his heart. *Lord, give me the words.*

Malcolm gripped her hands. "Jack, what is wrong? Speak to me, for I can make it right. I am lord now." He gave her a smile.

She shook her head, not able to think clearly with her hands encased in his.

Malcolm lifted her chin and stared into her eyes. She held her breath. Waiting … hoping.

He muttered something before pulling her to him, crushing his mouth to hers. Jocelyn tried to pull back, startled by his intensity, but his kiss gentled, and his arms came around her, pulling her closer.

Jocelyn lost all sense of time as she savored his kiss. So sweet, so gentle. Was this what 'twas like to be treasured? To be cherished?

Malcolm's hand cupped the back of her head, then tilted it as he deepened his kiss. Jocelyn pulled back, her chest heaving. "Nay," she whispered. "I must …" She needed distance to think, to form words and tell him the truth. She scrambled to her feet

Breathing labored, Malcolm reached for her. "Jack, we can manage a solution," he said, his voice hoarse. "Now that I am lord, we can be together. People overlook the actions of a lord."

Did she hear him aright? How could he suggest such a thing? That he had so little regard for her shook Jocelyn to the core. She shook her head. "I shall not become your mistress, and I am hurt that you would suggest I do so."

Confession forgotten, she ran from the room.

"Jack, come back!"

Jocelyn left the hut and ran toward their tent. Malcolm couldn't say anything to make her feel better. Pain and anger simmered within her.

And yet, if he had known the truth, he wouldn't have had to suggest such a plan. 'Twas her fault for not being honest with him. But to be thought of as a mistress—disappointment weighed heavy like armor, encasing her heart and drawing her down.

Did she still want to claim her inheritance and marry Malcolm, knowing he would suggest such a thing? She still had the option to leave Ramslea and find work or join another convent. But in truth she loved Malcolm. Any alternative without him was untenable, regardless of his feelings.

She stopped in the middle of the bailey, debating whether to return to Malcolm and tell him the truth. If she told him now, he would yell at her for keeping the truth from her. Dealing with his anger while mastering her own hurt would be disastrous. Nay, waiting until the feast would benefit them both. Malcolm could honestly say he knew nothing about her identity, and he couldn't berate her in Lord Talbot's presence.

Changing course, she headed toward the kitchens. Jocelyn had a feast to attend ... and an inheritance to claim.

CHAPTER 17

Jocelyn stepped into the hot, fragrant room, where servants scurried about like ants. Nelda stirred a pot set among the coals of a fire. "Elizabeth, make sure the bread is rising! Anne, don't cut the vegetables too thin." Her orders sent servants into frantic motion.

'Twould not be easy gaining Nelda's ear, but she was Jocelyn's best hope. Steeling her nerves, she shuffled through the busy workers and stood by the cook.

"What do you need, squire?" Nelda glanced across the room and frowned. "Nay! Do not use those greens. Use the ones picked this morning." She turned back to Jocelyn. "You need something?"

"Nelda, I know you are fraught with the task of cooking the celebration feast, but could I have a moment alone with you?"

"Can't you see how busy I am, lad?"

"I must confess something of importance, and I need your help." Jocelyn laid her hand on Nelda's arm. "I wouldn't ask unless 'twas urgent."

Nelda heaved a sigh and turned to Jocelyn. "What is on your mind?"

"Can we go to the cellarium for privacy?"

"Aye, but you must hurry. I can't leave these helpers for long." She exited the kitchen through the side door and Jocelyn followed. Grabbing a torch from the sconce in the wall, Nelda opened a door a few paces down the hall. Jocelyn went in after her and closed the door. Cool air hit her, a welcome relief from the heat of the kitchen. Baskets of food and spices lined the shelves of the storeroom, filling the air with a pungent, earthy aroma.

"Speak your mind, lad." Nelda lifted the torch high.

"I am not a lad. I am Jocelyn, daughter of Lord Ashburne." She breathed in deep and exhaled. It felt good to speak the truth.

"Nay, Jocelyn died more than a year past."

"'Twas a lie, for I have been at Lomkirk Abbey these past four years."

Nelda drew closer, peering at Jocelyn's face in the flickering light of the torch. Jocelyn pulled the binding from her hair, letting it spill to her shoulders. Nelda reached out and fingered the curls, shaking her head. "Can it be?"

"If you need proof, I recall the sweet cakes you baked for me before I left for the abbey. You made extra for me to take on my journey."

"Sweet Lord above!" Nelda grabbed Jocelyn with her free hand, pulling her into a tight embrace. Jocelyn wrapped her arms around Nelda's ample waist, relishing the warm reception.

Though she would have enjoyed receiving all of the comfort Nelda had to offer, Jocelyn stepped back. "I know 'tis a shock, but someone has been conspiring to keep me from Ramslea, and I haven't been able to determine who. I thought to keep in disguise while I unravel the mystery, but I've been unsuccessful. I have my suspicions, but they are just that."

"But you are heir to Ramslea! You cannot let Helen claim it."

"Aye, 'tis why I need your aid. Can you help me obtain a gown for tonight? I know 'tis only two hours away and you are busy. I also need to bathe in private somewhere before I present myself to Lord Talbot."

Nelda nodded, a grin spreading across her face. "I imagine the seamstress might have some extra gowns stashed away. As for a bath, the only rooms unoccupied would be in the far tower. I can have a tub sent up and filled with water. I'll bribe one of the kitchen lads to keep his mouth shut." Nelda chuckled. "Sweet cakes for a month should do the trick."

"I should say so." Jocelyn smiled and hugged Nelda once more.

Enveloped within her warm embrace, Jocelyn finally enjoyed the sense of coming home. "Thank you for everything."

"'Tis happy I am to know you are alive and well." Nelda pulled back. "Now we have work to do."

They left the cellarium and returned into the kitchen, where Nelda resumed command. "We've no time to spare. Let's keep working."

Jocelyn went out the back door and stood, hands on hips, gazing across the gardens. Her chest tightened at the emotions flooding through her. Tonight, all would be revealed. She'd be Lady Jocelyn, mistress of Ramslea, future wife of Malcolm. Not a mistress, but a wife. Malcolm should be pleased with the prospect. She'd create a home and family full of joy and love. 'Twas all she had ever wanted.

The sun had dropped in the western sky, so Jocelyn hurried through the bailey to attend her duties before she readied for the evening. She checked on Horse, then she hurried to Malcolm's tent and gathered his clothes for the feast. Garments in hand, she returned to the healer's hut and knocked. The healer opened the door and put a finger to her lips.

"Is Sir Malcolm asleep? I have clothes for him." Jocelyn walked in.

"He sleeps still."

Jocelyn peeked into the back room. Malcolm lay upon the bed snoring softly. Returning to the main area, she laid Malcolm's clothes on the table.

"Do you want me to awaken him for the feast?" The old woman went to her chair by the fire.

"Nay. If he sleeps through feast, then his body must need the rest. But if he awakens and wants to go, you will not be able to stop him."

"Aye, dearie. I shall see to him." She held out her wrinkled hands to the fire. "Don't fret. All will turn out as it should."

Jocelyn smiled. Though the healer uttered strange things at

times, she carried an air of contagious peace. They were the very words Jocelyn needed to hear.

All will turn out as it should.

"Thank you." Jocelyn opened the door, then turned back toward the healer. "Did Sir Rolland come to you for service?"

"Aye, he came in search of salve for the pain in his shoulder."

So Rolland was on his feet. Would he attend the celebration?

With no time to worry about Sir Rolland's appearance, Jocelyn made her way through the bailey and entered the hall. Servants threw fresh rushes and herbs on the floor while others banked the fires. She sneaked down the hallway toward the back stairs leading up the tower.

Though the torches barely lit the stairway, Jocelyn knew the way, climbing upward until she reached her room. She pushed against the wooden door, its creak echoing through the quietness of the empty tower. Dusky evening light filtered through the slits around the circular room. A torch thrust from the sconce by the door gave more light to the dim room. A tub filled with water sat near the wall to the right, with a towel and soap on the floor next to it. A gown hung over a nearby chair, along with a linen chemise and leather shoes.

Jocelyn entered the room, shut the door, and picked up the gown. Made of light-blue wool, dark-blue thread embroidered the neckline and hem. 'Twas lovely. She held it up to her body and smiled, ready to be in beautiful clothes again. She carefully laid the gown back on the chair lest her dirty hands leave a stain.

Jocelyn stuck a finger in the bath, pleased at its warmth. She had expected a cold bath since she had taken so long checking on Horse and Malcolm. Eager to enjoy a warm soak, she undressed, grabbed the soap, and climbed in. Scrubbing her skin and scalp, she reveled in the luxurious feel of a bath. Faith, 'twas good to feel clean.

After toweling dry, she donned the chemise and then the gown. She ran her hands over the soft fabric. The dress hung loosely around the waist but fit her perfectly through the shoulders, as well as the length. The shoes pinched, but she could endure the discomfort to reclaim her birthright.

Without the aid of a brush, Jocelyn combed her hair with her fingers as she walked to a window and looked out across Ramslea. From this vantage point, she could see much of the estate. The orange sun in the west cast a fiery glow along the battlements. Birds circled overhead, squawking as they prepared to roost for the night. Knights and ladies wove throughout the bailey visiting before the feast.

On the far side of the bailey sat the chapel. She hadn't stepped foot inside since arriving home. She'd been too busy. 'Twas something she would remedy soon enough. She and Malcolm would be married there tomorrow.

Married to a man she loved. It was something she longed for, but never had she imagined it turning out this way. She knew Malcolm cared for her—at least he desired her—but did he love her? How could he? He didn't really know her, not the real Jocelyn.

Truth be told, she didn't know him either. They hadn't discussed faith in God or things of true importance. If he thought her mistress material, then how strong could his faith be? She sighed.

Lord, thank you for seeing me home and giving me a man to love. Show me how to be a wife of noble character that I might be a light for him.

As the reality of what she was about to do descended upon her, Jocelyn fell to her knees and prayed for Malcolm, for herself, and for peace in remembering God was in control.

Malcolm threw back the covers and groaned as he sat up. The pale light from the window told him nightfall was near. "Jack!" Swinging his legs over the side of the bed, Malcolm caught his breath. By the saints, his strength had left him.

While used to the sharp pain across his chest, not having his strength was something altogether untoward. Truth be told, he didn't hurt as he ought to given all that had transpired. Mayhap he'd only needed a good nap. He stood, shaky on his feet, and made his way to the door.

"Och, dearie, you've a mind to be up and about," the healer croaked as she hung fresh herbs in front of the fire.

"Aye. I am quite refreshed."

"'Tis what you needed most, my lord. You will need your strength for what is ahead. Your squire brought you clothes." She hobbled to the table and picked up a stack of folded clothing. "You cannot be seen about the castle in your bloodied ones, can you?" She chuckled as if she had spoken a most humorous jest.

Malcolm took the garments. "Where is my squire?"

"I know not."

Malcolm frowned as he returned to the other room to change. Why wasn't Jack hovering over him, tending to his every need? Surely she didn't fault him for wanting to keep her close. He sighed. Couldn't she see what they felt for one another shouldn't be denied? Keeping Jack as his mistress was not ideal, but he couldn't bear to let her go. He'd grown accustomed to her presence, relished her ire, loved her smile. If only the prize included Jack instead of Helen.

What if he approached Lord Talbot about marrying another instead of Helen? The king could find a lord to marry her, and Malcolm would be free to marry Jack. She wasn't a commoner, so that was in his favor.

Aye, he would bend Talbot's ear this eve and hope for the best. The worst he could do was say nay.

Once dressed, Malcolm entered the healer's workroom. "Did Jack say where he was going?"

"Nay, my lord. You will find him soon enough. We always discover our heart's quest."

Malcolm frowned. Odd woman. Thanking her, he left to find Jack. How strange that no one, not even his betrothed, had come to visit him. He was the new Lord of Ramslea, was he not?

Malcolm stalked through the emptying field toward his tent. Many had been taken down as their inhabitants made ready to depart for home. He opened the flap and entered, but Jack wasn't there.

Mayhap she sought shelter in the keep or had found new friends to converse with. Neither idea sounded wise, yet Jack hadn't shown good judgment in the past. Malcolm didn't expect otherwise now.

Leaving the tent, he entered the castle gates and went into the bailey. Several young men stood by the blacksmith's stall comparing knives. Malcolm raised a hand to them. "Have you seen my squire, Jack? Scrawny lad?" The men shook their heads before turning back to their comparisons.

Malcolm neared the keep. Hopefully, Jack was ensconced in the kitchen, eating her fill. Out of sight and out of trouble.

As he entered the great hall, all eyes turned toward him, and the room grew silent. One by one, people stood, clapping. Soon the room filled with cheers. Malcolm paused and raised a hand. By the saints, he was Lord of Ramslea.

Sucking in a breath, he made his way to Lady Helen, who stood before the great fireplace. The flames cast an orange glow around her. Several knights surrounded her. Never taking her eyes off him, she laughed at something one of them whispered in her ear.

The light of the fire accentuated her curves in the rusty-hued gown she wore. Stopping before her, he bowed. He took the hand offered to him, kissing her fingers and smiling.

"My lord." Pulling her hand from his, she sat in a chair near the fireplace, facing away from him.

Malcolm pulled a chair next to hers. "I thought you might come to see me this afternoon at the healer's hut." He studied her profile for a sign of emotion, but her stony countenance held no clue to her feelings.

"I must confess, I dislike the healer and her quaint abode. I heard your wound was not mortal and thought to let you rest without interference."

"I appreciate your concern." Malcolm strove to keep the sarcasm from his voice. He looked around the hall, hoping to catch a glimpse of Jack. Where was she?

"Are you looking for someone, my lord?"

"Aye. My squire. He seems to have disappeared. Most likely into some mischief."

"As boys are wont to do." Helen glanced at the door across the hall. "I see Lord Talbot has arrived."

Malcolm stood, extending his arm to Helen. "Shall we join him for dinner, my lady?"

She placed her hand on his arm, accompanying him to the head table.

"Sir Malcolm and Lady Helen, the soon-to-be husband and wife. Come sit to my right." Lord Talbot smiled, lifting a goblet of wine to his lips.

Malcolm bowed while Helen sank into a low curtsy. He pulled out her chair for her. When she was situated, he sat beside Talbot.

Servants circulated the hall delivering goblets of wine to the guests. Once all had been served, Lord Talbot stood.

"In conclusion of the tournament, I congratulate Sir Malcolm Castillon of Berkham on winning the melee and the joust. As winner, I bestow on him the title of Baron, Lord of Ramslea. At noon on the morrow, Lord Malcolm will wed Lady Helen of Ramslea."

Malcolm glanced at Helen. She gave him a slight smile. At least she wasn't frowning. 'Twas a good sign. What would her thoughts be when he pleaded with Talbot to marry another? But now was not the time. After the feast.

Lord Talbot reached for his goblet and held it high. "Let us drink in celebration of Lord Malcolm and his new lady."

The guests raised their goblets and cheered. Malcolm lifted his drink and grinned. Lord Malcolm, a baron by order of the justiciar. His gaze traveled over the hall, taking in the crowd but not seeing the one face that mattered. He shook off his disappointment and brought the goblet to his lips.

A commotion drew everyone's attention.

Helen gaped. "Nay." Her face blanched white as she clutched her throat with one hand.

What had frightened her? He stood, his chair scraping across the floor as he followed her gaze across the hall.

Inside the door stood a woman dressed in blue. Familiar dark curls draped to her shoulders. Even with the fading bruise across her cheek, nothing hid the beauty of her countenance—the face of his squire.

Jack walked toward him, the gown flowing behind her. *What was going on?* Silently he urged her to turn around and walk out.

His little man Jack revealed herself as the beautiful Jacqueline. *But why?*

CHAPTER 18

Jocelyn's pulse raced as she walked into the great hall. She wended her way through the tables toward Lord Talbot. Her legs quaked, but she pressed on. Malcolm shook his head, but she planted one foot in front of the other. 'Twas for the best—for them both.

Jocelyn glanced at Helen, her face whiter than the first blanket of snow. 'Twould be interesting to see what transpired once the truth came out. Stopping a few paces away from Lord Talbot, Jocelyn sank into a curtsy, her eyes to the floor.

"Who do we have here?"

Jocelyn looked up to the justiciar, who smiled and motioned for her to stand. She rose and took a deep breath. "My lord, I am Jocelyn Ashburne of Ramslea." She let her gaze drift to Malcolm. His lips parted and brow furrowed, but he closed his mouth and remained silent. Except for the clench of his jaw, he stood still as stone. After a moment, he dropped his gaze and sat, taking a drink from his goblet.

She should have swallowed her anger and told him the truth earlier. *Lord, forgive me.*

"Jocelyn is dead. Is that not so, Lady Helen?" Lord Talbot looked to Helen.

"Aye, a year past." Helen turned to the justiciar, her back straight and hands in her lap. "This is not Ashburne's daughter."

"She's the very image of Lord Ashburne's first wife!" A voice called from across the hall. The guests began talking over one another.

"Cease!" Lord Talbot raised his hand, waiting for the crowd to quiet, then he addressed Jocelyn. "I would hear your tale."

She clasped her hands before her, lifting a silent prayer for words. "I was sent to Lomkirk Abbey four years ago after my father married Lady Helen. 'Twas late to go for an education, but I was told 'twould benefit my chatelaine duties once I married. After three years, I begged to come home, but received no more letters from Father."

"Had he written to you earlier whilst you were away?" Lord Talbot emptied his goblet and motioned a servant to bring more wine.

"Not often, but he did write. Up until a year ago. It was then that the abbess pressured me to take my vows. I did not feel called to the church and said as much. It wasn't long after that I overheard the abbess talking to a messenger. Someone was blackmailing her to have me take my vows or marry me off to any man willing to pay coin for a wife. That is when I escaped and came to Ramslea."

"Why did you not confront the abbess?"

"She was being blackmailed. She would not have answered my questions truthfully. Nor would she have let me return home. I had to escape and learn the cause of my father's silence." Jocelyn snuck a peek at Helen, who sat back in her chair, her face now flushed.

"How did you get to Ramslea? Did you have an escort?"

"I disguised myself as a boy but was accosted the first day and saved by Lord Malcolm." The guests once again murmured amongst themselves.

"Truly?" Lord Talbot turned to Malcolm, his brows raised. "You traveled with a woman the whole trip?"

"I did not know she was a woman, dressed as she was." Malcolm's lips pressed together. "She is—was—my squire."

"Your squire?" Lord Talbot threw back his head and laughed. "I find it hard to believe you did not discover her gender."

Malcolm shrugged. "She's been at the castle these past three days, and no one discovered her secret. Not even you, my lord."

Lord Talbot chuckled. "'Tis true, though I did wonder at your choosing such a scrawny squire."

Malcolm quirked a corner of his lip. "Aye, she wasn't much of a squire."

Jocelyn held her tongue. In the presence of the king's justiciar, she would mind her manners.

"I do find it hard to believe you didn't suspect her secret."

Malcolm reddened underneath his tanned skin. "Two days into our journey she was injured, and I discovered her gender then."

"You did knowingly travel with a woman?"

"Aye." Malcolm turned and looked at Jocelyn, his gaze unreadable. "She told me she was running away from a forced marriage and wanted to find work as a maid at Ramslea." He looked at the justiciar. "'Tis my chivalrous duty to aid those in need."

The king grunted and turned back to Jocelyn. "You concur with Sir Malcolm's statement?"

Jocelyn nodded. "I agreed to squire Sir Malcolm for the tournament in exchange for safe passage to Ramslea."

"Why did you not reveal yourself once at Ramslea?"

Jocelyn hesitated, wondering how much to share. "I considered it but thought I could gain more information in disguise. I didn't know why my father hadn't written, and I suspected 'twas someone here at Ramslea who was blackmailing the abbess. I didn't think anyone would be forthcoming to Ramslea's heir."

"Were you successful in obtaining information?"

"I was not. While I had a conversation with a maid and the cook, I was too busy squiring to ferret out the information I wanted."

The crowd twittered with laughter and Jocelyn glanced at Malcolm. Still no smile, no joy at her revelation. Jocelyn's heart sank, wishing she could pull him aside, tell him she loved him and how good their life would be as husband and wife.

"What made you come forward now?"

Not wanting to share her heart with the whole of Ramslea, she offered another truth instead. "I … I couldn't let Malcolm marry the wrong woman. Even though I did not discover the abbess's blackmailer, I couldn't stay hidden. I am the heir."

Lord Talbot steepled his fingers and pursed his lips. Stillness filled the hall. Jocelyn looked from the justiciar to Malcolm to Helen. All silent. All solemn.

"You have no proof of your parentage?"

"Nay. To travel light, I left my personal belongings at the abbey. I have a small portrait of my parents but didn't want to risk damaging it on the journey."

"Lady Helen says you are not Jocelyn. How can you prove otherwise?"

Helen raised an eyebrow, a challenge in her gaze. She had to be involved in this mess.

Jocelyn had no physical proof of her own identity, only the testimony of those who remembered her. "Ramslea's cook, Nelda, will remember me."

"And I," a voice called.

"Come forward." Lord Talbot motioned the caller forward.

The man who spoke up stood by Jocelyn and bowed before Lord Talbot.

"State your name and how you know this to be Ashburne's heir."

"I am Sir John Williamson, knight to Lord Cottilde. I squired under Lord Ashburne and knew his lady when Jocelyn was only a small lass." He gestured toward Jocelyn. "Anyone who knew the Lady Ashburne can see this woman here is the very image of her mother."

Lord Talbot nodded. "Thank you. You are free to go." He motioned to Jocelyn. "Face the guests." He waited while Jocelyn turned, then addressed the room. "If you recognize this woman as being Jocelyn, daughter of Lord and Lady Ashburne, please rise."

One by one, men and women stood, twenty in all. Jocelyn's chin quivered, grateful so many people knew her mother and could see the resemblance.

"You all may be seated."

Jocelyn turned back to Lord Talbot, hope surging through her.

"Many seem to think you Ashburne's heir." Lord Talbot turned to Helen. "Are you sure about this not being Jocelyn?"

Helen stared at Jocelyn. She tilted her head, squinting. "I can see how others might think she is Jocelyn. The eyes, the mouth. But what about the reports of her death? Who would falsify such a report?"

Who, indeed? Jocelyn could think of only one person with motive to do so, but she had no proof.

Lord Talbot frowned. "I wonder the same thing." He folded his arms across his chest, silent for a long moment. The crowd's whispers tapered off. "I only met the late Lady Ashburne once, but from what I remember, I can see her face in yours. I concur with the testimony given and those who vouched for your identity. You are Jocelyn, daughter of Lord Ashburne."

The guests cheered, coming to their feet. Jocelyn placed a hand over her heart, bowing her head to Lord Talbot. Then she looked at Malcolm, who remained stone-faced in light of the declaration. Would that he could see the possibilities along their new path. Surely time would heal him of his anger.

As for Helen, what did the future hold? Her pinched face reflected no joy at Lord Talbot's words. Jocelyn couldn't fault her, as her life had just been turned upside down. Of course, 'twas likely due to her own scheming.

Lord Talbot addressed Malcolm. "With Lady Jocelyn's return, she will now be your bride. The wedding will take place on the morrow."

Malcolm nodded. "As you say, my lord." His gaze traveled the hall, and she sensed his … reluctance? Anger? Pain? What was going through his mind?

Lord Talbot looked at Helen. "As for you, Lady Helen, I am sorry for this upheaval. But I will speak to the king and find you a husband. One of good standing and rank. You shall remain at Ramslea until one is found."

Helen's face relaxed. "Thank you, my lord. You are too generous."

Though not thrilled with the news of Helen's continued presence at Ramslea, 'twould give Jocelyn the time to determine Helen's involvement in the plot against her.

Lord Talbot nodded at Jocelyn "As for the strange actions against you—the blackmail and your supposed death—I shall begin an investigation into the matter."

"Thank you." She breathed deeply, grateful to have help.

"Now come, sit and eat. Our food is getting cold." He turned to Helen. "Lady Helen, come sit to my left while Lady Jocelyn sits beside her intended."

Helen stiffened, but rose and sat by the justiciar. Jocelyn walked around the table and slid into the chair beside Malcolm. He kept his gaze averted, picking a piece of meat from the trencher.

"Malcolm," she whispered. He watched the guests before him as he continued eating. She placed a hand on his arm, and he tensed. "Please understand—"

"We shall discuss this later." He pulled his arm away, grabbing his goblet and taking a long drink.

She'd expected his anger, but his dismissive attitude stung. How daft she was to think he would be overjoyed, even relieved, at discovering her identity.

They ate the rest of their meal cordially, listening to Lord Talbot and answering his questions. Did others notice Malcolm's indifference toward her? 'Twould be difficult not to.

Lord Talbot pushed back from the table. "Let the musicians play, and the dancing commence."

Servants cleared the tables, pushing them against the walls. Musicians readied themselves in the back of the hall and then struck up a cheerful tune.

Lord Talbot turned to Helen. "Partner with me in the dance." He rose and held out his hand. She took it, and they walked around the table toward the open area. He glanced at Malcolm. "Lead your new lady to dance."

Malcolm looked at Jocelyn, and her heart stuttered, his eyes intense. Would he defy Lord Talbot? His gaze traveled over her face, then he stood, extending his hand.

Jocelyn placed her fingers against his palm, its warmth seeping into her, sojourning through her limbs as he led her to the edge of the hall. They joined those already dancing. Malcolm moved through the steps keeping his gaze above her head. 'Twas an active dance and much laughter ensued. But not from Malcolm. His jaw continued to clench, and his grip tightened when they occasioned to touch in passing.

The dance ended, and another set formed while the musicians played a slower tune. Malcolm stood across from Jocelyn as two lines formed. His hands clenched at his sides, then released, splaying his fingers as if releasing the pent-up stress of the evening. All caused by her doing.

Would he—could he—forgive her? *Lord, ease his heart. Let him be receptive to my pleas for forgiveness.* Determination filling her, she vowed to earn his trust once more. She didn't know how, but God would show her the way.

CHAPTER 19

Malcolm stood across from Jocelyn waiting for the dance to begin. Her gown clung to her curves, the loose gold belt accentuating her small waist. The bruising on her cheek had faded to a pale yellow while her dark hair gleamed, the large curls hitting her shoulders in abandon.

She was his, along with the land. And she was a liar, her deceit inducing all manner of turmoil within his chest. After the betrayal of his betrothed with his brother seven years past, he had vowed never to align himself with duplicitous women. In fact, he had assumed he'd never marry. No wife or children meant peace and quiet.

While gaining Ramslea necessitated marriage, his disappointment in Jocelyn's mendacious actions rivaled his anger at her unwillingness to trust him. Had he not proven himself trustworthy?

The music began, and he moved toward her, his hand sliding around her waist as he twirled her around. They parted, circled the dancers to their right, then came back together. Palm to palm they walked in a circle, their faces but a breath apart. His intention to not look at her all but forgotten in the heady closeness of her body. Her lips parted, and her chest rose, straining against the snug fabric.

By the saints, she would be his undoing. A duplicitous temptation, indeed.

They parted, circling the dancers on their left, then drawing close once more.

"I am sorry," said Jocelyn, her hand fluttering in his during the pass.

"Save your explanations until later." His words rattled harsh even to his own ears. As they promenaded down the middle of the two lines, her hand on his arm, he tried to soften his response. "I would hear your tale." He looked into her misty eyes. "Your truthful tale."

They stepped in time to the music, coming to face one another across the lines. The song ended, and he bowed while she curtsied. Several men gathered around Jocelyn vying for a dance. Malcolm left her to her admirers and sat back at the head table, gulping down a swallow of wine.

What should have been the biggest celebration of his life had soured, leaving him in a foul mood. Watching Ja—*Jocelyn*—dance with others, her smile bestowed on her partners, only deepened his anger. He resented her for taking the joy out of his night.

Enough! He set down his empty cup and went to his bride. "Gentlemen, I request the presence of my lady." The men nodded. Malcolm extended his hand to Jocelyn. She hesitated several long heartbeats, then put her hand in his. He led her toward the hall door.

"Are we not going to dance?" She hurried, trying to keep in step with him.

"Nay, I shall hear your tale." A servant opened the door, and they walked out to the bailey. A stiff breeze cooled Malcolm's heated body, calming his nerves with every step.

Jocelyn jogged beside him, one hand struggling to keep her skirts out of the way, as he strode toward the stairway leading to the parapet. 'Twould be quiet there, with only a few posted guards around the castle walls.

The stairs rose beside the guardhouse near the castle gate. With no railing overlooking the bailey, Jocelyn kept close to the outer wall as he led her upward.

"My lord and lady." A guard met them at the top of the stairs and bowed.

"Carry on. We shall walk the parapet."

Malcolm led Jocelyn around the wide path of the battlement. The half-moon in the sky and the torches below gave light to life within the castle walls. A few souls walked the grounds. Some retired to their tents outside the castle, some closed the doors to their shops, and some merely strolled the grounds enjoying the company of others.

Stopping a good way from the guard, Malcolm released Jocelyn's hand. He leaned against the wall and crossed his arms. "I want to know why you did not tell me the truth."

The wind blew a curl across Jocelyn's face, and she tucked it behind her ear. "'Tis complicated."

"I am not simpleminded."

"Nay, that you are not, but the reasons I have sound daft even to my ears."

"I would hear them regardless."

She clasped her hands together and sighed. "When you found out I was a woman, I didn't tell you who I was because I would have slowed you down as you would have been obligated to find a chaperone. I also feared you might leave me at a village and have my father send an entourage for me."

"You were the daft nun those men were looking for!" Malcolm uncrossed his arms and pushed away from the wall.

"Aye, that too." Jocelyn pushed back her shoulders. "I was being hunted."

"I would have avoided those men had I known." He would have protected her better.

"And leave that poor maid on the road in their hands? I think not." Jocelyn smiled, shaking her head.

"True, but—"

"I was going to reveal myself to my father, but when I learned of his death, I decided to stay in disguise and find out who was behind all my trouble. The more I've learned, the more I suspect Helen may be involved."

"Helen? Surely not." While Helen had no love of him, he did

not think her capable of blackmail, much less deceiving an entire castle about Jocelyn's death.

"Who else would have motive? 'Twas her idea for me to go to Lomkirk. Seems likely she would want to keep me there." A frown furrowed her forehead. "Though what she holds over the abbess, I cannot fathom."

"But the news of your death came a year ago. If what you say is true, then she planned for you to be away forever." Malcolm grew uneasy, Jocelyn's suspicions dousing his anger over her deception.

"Aye, it seems she wanted my father to herself." Jocelyn's eyes saddened.

Malcolm remembered gossip from the bath house. "I heard tales that Helen sought the attention of other men. If she loved your father, would she have wooed them under his nose?"

Jocelyn bit her thumbnail, then gasped. "What if she tired of my father and killed him?"

"Nay, he died a slow sickness." Malcolm did not believe Helen capable of such a thing.

"Poison could do that over time." Jocelyn put a hand to her temple and began to pace in front of him. He admired her keen observations but needed to put a stop to her vivid imagination.

"Jack—Jocelyn—you cannot think Helen guilty of such a thing. And for what? A new husband? Ramslea itself?"

Jocelyn stopped and put her hands on her hips. "*You* were willing to marry for such a land."

Malcolm leaned against the wall. She spoke truth. "Aye, but murder?" He shook his head. "I can believe she wanted your father to herself, but murder? Nay."

"What if I can find proof?"

Malcolm didn't respond. His head still ached from finding out Jack was Jocelyn. He didn't want to think about the possibility of a murderer within the castle. He pushed away from the wall and stood in front of Jocelyn. Other matters required his immediate attention. "Why did you not trust me with your secret?" He spoke low, almost a whisper.

She stepped back, but he caught her, both hands holding her at the waist. She sucked in a breath. Her eyes grew wide, her gaze searching his.

"Why, Jocelyn?"

She slowly shook her head. "I ... I didn't know you to be trustworthy."

He tightened his grip on her waist, pulling her closer. She pushed against him, trying to keep distance between them.

"Didn't I prove myself by saving you, not once, but twice? I let you travel with me to keep you safe. I kept up your ruse at Ramslea while surrounded by nobility, even the justiciar. Surely that makes me worthy of your secret."

Jocelyn lifted the corner of her mouth in a half smile. "I know it does not make sense. My quest for the truth blinded me. So much time had passed since I'd started lying. I knew you would be angry."

"I am angry." His blood boiled thinking about what could have been had she told the truth. Knowing she was part of the prize would have made winning so much sweeter. And he wouldn't have insulted her by suggesting she become his mistress. His anger simmered as he gripped her tighter.

"Malcolm, I am sorry. Please forgive me," she whispered, her face close to his.

Forgive her? Forgiving her would mean releasing his anger. Accepting her deceit. Trusting her. He took in her eyes glistening with unshed tears, her full lips waiting for his assault. By the saints! She'd deceived him twice. How could he trust her?

He let go of her waist and stepped away. She stumbled backward, pressing a hand to her heaving chest. Nay, he couldn't forgive her.

"I am sorry for all that has happened to you, but you fooled me twice." He shook his head. "I cannot trust you." He walked away, Jocelyn's footsteps padding behind him.

"Malcolm, wait!"

He reached the stairs and the guard at his post. "See the Lady Jocelyn back to the hall."

"Aye, m'lord."

He descended the stairs but walked away from the hall and across the bailey. He had to clear his head and let his blood cool. His body heated with the emotions coursing through him. From anger to shock, disappoint to desire, his mind was so jumbled he knew not what to think.

Malcolm dragged his feet as if walking through marshland, his circumstances sucking him down into chaos, uncertainty, and pain. He acknowledged those who greeted him, yet kept trudging along not knowing his destination. Not caring.

He ran his hands through his hair. He'd marry Jocelyn on the morrow. A woman he desired but couldn't trust. While 'twasn't the same kind of betrayal as his previously betrothed, the lies Jocelyn told cut deep.

He rounded the keep, revealing the stone chapel further down the bailey. A wooden steeple adorned the top of the steep wooden roof. He plodded toward it, pausing on the front step. It had been years since he'd been near a chapel, much less inside one. But his mother found comfort in God's house. Perhaps he would as well.

Malcolm opened the door and stepped inside. Torches on either side of the doorway gave light to the room. A wide aisle separated rows of benches. Tapestries stitched with every color of the rainbow told the story of the wonders of heaven as they hung along each wall. The front of the chapel housed a wooden statue of Jesus on the cross that reached almost to the ceiling. Tables covered with burning candles sat on either side of the statue, giving it an unearthly glow. He moved forward, his footsteps echoing against the stone.

An air of reverence filled the place touching even Malcolm, a heathen, deep in his soul. Stained-glass windows set high in the walls would no doubt scatter a collage of color across the room on a sunny day.

Stopping halfway down the aisle, Malcolm sat on a bench and bowed his head, breathing deeply.

Peace filled this place. 'Twas as if he could reach out and grab a wisp of solitude, easing both body and soul. His troubles seemed to melt away, insignificant in the presence of such tranquility.

His mother had been a woman of faith, yet it had not spared her the pain and suffering of her marriage. Her devotion did not keep her from wasting away under his father's verbal abuse. Malcolm had no use for a God who didn't protect His own. He hadn't entered a chapel since her passing.

The door to the left of the candles opened and the priest entered, his long black robe rustling in the silence. A smile bloomed across his wrinkled face. "Good evening, my lord. May I be of service to you?"

"Nay, Father." Malcolm ran his hands through his hair. "I am not sure why I came. I ... it has been a long while since ..." He tapered off, not wanting to offend the priest.

The priest took a seat beside Malcolm. "Sometimes God draws us, and we do not understand why. 'Tis good to come and be near. To sit. To listen. To be at rest in His presence."

Malcolm nodded, knowing full well the truth of the priest's words. The tangible peace had already eased his troubled soul.

Several moments passed, silence filling the space between them. Would the priest have advice on how to proceed with Jocelyn? On how to marry someone he didn't trust?

"Father, might I ask you for advice?"

"I may not have the answers you want to hear."

"I am to marry Lady Jocelyn tomorrow."

"Aye, I heard such news."

"I have been deceived once before by my betrothed. She lied about intimacies with my brother. How can I trust Jocelyn when she has lied to me twice already?" Malcolm slumped over and rested his elbows on his knees, the reality of his situation weighing on him.

"It seems to me God has drawn the two of you together for a reason. The circumstances from beginning to end have kept you bound in such a way that hints of a destiny designed by Him." The priest laid a hand on Malcolm's shoulder. "Do you love Jocelyn?"

Malcolm rubbed his hands over his face and stood. "In truth, I do not know. What is love?" He walked to the window and touched the colorful panes of glass. "She makes me daft. I enjoy sparring with her and seeing her riled. I like her smile and laughter. I want to protect her and keep her safe, yet she tries my patience daily and finds trouble wherever she goes. She is so beautiful she fair takes my breath away." He turned to the priest. "Is that love?"

"It rings of love to me."

"But how can I love her, if I don't trust her?"

"Do not fear what God is doing, my lord. Marry her. In time she will earn your trust."

Malcolm nodded as he pondered the priest's words. Aye, time was on his side. He could keep his distance while she proved herself trustworthy. He wasn't sure what that looked like, but surely he would feel when he was ready to trust again. "Thank you, Father. You have been most helpful." Malcolm bowed before turning to go. When he reached the door, he glanced back. "I suppose I shall see you on the morrow. With my bride."

Malcolm left the chapel and headed for the hall. Talking with the priest had eased his mind. In fact, the chapel itself had given him a sense of tranquility. Mayhap attending services regularly would help him learn more about the God who gave the peace he desperately needed. 'Twould also be a good beginning for Jocelyn and him as they built a family together.

Malcolm stopped in his tracks.

A family. 'Twould be his right as husband, but did he want to bed a liar? He had never considered siring a passel of babes. Surprisingly, he rather looked forward to the idea.

By the saints, it had been a most tiresome day. What he needed was a good night's sleep. As lord of Ramslea, he wouldn't have to sleep in a tent, would he? But with the justiciar still present, the lord's bedchambers would be occupied.

Malcolm entered the hall. Jocelyn sat by the fire with Lord Talbot. Malcolm approached them, glancing about the hall for Helen. She danced with one of the neighboring knights.

"Lord Malcolm, I've been conversing with your bride." Lord Talbot grinned. "She is quite an interesting woman."

"Aye, I've much to learn, I'm sure." Malcolm raised a brow. Her smile faltered.

"Now that you have returned, I shall take my leave and retire for the night." As Lord Talbot rose, several of his guards came up behind him.

Malcolm cleared his throat. "My lord, about accommodations—"

"Of course, Lady Jocelyn cannot stay in a tent, can she?" Lord Talbot chuckled. "I am in the lord's chamber, which you shall both have once I leave Ramslea. Several barons left after the joust, so you may take their rooms."

"Thank you, my lord." Malcolm waited until Lord Talbot disappeared through the doorway, then turned to Jocelyn. Darkness shadowed under her eyes. "Are you ready to retire?"

She rose from her chair. "I am."

He held out his arm, and she looked at him, her gaze questioning. "I thought you were angry with me. Couldn't trust me were the words you used."

He dropped his arm. "I am angry, and trust is an issue. But I was rude earlier, and I apologize for how I left you."

Jocelyn lifted her lips in a small smile. "Apology accepted. Now if you will excuse me, I am weary and would like to find a place to sleep." She stepped around him and walked toward the stairway in the far back corner of the hall. Malcolm followed her.

A servant stood at the base of the stairs. Jocelyn drew near to the lad. "Could you show me to an available room for the night?" Though she walked gracefully, her shoulders drooped. Malcolm fought the urge to whisk her into his arms and carry her up the stairs.

The servant bowed. "Aye, m'lady. Follow me."

Malcolm followed them up the stairs and down the dark hallway. He'd not yet been on the upper floors of the keep. The intricate masonry of the walls and the sturdy wood floors impressed him. 'Twas better constructed than his father's keep.

The servant stopped at an open doorway near the end of the hall. "Will this do for the night, m'lady?"

"Aye, thank you."

"Your room is across the hall, m'lord. I will send someone to bank the fires." The lad bobbed his head before hurrying back down the hall.

Jocelyn turned to Malcolm. Her eyes glistened in the torchlight. He wanted to touch the creamy skin of her cheek. He ached to pull her into his arms and kiss her full lips.

"Did you need something more, my lord?"

Hearing her say *my lord* flipped his heart like a fish on a dry bank. She referred to him as her lord, as she was his lady.

He didn't want his heart reacting to such things. By the saints, he didn't trust her!

He pushed his shoulders back. "Nay, I do not. Rest well." He turned his back to her, entering his room without a backward glance. Shutting the door, he leaned against it as he rubbed his hands over his face.

Saints, he desired his bride. 'Twould be difficult to put distance between them while he learned to trust her.

CHAPTER 20

Jocelyn lounged in the large wooden tub in the middle of her room. A servant girl poured more hot water into the bath. Steam rose around them. Jocelyn had slept well on the soft mattress, then a servant banked the fire before dawn. She relished waking up warm.

Though she'd bathed yesterday, today was her wedding day. She wanted to start her new life fresh and clean. Leaning against the tub, she let the warm water relax her, wishing it could settle her anxious heart. Though her muscles loosened, her mind churned with all the happenings of the previous day.

Jocelyn hugged her knees and closed her eyes. Her wedding would take place soon—and her groom still held on to his anger. He had not appeared at breakfast. She'd been told he'd foregone eating in favor of swordplay, with no care to his wound. Swordplay on his wedding day.

Despite his absence, she resolved to be strong. In time, she'd earn his trust and, ultimately, his love. For now, she would entrust to him her heart and body, praying 'twould be enough to sustain her. If not, perhaps God would bless her with children to love her in return.

She heaved a sigh.

The water had cooled, so she rose from the tub. The servant girl held up a toweling cloth.

Jocelyn took it and dried herself. "I've spent years in a convent. It has been a long while since anyone assisted with my bath." She smiled at the girl. "What is your name?"

"Ida, my lady." She gathered Jocelyn's discarded clothing from the bed. A knock sounded. "Who's there?"

"Margaret. I have m'lady's dress and chemise."

Jocelyn wrapped herself with the towel while Ida saw to Margaret. After trading Jocelyn's clothing for the dress, she shut the door.

Jocelyn gasped at the gown. White and gold embroidery edged the sleeves, hem, and neck of the dark crimson fabric. She fingered the exquisite stitching, marveling at the handiwork. "I've seen nothing so lovely. How did you obtain this?"

"The Lady Helen was havin' dresses made, and she didn't care for this one. Methinks 'twill look ever so lovely on you, though it may be a trifle long."

"This shall make a beautiful bridal gown." Jocelyn smiled, holding the garment close.

"Indeed. 'Tis time to get ready." Ida took the dress, laying it on the bed, then helped Jocelyn into the chemise. Ida slid the garment over Jocelyn's upheld arms, pausing when she reached Jocelyn's waist. "My lady! What happened to ye?"

Jocelyn put a hand to the scar on her side. "I attempted to help Lord Malcolm fight off an attacker and was wounded."

"Och, my lady, it looks like a fresh one, it does." Ida's brow wrinkled as she pulled the chemise down over Jocelyn.

"'Twas not so long ago, though I am much better. 'Tis only a little sore."

The girl helped Jocelyn into the gown, her touch gentle. "Ye've been through much, m'lady."

"Aye, but 'tis wonderful to finally be home." She ran her hands across the gown, marveling at its silkiness and rich hue. She'd missed wearing lady's clothing. It brought a sense of normalcy to her chaotic life.

Tracing the edge of her sleeve, she admired the delicate stitching. The soft fabric skimmed her body like a caress. With a thin belt draped around her hips, she looked like a princess.

Once she was dressed, Jocelyn sat on the small bench near the bed and allowed Ida to brush her hair. The girl let the curls hang loose to Jocelyn's shoulders, then placed a small circle of gold around her head.

A memory tugged her heart. "Where did that come from?"

"'Twas your own mother's, my lady. When I heard the tale of your return, I went to her trunk. She had some mighty pretty things."

Jocelyn touched the circlet, her eyes misting. She remembered. Her mother wore it when the king came to visit. Jocelyn had been a young child. She'd climbed onto her mother's lap while she finished getting ready to greet their guests. Jocelyn closed her eyes as she remembered the sweet scent of roses and the warmth of her mother's embrace. "I would love to see my mother's belongings."

"An' so you shall, my lady." Ida patted Jocelyn's hair. "My, 'tis beautiful you are."

Jocelyn pulled on a curl, wishing for her long tresses. "Thank you, Ida."

Needing to shake off the melancholy of the past, she walked to the window, gazing at the green, rolling hills in the distance. The bailey below bustled with people dressed in their finest for the wedding and feast. Was Malcolm already at the chapel? Or was he getting dressed, pondering their marriage as she was? *Lord, help me through the day. Show me how to love Malcolm as I should.*

Jocelyn took a shaky breath and released it slowly. Her fingers trembled. Why was she nervous? She was marrying the man she loved, a far better fate than she had expected. He would run the large estate, and together they would build a family. A dream come true, really.

A quiet knock interrupted her.

"Enter." Jocelyn clasped her hands in front of her.

The door opened, and a guard dipped his head. "My Lord Castillon awaits your presence."

His words straightened Jocelyn's spine. 'Twas time to face Malcolm … at the chapel. She offered a weak smile. "I am ready."

Her shaky legs belied her words.

Jocelyn followed the guard through the keep to the bailey. As she stepped into the sunshine, people cheered. Many lined the walls as she walked to the chapel. Musicians with flutes and lyres played a happy tune, walking along behind her. The people joined in the procession, clapping to the music.

Chain mail clinked behind her. She glanced over her shoulder. Four hulking guardsmen followed her, all solemn except for Ian. A grin spanned his face as he winked at her. She couldn't help but smile. But why would she need guards? Protection in light of the strange events surrounding her? Her heart warmed that Malcolm might be concerned for her safety.

Jocelyn slowed as she drew near the chapel. Garlands decorated the door and eaves. Along the left wall sat a table with quill, ink, and the marriage contract. A stone lay atop the papers to keep them in place against the wind. The priest, Lord Talbot, and Malcolm waited outside the door. Malcolm stood tallest among them, dressed in dark hose and tunic with a navy-blue surcoat. No smile issued forth as his jaw clenched.

Panic forced her heart into an erratic beat as she struggled for breath. Could he ever come to trust her? Love her? She took a step back, only to bump into a solid wall of muscle. She yelped in surprise.

"You go the wrong way, my lady." Ian's whispered words rallied her courage. She pulled her shoulders back and smiled at her future husband. *Love him until he thaws.* She stepped forward and stood to his left. A cool breeze blew her hair across her face, and she wished the ceremony could be held inside the church.

Jocelyn glanced at Malcolm, and his eyes finally met hers. Her heart stuttered. He reached for her. Swallowing hard, she placed her hand in his, luxuriating in the sense of security his presence brought.

The priest cleared his throat, and Jocelyn looked into his kind eyes. "We are gathered today to witness the joining of Lady Jocelyn

Ashburne to Lord Malcolm Castillon. Though their joining is by duty to the king, may God bind their hearts with His love."

Jocelyn glanced at Malcolm. He stared at the priest.

"Lady Jocelyn?"

Facing the priest, Jocelyn frowned. What had she missed?

The priest smiled. "Do you, Jocelyn Marie Ashburne, take Malcolm John Castillon to be your husband?"

"Aye. I do."

"Do you, Malcolm John Castillon, take Jocelyn Marie Ashburne to be your wife?"

"I do." Malcolm's voice rang strong and sure.

The priest placed a small gold ring in Malcolm's free hand. "The circle of gold in your hand is the symbol of never-ending love, the infinite love for one another and for God. May it be a reminder to love as God has loved you. You may place the ring on your bride's finger."

Malcolm faced Jocelyn and guided the ring onto her finger. The clear blue stone sparkled in the light.

Glancing up, she smiled at the questioning look in Malcolm's eyes. "Thank you. 'Tis beautiful," she whispered. He nodded, then turned back to the priest.

"Now we shall proceed to the marriage papers." The priest led them to the table, then reviewed the holdings of both parties.

Malcolm brought nothing to the marriage but his gold and his sword. And the strength to wield it. It mattered not his lack of wealth. He would be good for Ramslea and, hopefully, for her as well.

After signing the marriage contract, they returned to their place in front of the chapel door. Malcolm tightened his hold on Jocelyn's hand as the crowd tittered. He looked at her, his eyebrows raised.

Jocelyn shook her head, not understanding. The priest cleared his throat. Heat crept up her neck.

Malcolm turned her to face him. With a grim smile, his hand slid to the small of her back and drew her close. His other hand slipped through her curls, cupping her head.

He hesitated, his gaze flickering over her face before his lips touched hers, light and teasing. She gripped his arms as her knees weakened. The crowd cheered. Malcolm pulled away, their breath mingling as his lips hovered over hers.

Jocelyn's eyes burned at the sweetness of his touch, and a tear slipped down her cheek. Hope bloomed within her.

He wiped her tear with the pad of his thumb, his brow furrowed. "Our people shall think you care not for this marriage," he whispered. "Fear not. I shall give you freedom from my presence as much as I can."

"But that is not—"

Malcolm turned to the people and raised his fist high. The crowd cheered for the new lord of Ramslea and his bride.

Jocelyn took his arm, frustrated at his words. She did not want freedom from him. How could she woo him if he kept his distance?

They followed the priest into the chapel for the nuptial mass. After the priest's blessing, they headed to the great hall for the wedding feast. The justiciar walked before them while the musicians played, the crowd parting as they surged through the bailey.

Jocelyn glanced around for Helen. Had she attended the wedding? Jocelyn wouldn't blame her if she hadn't. Being set aside as she had been would be a difficult thing. Truth be told, Jocelyn was glad of her absence, as Helen's presence would only add tension to the atmosphere.

When they entered the hall, more garlands decorated the walls and fireplaces. A servant led them to the head table.

Trenchers piled with meats and vegetables, goblets of wine, loaves of bread, and a variety of sweet cakes covered the table. A feast she wished she hungered for. With trembling fingers, she reached for her wine and gulped it down, more to calm her nerves than to quench her thirst.

Jocelyn picked at the food while Malcolm ate heartily. He conversed with Lord Talbot and those around him, laughing and enjoying himself. He all but ignored her, not once turning to have speech with her.

A servant refilled her cup, and she swallowed hard, trying to drown the anger building in her heart. Anger would not facilitate the wooing of her husband. *Lord, take this anger from me.*

Jocelyn placed a hand on Malcolm's arm. "You look handsome in your blue surcoat."

Malcolm stiffened, glancing at her hand. "Thank you." His gaze turned to hers, then traveled down over her bodice. "That gown is lovely on you."

Heat traveled up Jocelyn's neck at his perusal. Faith, 'twouldn't be long until she would climb into her marriage bed. A mixture of excitement and anxiety washed over her. "Thank you. I confess that wearing Helen's castoff is a bit deflating."

"Where is she?" Malcolm's gaze searched the room.

"I know not and, truth be told, I care not."

Malcolm's lips twisted, and he leaned toward her. "I hope the king finds a husband for her in short order."

"Aye, she makes me uncomfortable." Jocelyn smiled. At least they had that in common, wanting Helen gone from Ramslea.

Malcolm sat back and turned to Lord Talbot, rejoining the conversation about France and political intrigues.

Jocelyn sighed and picked up a piece of cheese. She needed sustenance, but her stomach fluttered too much to eat. Music played while the feasting ensued. The chatter and laughter reminded her of when her parents were alive. They often held parties with games and dancing. How she missed them.

They would have liked Malcolm. Father would have respected his strength and determination. Mother would have enjoyed his kind chivalry. They'd have welcomed him with open arms.

As the guests finished eating, servants pushed back the tables and dancing commenced. Jocelyn smiled at the celebration, tapping her toes to the happy music.

"Malcolm, you must take your beautiful bride out to dance."

Lord Talbot rose. "I aim to find a comely lady to dance with myself."

Malcolm pushed back his chair. "I suppose I shall." Taking Jocelyn by the hand, he escorted her to the middle of the hall while the guests called out their approval.

Once they reached the center of the room, he faced her. His hand tightened on hers before beginning the intricate steps. While he did not frown or glare at her, neither did he smile. She had anticipated his displeasure regarding the wedding, yet she'd expected more joy at having gained Ramslea.

"Are you happy, my lord?"

Malcolm tilted his head and frowned. "What do you mean?"

"You have Ramslea, a better land than your tourney wins could ever produce. 'Twas your dream, was it not?"

He pursed his lips. The lightness of his feet belied the heaviness in his eyes. "Aye, I am happy about the land."

"Yet not about your new wife."

"I daresay, I do not understand what you mean." He raised a brow.

"I daresay you do." Jocelyn smiled as they passed one another during a turn.

"I told you last night my feelings. It shall take time for you to earn my trust." His hand gripped her waist as he twirled her to his other side. "Fooled by women is not something I shall succumb to again."

Jocelyn took in Malcolm's thinned lips and furrowed brow. "Women? As in more than just me?"

"You would do well to keep your questions to yourself."

"You do not frighten me in the least, my lord."

"Perhaps I should remedy that."

When the dance ended Malcolm bowed, and she curtsied. Lord Talbot came to stand before them. "Might I dance with the new lady of Ramslea?"

Malcolm nodded. "Of course, my lord." He bowed, then left

the dance floor.

"My lady?"

Jocelyn tore her gaze from Malcolm's retreating back to focus on her partner. She placed a smile on her face and put her hand in his. A good dancer, he led her through the steps effortlessly.

"Much has transpired in the past weeks. How do you fare?" Lord Talbot's gentle smile nearly did her in.

"I am well. Except for losing my father and suspecting Helen of subterfuge."

"Helen?" His brows rose. "On what grounds?"

Jocelyn regretted her words. "I have no proof—at least not yet. I merely suspect her of conspiring to keep me from Ramslea."

"Why did you not mention this yesterday?"

"I do not know why she would plot against me, and 'twould be my word against hers."

"I've sent an official to question the abbess at Lomkirk. We shall discover who conspired against you."

Relief washed through Jocelyn. "Thank you for your assistance. It eases my mind."

When the dance ended, men surrounded Jocelyn wanting to claim a dance. She spent the rest of the evening on her feet, dancing, smiling, and enjoying the festivities.

Malcolm danced with many women yet did not claim her hand. She envied the smile and easy laugh he bestowed upon his partners. One day she would bring about such a laugh.

The music ended, and she turned to her most recent partner. "Would you take me to rest by the fire? I am in need of refreshment."

"Of course, my lady." He offered his arm and escorted her to a chair by the fire. "I shall return with a drink."

"Thank you." Jocelyn sat back, wishing she could take off her shoes and rub her feet. As she rested, she spotted Malcolm walking his partner off the floor across the room. While they conversed, a woman in a pale-rose gown entered the hall and approached him. *Helen!*

Jocelyn came to her feet to gain a clearer view. Helen curtsied as Malcolm held out his hand. Nay! After all that Jocelyn had shared with him, how could he dance with her stepmother? She stepped toward them, determined to intervene.

"Here is your drink, my lady."

Jocelyn smiled at the knight who stepped in front of her, a goblet in his hand. She looked past him to Malcolm. He and Helen were already on the dance floor. Music began. Faith! Jocelyn couldn't interrupt a dance already begun.

Reluctantly, she turned back to the knight and took the goblet. She gulped the liquid, cooling her heated body and heart. Why had Helen made an appearance now?

Jocelyn watched her husband and stepmother dance. Though older by ten years, Helen remained beautiful, her face unlined and her plaited blonde hair like spun gold. She laughed at something Malcolm said.

Jocelyn strolled around the edge of the dance floor, drawing closer to where they danced. She sipped from her goblet while she watched. Malcolm caught her gaze, and she raised her brows. He gave a slight shake of his head. Helen must have noticed, for she glanced over her shoulder. Seeing Jocelyn, her lips curved into a slow smile.

Jocelyn snorted. Helen was most certainly up to something, and Jocelyn determined to find out what.

After the dance, Malcolm escorted Helen to the head table, where Lord Talbot conversed with members of the king's court. Jocelyn moved to intercept them. She reached them several paces from the table.

"Lady Helen, what a pleasant surprise." Jocelyn nodded to her stepmother. "I did not see you at the wedding."

"Alas, an ache in the head kept me from your nuptials." Helen put her fingers to her temple.

"I trust you are feeling better."

"Aye, that I am." Helen looked at Malcolm and smiled, squeezing the arm she still clung to. "I believe dancing with a handsome man was the very thing needed."

Malcolm patted her hand, then extracted his arm from her grip. "I'm glad you are feeling better. Why don't you sit? I will have a servant bring you food." He gestured to the table.

"You are most thoughtful, Malcolm." Helen walked around the table and sat next to Lord Talbot.

Jocelyn held her tongue. Helen used Malcolm's given name, then took his seat of honor. How rude and presumptuous.

Lord Talbot turned from his conversation. "Ah, Lady Helen. I'm sure Lord Malcolm won't care if you sit there whilst he dances."

"I have an errand to attend to and more ladies to dance with." Malcolm bowed, then walked toward a servant refilling drinks.

"Lady Joshelyn, will you do me the honor of a dansh?"

Jocelyn turned to the large knight at her side. She had danced with him earlier when he stood steady and too many drinks did not slur his words

The knight held out his hand. "My lady?"

She hesitated. She didn't want to be rude, but the knight hardly seemed fit to dance. Propriety defeated caution, so she placed her hand in his and let him lead her to the floor.

A broad smile filled his face. "I am honored that you would choosh me for yet another dansh. May I be so bold as to think you might favor me?"

"Sir, I didn't choose you. You asked me for the dance." Jocelyn frowned. The man's steps faltered several times.

"But you said *aye*. It must count for shomething." He clutched her closer than the dance required. Jocelyn stiffened in protest. Then he leaned close to her ear, whispering, "'Tis no secret you and the Lord Ramslea were forced to marry, and I could give you—"

Jocelyn gasped and pushed against the man, his foul breath turning her stomach. "You—"

The knight lurched back, pulled away by Malcolm. He stepped between Jocelyn and the knight, his hands clenched at his side. "I fear you have had the pleasure of my lady's company far too long."

"My lord, I—"

"You will cease with your attentions toward my wife. Do not come near her again."

The man stumbled through the crowd and out of the great hall.

Jocelyn pressed a hand to Malcolm's back, warmed that he had come to save her yet again. "Thank you. He was most—"

He spun around, his eyes wild. "What were you thinking dancing with a drunkard such as he?"

"I didn't want to be rude in front of our guests."

"Instead, you allow a situation to occur that forces *me* to cause a scene."

Jocelyn swallowed. 'Twas true. "I am sorry, but I appreciate your rescuing me."

"I do not expect there to be cause to rescue you again." He folded his arms across his chest.

She glanced around them, realizing the music had stopped, and the guests watched them. Heat rolled through her. She needed air, space to breathe and be free of the quiet stares. She walked past him. A grip on her arm stopped her. She looked from Malcolm's hand to his face. "We are watched by all. Unhand me, sir."

Malcolm pulled her flush against his hard body. "I believe you are the one causing the scene. As the new lord, I will not have you walk away from me." His grip loosened. "Now, you will smile."

"Why?"

"Smile, Jocelyn."

Her name on his lips thrilled her, his deep raspy voice feathering her curls. She couldn't help but smile then. "But why?"

"I am about to cause a scene that will please the guests." He let go of her arm and scooped her up into his arms. Startled, she flung her arms around his neck. "Malcolm!"

The guests cheered.

Malcolm spun around. "I thank you for your presence this eve. As this is my wedding night, I shall take my leave."

Lord Talbot rose and spread his arms wide. "May your marriage bed be blessed with many sons to defend England for years to come."

Malcolm bowed, then turned and walked across the hall.

"Kiss! Kiss! Kiss!" The crowd chanted as Malcolm neared the stairs.

He paused at the foot of the stairs and gazed at Jocelyn. His brow furrowed for a moment before he turned them around to face their guests, a slow smile spreading across his face. Jocelyn's pulse quickened, and she licked her lips. Two kisses in one day, with more to come later. She sucked in a breath as Malcolm lowered his head, ready for his touch.

His lips pressed hard against hers as he pulled her closer, his arm about her waist gripping her tightly. She moved her lips against his, and he groaned, slanting his mouth over hers. He kissed her deep and long, like a man thirsty, needing more. Jocelyn's toes tingled, and she moved one of her hands along his neck, threading her fingers through his hair. She wanted him, needed him.

Malcolm pulled back, his breathing labored. His eyes. They gazed at her with … longing? Then he blinked, shuttering his emotions. Lifting his head, he grinned at the guests. Whoops and hollers bellowed about the hall as Malcolm turned and took the stairs two at a time.

Lord help her if the rest of the night was anything like that kiss.

Malcolm ran up the stone stairs holding Jocelyn close, her soft body against his. Her small waist, the swell of her hips. By the saints, he wanted to bed his wife. 'Twas his right.

And yet, he could not. He could not bed her while not trusting her.

What if he gave in to his feelings and she betrayed him like his first betrothed? Therein lay the problem. He feared giving her his heart.

Malcolm carried her down the long hallway and stopped at her room. He lifted his foot and pushed against the door. Like his room, hers housed a large bed with a wooden chest along the wall to the right. Two chairs sat near the fireplace on the opposite wall. A jug and two cups sat on a small table in between the chairs. A fire burned brightly, warming the room. He stepped inside and set Jocelyn on a chair.

She gazed at him, her lips curling in a small smile. She smoothed her dress. "Would you care for a drink?"

"Nay." He walked to the fire, holding his hands to its warmth. He wasn't cold, but nervous ... uncertain. He would never admit that to Jocelyn—to anyone. How did one turn away his bride?

"Would you like to sit for a while?"

"Nay."

Jocelyn came to stand next to him, the scent of rose mingling with the smoky scent of the fire. A heady aroma.

"Are you feeling well? Does your wound ... " She placed a hand on his arm, her touch like the coals that glowed red in the fire below. He fought the urge to yank his arm away. Instead, he dropped his hands to his sides.

Just tell her and be done with it.

"Jocelyn, I am not going to bed you." He glanced at her, gauging her reaction.

Her brows drew together. "Why not?"

"I can scarce stomach the idea of bedding a liar."

"But I told you the reasons for my disguise. 'Twas for my safety and to gather information. 'Twasn't to hurt you." She clasped her hands in front of her and took a step closer. "Malcolm, I will not lie to you again."

Would that he could believe her. What if a traveling knight came through and stole her heart? Or even one of Ramslea's guards? "You cannot know that for certain."

Jocelyn took his hand in hers, covering it with her other. "Malcolm," she whispered. "Who has lied to you in the past that you do not trust me?"

How could he share his story with her? 'Twas his own shame to carry that he wasn't man enough to keep his betrothed. He heaved a sigh.

She squeezed his hand. "Malcolm, tell me. I will not be like that person."

He pulled his hand from hers. "You cannot promise such a thing. Two years ago, my betrothed vowed she loved me, then she betrayed me with my brother and had the gall to lie about her intimacies." He went to a chair and sat, staring into the fire. "You have already shown that you are capable of lying. *You*—educated by nuns."

Jocelyn pulled the other chair close to his and sat. "I am truly sorry you were hurt by that woman. Betrayal is a terrible injustice. But I am not her. Aye, I lied about who I was, but I was not bound to you as I am now. I am yours, and you are mine. I *will* be true to you."

"You cannot guarantee your faithfulness."

"But I can. I don't know what your betrothed's spiritual life was like, but I believe in God and His precepts. Marriage is binding, and I will not stray. There may be men like the knight tonight who will try their wiles on me, but I am in a covenant with you. I choose you. For always."

Malcolm gazed at this woman sitting beside him. His wife. Bound to him? His betrothed had never spoken thusly. Could he truly trust Jocelyn?

She smiled as she rose, then sat on his lap, placing a hand on his chest.

His blood heated as his heart beat a heavy cadence.

"Malcolm, I am your wife. I am willing."

Who was he to deny his wife? Trust or no, he would give his wife what she desired. He dove off the cliff of uncertainty and slid his hand around Jocelyn's waist, his other hand sliding along her neck and into her thick curls. He pulled her face toward his, pressing his lips to hers.

Soft and yielding, he tasted of her sweetness. Jocelyn's hand moved around his neck, pulling him closer. Her lips moved against his, and he lifted her, carrying her to the bed. Laying her on the covers, Malcolm paused.

He didn't need to trust her in order to bed her. But how long could he keep his heart intact?

Jocelyn reached for him. By the saints, he would not deny her. Not tonight.

CHAPTER 21

Jocelyn stretched in the bed she had shared with Malcolm. Morning light shone through the cracks in the shutters as she smiled. What a glorious night with her husband. He'd been so gentle yet masterful. She nearly swooned with delight. Already marriage to Malcolm exceeded her dreams—at least in the marriage bed.

She looked at the indention on his pillow, disappointed by his absence. She'd hoped for more of his kisses before starting the new day. No matter. A lifetime of his kisses awaited her.

Throwing back the covers, she donned her chemise, then went to the trunk and searched the gowns inside. With only four to choose from, she quickly selected a purple woolen gown. 'Twas simple with no decorative stitching. Perfect for a day of inspecting the castle and beginning her work as chatelaine. She looked forward to examining her home and taking on the responsibility of running the household operations.

Without the aid of a maid, Jocelyn pulled the dress over her head and smoothed it over her hips. Donning leather shoes, she proceeded to the great hall.

Knights, ladies, and guardsmen littered the hall, a fraction of those present the night before. Helen sat at the head table with a few of the king's officials, but no Malcolm or Lord Talbot. Jocelyn paused in the doorway, not wanting to eat near Helen. But she was the lady of Ramslea now, not her stepmother. Jocelyn lifted her chin and crossed the hall. Helen sat in the middle chair, the place of honor where Lord Talbot—or Malcolm—should sit. Jocelyn slid onto the empty chair next to her.

"Good morning, Jocelyn." Helen smiled, her gaze traveling over Jocelyn's attire. "I trust you managed to sleep some last night?"

Jocelyn frowned. How rude to refer to her wedding night. Still, she would not respond thusly. "Aye, thank you." A servant set a bowl of porridge and a cup of ale in front of her, saving her from having to respond further. She tasted the warm mixture, its spiced aroma melding with the delicious taste.

"The justiciar is set to leave today." Helen sat back in her chair and sipped her drink.

"I've heard."

"'Twill ease our larder and cellar with company gone."

Jocelyn made a note to check the food stores. She continued eating, hoping Helen would cease her speech. Though now, with Malcolm and Lord Talbot absent, seemed the perfect opportunity to question the woman. "With all that has happened since I've returned, we've yet to converse. The sisters at Lomkirk were most gracious, though—as I suspected four years ago—Mother had already taught me most of what I needed to know to run Ramslea."

"My dear, you needed more structure. With an estate such as Ramslea, discipline and hard work are essential, not to mention the specialty skills gained at the abbey. You learned illumination, did you not?"

"Aye, but 'tis hardly the education needed to run a home." Jocelyn sat back in her chair and faced Helen. "I heard Father regretted sending me away. Why did he not send for me?"

Helen's lips pressed together. "He had no regrets. He was proud of your education. Who would tell you such a thing?"

Jocelyn wouldn't betray Lisbet, and yet she needed more information "There are so many new servants, I do not know who I heard. Something about his regret, and something else about the abbess. Do you know her?"

A crease formed between Helen's brows. "I do not. Why do you ask?"

"A woman blackmailed the abbess." Jocelyn lowered her voice, aware of the man seated on the other side of Helen. "I thought perhaps those in her confidence should be warned, in case the plot extended beyond the convent. 'Tis fortunate for you that you do not know her."

"Most fortunate," Helen murmured.

"Though I do wonder about the rumors of my father. Do you suppose someone was trying to keep me away from him?"

Helen's face reddened. "As I do not know the abbess, I couldn't say."

"But you were his wife. Surely you shared his confidences."

"'Twas an advantageous match. He received a young wife." Her countenance relaxed. "And I became Lady of Ramslea."

Lady of Ramslea. Could that be Helen's motive? How should Jocelyn respond to that? She couldn't accuse Helen without proof.

Helen pushed her porridge aside and stood. "Jocelyn, I suggest you ignore the servants' gossip. As the Lomkirk-educated lady of the house, such actions are beneath you. Now, I must see to dinner preparations with the cook."

"Nay, I am chatelaine now and will see to Ramslea's needs."

Helen stopped, her back to Jocelyn. Without a word, she strode across the hall and out to the bailey.

Jocelyn blew out a breath and relaxed into her chair. Faith, her suspicions about Helen deepened. But how to gain proof?

Perhaps she should seek aid from Malcolm, include him in her plans. 'Twould help in gaining his trust. She'd glean information from more servants while Malcolm talked with the guards. Who knew what they might have overheard while standing guard.

As she plotted, Jocelyn swallowed a spoonful of porridge, savoring its spiced warmth. After the meal, she'd speak with Nelda about the menu for the noonday and evening meals. 'Twould be the first of many tasks she would see to today, one of which would be stealing a kiss from her new husband.

Malcolm wiped the sweat off his brow, stuck his sword in the ground, and grinned at Ian. The Scotsman brandished his sword once, then slid it into its scabbard. Guardsmen filled the lists, training and engaging in swordplay.

"'Tis glad I am you are lord of Ramslea." Ian took the towel offered by a young servant and wiped his face and neck. "Your youth and ability with the sword work in your favor."

"I appreciate your confidence. I will need advisors as I take on this role." Another servant handed Malcolm a drink, and he downed it. "I hope you are up to the challenge."

"I've been here four years, and only recently made chief guard, but I will answer any questions you have."

"Well said." The sun rose high in the sky above the castle. 'Twas close to midday. "I am off to the baths before partaking of the midday meal."

"I will see to the rest of the men and push them a little longer." Ian wiggled his brows. "We do not want them going to fat."

Malcolm chuckled. "Be kind. I don't want my guards thinking I'm an ogre of a lord."

"I'm the epitome of kindness, my lord. Firmness with a smile is my life's platitude." Ian winked as he turned and bellowed. "You fight like maids! Stronger! Harder! Your lord watches!" He glanced over his shoulder and grinned at Malcolm.

Malcolm laughed. He pulled his sword from the ground and made for the baths. With the tournament over, the crowds had thinned, making the bailey easier to navigate.

Free of the many knights from the tournament, the servants at the bathhouse worked together to arrange a bath for Malcolm. In no time, he'd cleaned and changed, then made his way to the hall to eat. Saints, he had worked up an appetite.

Lord Talbot and his entourage exited the hall as Malcolm drew near. Two wagons piled high with luggage, food stores, and bedding waited in the bailey. Servants harnessed the horses, hitching them to the wagons. More horses awaited, ready for the justiciar's party.

"Lord Malcolm, I'd hoped to see you before I left."

As Lord Talbot walked toward him, Malcolm bowed.

"I wanted to congratulate you on your win and urge you to keep a firm hold on Ramslea and your knights' training. The king may have use of your forces in the coming days."

"I shall, my lord. Won't you stay for the noon meal?"

"Nay, I must not tarry. I am due in Middlesbrough two days hence. Your cook provided us with sufficient food for our journey." Lord Talbot clasped Malcolm on the shoulder. "I assure you I am checking into the strange dealings with Lady Jocelyn at the abbey. I've already sent an official on my behalf. I'll send information as I receive it. As for Lady Helen, I have someone in mind for her. Once the king approves and the arrangements have been made, I shall send for her."

Malcolm nodded. "Thank you. Godspeed, my lord." Talbot and his men mounted. Malcolm glanced at the crowd forming outside the hall. Jocelyn stood at the front, hands clasped in front of a lovely purple gown. The wind blew the skirt across her curves, reminding him of last night. By the saints, she fair took his breath away. Last night had been …

He tore his gaze away and focused on Lord Talbot and his company. Once they disappeared from sight, he released a slow breath and turned to the dispersing crowd. Among them, Jocelyn stood tall with a smile spread wide across her lovely face.

When he reached her, he offered his arm. "My lady."

She accepted his arm, and he led her into the hall. The greenery from the wedding feast still decorated the walls. 'Twasn't as noisy as the past few days, so Malcolm relaxed.

"I missed you this morning." She slid into her chair at the head table.

Malcolm paused as he pulled out the chair next to her. Though he had determined to keep his distance from her, he didn't want to explain his reasons why. "I spent the morning in the lists, working out the soreness from the tournament."

"Are you going to sit?" She looked at him, a small crease puckered between her eyes.

Malcolm didn't want to stay if it meant continuing this discussion, and he doubted his ability to deny Jocelyn should she ask. "Nay, I want to tour the estate this afternoon. I shall grab some bread and cheese from the kitchens."

She rose. "I shall go with you."

"Nay. Stay and eat. I shall return for the evening meal."

"But I would love to see my family home again." She smiled.

"This is not a pleasure trip. 'Twill be fast and informative. One of your father's lead servants will teach me what I need to know." Guilt riddled Malcolm as Jocelyn's countenance drooped. He could understand her desire to revisit her home land, but his feelings and thoughts jumbled together making it difficult to think around her. He wanted to clear his head and focus on his land. "I shall take you soon." A small concession to ease his conscience.

Jocelyn nodded and sat, pulling her bowl of soup closer. By the saints, keeping his distance would not be easy. He didn't want to treat her badly but needed to resist the pull she had on him until she gained his trust. Before he could change his mind, he left for the kitchens.

In the hallway, he stopped two young servants. "Who was your previous lord's most trusted estate servant?"

"That would be Tom, sir. He oversees the farms and castle grounds."

"Find him and let him know I would tour Ramslea this afternoon. I request his presence. And you"—Malcolm pointed to the other lad—"let a stable hand know I will need my horse and one other saddled promptly."

"Yes, my lord." The young men bowed before rushing away in opposite directions. Malcolm gathered food, giving them both time to complete their tasks. By the time he reached the stables, Tom stood ready for him with two readied horses.

Malcolm mounted Horse and followed his guide past the

paddock toward the gate. The thumping of hoofbeats sounded behind him. He glanced over his shoulder. Helen pulled up beside him sitting atop a brown mare.

"Off on an adventure, my lord?" Her small smile widened.

"I am touring the estate. No adventure, only business."

"I shall attend you. There is much I can voice on the matter of the land."

As they passed the keep, Jocelyn stood at the entrance, speaking with one of the servants. When she glanced up, her brows rose. By the saints, she would think he'd invited Helen.

He looked at the former lady of the castle. "I do not need your aid for I have Tom to inform me. You shall remain here."

"I think not." Helen kicked her heels, spurring her horse next to Tom's.

Malcolm growled, frustrated at her rudeness but unwilling to make a scene. Instead, they rode through the barbican and outside the castle walls. Then he spurred Horse next to Helen, grabbed her reins, and stopped. "You are not going."

"Malcolm, please," she whispered. Tears filled her eyes as her chin quivered. "I have been through so much. First my husband, then Jocelyn's blessed return, only to be forced out of Ramslea and into a new marriage. Please, let me have this last look at the land I've come to love." A tear streaked down her face.

Saints! Was he to make every woman miserable today? He handed Helen her reins. "You may come but must keep up." He urged Horse forward. "And keep silent whilst I do business."

"Thank you, my lord." Helen brought her horse beside his. "I shall try to remain quiet."

Malcolm turned his attention to Tom. "Will we be able to tour all of Ramslea in a day?"

"Nay, but we'll go to the northern hill where ye can see the whole of the land."

They discussed Ramslea as they rode around the property. The estate included approximately 1,200 acres, ten times more than his father's land. 'Twas infinitely more than he could have earned by winning tournaments. Malcolm marveled at his good fortune.

As promised, Tom led them up the hill to the north of Ramslea. Once they reached the peak, they dismounted and walked to the edge of a cliff. The drop appeared to be about thirty feet with shrubs and trees below. With the sun in full force, the land sat in vivid focus—rolling hills, flat farmland, and forests as far as Malcolm could see. Bits of fall color dotted the trees, giving the land an artist's touch.

His castle stood on a smaller hill that plateaued for several acres, leaving room for gardens and the tournament field. It also provided a clear view of approaching visitors, friend or foe.

He breathed in. The quiet surrounding him, coupled with the majestic view before him, swept him into a sacred moment. 'Twas a moment of peace and fulfillment. A calling of destiny as lord of this land.

A hand slid around Malcolm's arm. Helen pressed her body against his. "'Tis beautiful, is it not?"

Malcolm moved, putting space between them. "Aye."

"I shall miss it." She squeezed his arm. "Are you sure you wouldn't want me to stay? To give you personal tours of the estate? I could be of great assistance."

"I'm sure Jocelyn will suffice."

Helen placed her other hand on his arm, pulling close once more. "I'm sure Jocelyn doesn't have as much experience as I."

Malcolm stiffened. The woman's audacity unnerved him. He pulled from her grasp and stepped away. "I'm sure your experience will be welcomed by your new husband."

A fleeting frown graced Helen's face, then she raised one brow. "Naturally."

Malcolm turned to the man next to him. "Show me Ramslea's reach."

Tom pointed at the farthest visible mountain. "If you look to the right of the castle, the land goes up to the next tallest peak.

To the left, the wooded land spreads past the lake up to craggy mounds a few miles over."

Helen moved closer to Malcolm. "Directly past the castle, the land flattens, and many serfs farm the land. I had to become knowledgeable when Ashburne turned ill."

"How much farmland is there?"

"About 100 acres," said Helen.

"Tom, is that correct?"

"Aye, my lord."

"What else is there to see?"

Tom scratched his head. "Only the village a couple of miles from the castle. Beyond that, there are tenant homes around the farmland."

"Good. Let's move on."

Returning to their horses, Helen stumbled and grabbed hold of Malcolm's arm. "Oh, my ankle!" She clutched her foot, her face pinched. "I turned it on the uneven ground."

Malcolm knelt beside her. "Can you walk?"

"Nay, can you get me to my horse?" Tears pooled in her eyes.

Once again, Malcolm regretted his decision to let her come. He picked her up and carried her to her horse. Her hands gripped his shoulders as he lifted her onto the mare. "Thank you," she whispered.

Something about the woman made him want to run. Her gaze reminded him of a cat closing in on its prey. Returning to Horse, he mounted. "Since we must pass the castle on our way to the village, you can return and see the healer."

"Will you help me when I arrive?"

"There are plenty of servants to give you aid." Malcolm ignored her pout, guiding Horse away from the cliff. "Let's be off."

They made their way down the hill, then found the road leading home. As they neared the castle, Helen veered away from them. Malcolm followed Tom to the village as he watched to ensure that Helen made it safely through the castle gates.

As she disappeared, he sighed. After an afternoon in Helen's company, the difficulty of being around Jocelyn seemed as easy as … breathing. Mayhap not that easy, for with Jocelyn his breathing hitched from time to time, but 'twas definitely preferable.

And definitely desirable.

CHAPTER 22

Jocelyn supervised the servants as they cleaned the main bedroom, hands on her hips. After watching Malcolm ride off with Helen, she'd thrown herself into her castle duties, determined to work out her frustration.

He took Helen after telling Jocelyn nay! The pain sank deep into her heart like a stone thrown into dark waters, heavy and suffocating. How could she gain his trust if he avoided her? Somehow, she must find time with him. Not only would she win his trust, she needed his aid in gaining proof against Helen.

Unwilling to think on it any longer, Jocelyn stepped into the spacious bedroom. Two servants cleaned the floor while another swept ash from the fireplace. "Thank you for your hard work. Once the room is clean, bring in my trunk, as well as Lord Malcolm's."

"Aye, my lady. We shall make sure all is ready."

Confident in their abilities, she left the room and walked next door to the solar. With the recent festivities, she hadn't had time to enjoy it. Padded benches and pillowed chairs filled the large room. Small tables had been placed among the seats, some holding games, some empty. She ran a hand over the stone casing of the fireplace as she walked to a trunk sitting in the corner and opened the lid. A basket of embroidery supplies, a sharpening stone, and a lyre.

Memories washed over her of times spent in this room with her parents. Mother stitched tapestries, Father sharpened knives, and Jocelyn played with her dolls. Sometimes Father would play the lyre and sing love songs to Mother. The music often lulled Jocelyn to sleep, so Father would carry her to bed. He'd smelled of leather and smoke. She missed her parents and the security their love brought and hoped she'd experience that sense of belonging once more with Malcolm. Perhaps one day she and Malcolm would make memories here with their own children. One day, when he quit running from her.

Lord, help me to quench my anger and forgive Malcolm.

She sighed, wishing she could stay and reminisce, but there was much to do. Leaving the room, she headed downstairs and into the hall. Servants tended the fires and cleaned tables, tidying after the noon meal. Her foot slid out from under her, and she caught herself against a table. Inspecting the floor, she discovered food in the rushes from the past few days of feasting.

"You there, I need your aid." Jocelyn smiled at the servant girl who hurried to her. "I would like these dirty rushes removed and fresh ones laid today. Can you see that 'tis accomplished?"

The girl curtsied. "Aye, m'lady. I will gather help now." She ran off to the kitchens.

That task begun, Jocelyn went to the storeroom and cellarium, checking the food stock and making note of items in short supply. When she left the keep, she inspected the washroom nestled against the castle wall, then went to the seamstress's hut next door. While thankful to have worn Helen's unwanted gowns, she desired dresses of her own choosing.

After knocking on the door, Jocelyn stepped back. The mortar around several stones needed replacing, though the thatched roof looked in good condition.

The door opened, revealing a middle-aged woman, her hair streaked with gray. Her face brightened, and she curtsied. "My lady, I'm delighted you've come. Please, come in." She stepped back, letting Jocelyn in.

"Thank you." She entered and took in the small room. Fabrics and clothes covered the table next to a chair holding a basket full of needles, threads, and yarn. "Your name is Matilda, correct?"

"Aye, 'tis so."

"I would like three dresses. A simple gown to work in, and two ornate gowns, perhaps with decorative stitching. Can you have the work dress completed in a day or two?"

"To be sure, m'lady. I can have a plain dress ready tomorrow. Let me get you measured." Matilda cut a piece of twine and took Jocelyn's measurements, making a knot as a guide. After discussing colors for the dresses and thread for the embroidery, Jocelyn left for the keep.

'Twas midafternoon. Surely her new bedroom would be finished. Eager to inspect it, she quickened her steps. She and Malcolm would share that room—the room where they would create and bear life.

Pushing through the door to the bedroom, Jocelyn halted. Helen lay on the bed, curled on her side. On Jocelyn's bed! How dare the woman?

"What are you doing in here?" Anger propelled her forward, stopping her at the foot of the bed.

Helen pushed up on an elbow and yawned. "Taking a nap after a wonderful ride." She glanced around the room. "Thank you for having the room cleaned. I missed it whilst Lord Talbot was here."

Jocelyn fought the urge to raise her voice. "This is no longer your room. This room belongs to the new lord and lady."

Helen sat and stretched, her lips turning up at the corners. She rose, brushing her rumpled gown, then sauntered past Jocelyn, her fingers trailing across one of the chairs. "I suppose you are right, though in truth I should have remained the lady." She fluffed a pillow on the chair. "'Tis a shame you returned."

"But return I have." Jocelyn pushed her shoulders back, stunned at Helen's admission yet refusing to let her intimidate her. "You may remain in your current room if you wish—"

"If I wish?" Helen tilted her head. "I wish so many things. Things I cannot obtain with you in the way."

A chill settled over Jocelyn. She lifted her chin and moved toward Helen. "Leave this room at once, or I shall call a guard to have you removed."

Helen laughed. "My dear, there's no need for force." She strolled toward the door. "I hope you enjoy your time at Ramslea. We shall see how you fare as its keeper." Her soft laughter faded as she walked down the hall.

Jocelyn shook with frustration at Helen's audacity. The woman's disrespect wreaked havoc on her peace of mind like a whirlwind inflicted destruction in its path. Jocelyn straightened the rumpled bedding, resisting the urge to strip it and give it a good scrub.

Sitting on the edge of the bed, she plopped back and stared at the wood planks of the ceiling. Faith, her life turned more complicated with each passing day. While she relished being home, the relational issues wearied her heart.

Consider it pure joy whenever you face trials.

Humph. 'Twas difficult to embrace joy in this situation. But perhaps if she relied on the Lord instead of trusting in her own abilities, she could find the joy in God's plan for her—no matter what transpired or who bothered her. She'd pray for wisdom, glean information, and trust the Lord to reveal the truth in time.

As she prayed, hope threaded its way into her heart, binding the fear of the unknown and releasing a peace only God could provide.

After touring the villages with Tom, Malcolm left Horse at the stables, then headed for the great hall. As the sun set behind the western hills, servants lit torches near the hall's entrance. He marveled at how efficiently his new home ran.

When he entered the hall, disappointment smote him. Helen sat at the head table. He'd hoped her injury would keep her abed. Jocelyn sat two chairs down, an empty chair between them. Neither woman smiled as he approached. 'Twould be a long evening.

Sliding onto his chair, Malcolm turned to Jocelyn. "Did you have a pleasant day?"

"I've had a productive day, though not all pleasant."

"Dare I ask?"

"The details would bore you, I'm sure. Did you enjoy seeing the estate?"

Malcolm winced. "About that … I did not invite her to join me."

"I should think not since you refused to take me."

"I know you are angry, but I tried to make her stay."

One of Jocelyn's brows rose, but she didn't respond.

Malcolm ran a hand over the back of his neck, attempting to ease the tight muscles. Where was the food and drink? While he waited, he should at least endeavor to explain. "She seemed sad with all that has transpired." He lowered his voice. "The tears—"

"Did you offer her a kiss of comfort?" Jocelyn reached for the goblet a servant set before her.

Malcolm's ears grew warm, once again regretting his explanation of their first kiss. "Nay, Jocelyn. There was no kiss."

A servant poured Malcolm a drink. "Leave the jug here, please," he said. The servant set it on the table. Malcolm drained his goblet, then poured more. "I *will* say that Helen's tears looked real to me."

"Many women can cry on command." Jocelyn sat back in her chair and gazed out over the hall.

"Such as yourself?"

Jocelyn gasped. "Nay! I never have, nor shall I ever, use tears to wield influence."

"Never?" Malcolm cocked his head.

"Mayhap as a small child crying for my doll." A smile curved her lips. Malcolm's gaze traveled over her face and down her neck, remembering her smile last night—nay, focus on her words.

"My lord, if I may have a word." Helen placed a hand on Malcolm's arm, drawing his attention. "I assure you, my tears were real."

Jocelyn snorted.

Helen frowned.

By the saints! 'Twas as if he were caught between two armies at war, arrows flying from every direction. Malcolm breathed in the hearty aroma beef, onion, and spice as servants carried in bowls from the kitchen. His stomach rumbled. The bowls of soup were placed in front of them, and Jocelyn's brows drew together. "You do not care for the meal?"

"'Tis not the meal I requested. This was served at the noon meal." Jocelyn motioned to a servant girl. "Do you know why we are having soup tonight? We were to have venison."

The girl's eyes widened. "The cook said you requested the soup again, m'lady."

"I did no such thing."

The girl glanced at Helen, then focused on the ground. "I believe 'twas the Lady Helen who delivered the message, m'lady."

Jocelyn's face reddened. "Thank you. You may continue your service." She placed the palms of her hands on the table and leaned forward, looking around Malcolm.

Malcolm sat back in his chair. He glanced from Jocelyn to Helen. The former lady of Ramslea sipped her soup.

"Did you tell Nelda I wanted soup again this eve?"

Helen's brows rose. "You told me you wanted soup again."

"I did not."

Helen dabbed her mouth with her finger. "I know not what you speak of."

Jocelyn leaned close to Malcolm. "She lies and is deliberately undermining my authority. She is not as innocent as—"

Helen twisted to face Jocelyn. "I demand to know what you are saying."

"Cease!" Malcolm raised his hands. "Enough of this bickering. Let us eat. The soup will be fine. Speak not another word." He wearied of the tension between the two women. Where was the peace he so desired?

"Malcolm, I—"

He held up a hand to his wife. "Nay, utter not another word."

The rest of the meal progressed in blessed silence as Malcolm filled his belly, relishing the quiet on either side of him. Around them, the guardsmen's conversed and joked with one another as they ate. *That* was how a meal should be eaten.

Satisfied, he pushed back from the table. "I shall leave you ladies and retire for the night. It has been a long day." He moved toward the stairs.

"Malcolm, I need—"

He held up his hand, not glancing back to see the frown that most likely adorned his wife's countenance. He needed quiet. He needed peace. He needed sleep.

Taking the stairs at a run, he gained the hallway, and he stepped into a cold, dark room. Where was his fire? He walked to the far side of the room, but his trunk was missing.

"I tried to tell you earlier." Jocelyn walked in behind him, torch in hand. "I had our things moved to the main bedroom."

Torn between wanting to sleep and wanting Jocelyn, Malcolm remained silent. If he moved to the main bedroom, sleep would not be a priority. He would gain more rest if he bedded here, but then he'd hurt Jocelyn's feelings. Of course, he'd already angered her by riding out with Helen, so one more slight would hardly matter. Castle gossip, however, would give Helen fodder for more taunting.

Nay, he couldn't do that to Jocelyn, no matter how much he desired peace.

"Malcolm?" Jocelyn stepped in front of him, her questioning gaze sealing his decision. Saints, she was beautiful in the flickering torchlight.

"Aye." He took the torch from her hand. With his other hand, he twisted a curl that lay against her cheek. So soft.

She took his hand and smiled, pulling him into the hallway. She led him to a room near the solar. A smile teased her full lips as she led him inside.

A fire lit and warmed the spacious room. Two padded chairs

sat before the fire with a table in between. Two cups and a jug sat on the table. His trunk rested next to another that must be hers. Tapestries hung on the walls. The room invited him in.

Malcolm released her hand and set the torch in the wall.

"Shall I pour you spiced mead?" She went to the table, her hand poised over the pitcher.

"Nay."

"Do you wish to sit by the fire?"

"Nay, I do not want to sit, and I do not want talk." He didn't try to stop himself as he went to her, sliding his hands around her waist and pulling her to him. She came willingly, looping her arms around his neck and lifting her face to his. His lips hovered over hers, and she sighed, trembling in his embrace.

He kissed her, teasing her lips before kissing a trail along her jawline. She sucked in a breath as he nipped her earlobe. Scooping her into his arms, he walked to the bed and gently laid her down. His beautiful, passionate wife.

A languid calm rippled through him, releasing the tension from his body. Within her arms, the tranquility he longed for found a home. There, he had peace.

CHAPTER 23

Jocelyn smoothed the bedding over the mattress, then plumped the pillows. Once again, she'd woken up alone. She tried to ease the sting by dressing and straightening the room, but she wrestled with the hurt of his avoidance and the need to find a way to gain his trust.

"Oh, m'lady." Ida entered the room. "I didn't know you were still here, it bein' so late."

Jocelyn set the pillow on the bed. "I'm lazy this morn, it seems."

"Lazy? You be doin' my chores!"

"There is plenty of work still to do." Jocelyn took her night shift from the end of the bed and put it in the trunk. "Do you know where Lord Malcolm is this morning?"

"Nay, though I did hear talk of a hunting party going out later."

A hunting party? They had plenty of meat in the salt house.

"Shall I bring you something from the kitchen? The morning meal has already been served." Ida gathered the cups and jug.

"Nay, I shall get something later. I'm going to check on some of the tasks I assigned yesterday."

"Very good, m'lady." Ida curtsied and left the room.

Jocelyn followed her out, then headed the other direction to check the rooms the servants cleaned yesterday. She opened the first door. The bed had been stripped, but ash filled the fireplace and covered part of the floor. She checked the other three rooms with the same results. Odd.

Shutting the door to the last room, she looked for a servant. Not seeing any in the hall, she entered the kitchen, blinking against the smoky haze. Nelda stood by the open back door, fanning the room with her apron.

Jocelyn rushed to the cook. "What happened?"

"I was teaching Lisbet how to make bread and forgot about the sauces cooking in the coals. Me and my addled brain."

"We've all had much on our minds recently. Don't worry your addled head about it."

Nelda chuckled. "You are kind like your mother."

"I'm honored you would say that." Jocelyn didn't feel kind, at least not in her dealings with Helen.

Nelda continued her fanning. "Did you need me, m'lady?"

"I was looking for Ida or any of the housemaids."

"Today is wash day, so you might try the washroom or down by the river."

Surely not all the castle servants did the wash. If so, a change of plan was in order. "Thank you, Nelda." She left through the back door. When she spotted a servant girl carrying a basket of wet clothing across the bailey, she waved and walked toward the girl.

"Good mornin' to ye, m'lady."

"Good morning. Do you know anything about the cleaning of the rooms upstairs?"

"Aye, we started yesterday, then went to weed the garden as Lady Helen instructed." The girl cocked her head. "Were we wrong to do so?"

Jocelyn forced a smile. It wasn't the girl's fault. "Nay, 'tis all right. Thank you for clarifying, but tomorrow would you see that the cleaning gets finished?"

"Aye, m'lady. 'Twill be done first thing."

"That is all. Thank you." Jocelyn made her way to Matilda's, frustrated at Helen's interference. First changing the menu, now changing Jocelyn's orders. How else could she make herself clear to Helen? Or was she intentionally undoing Jocelyn's work? After knocking on the seamstress's door, Jocelyn smiled when Matilda opened the door. "Is the work dress ready?"

"Aye, my lady, enter."

The woman lifted a gray gown from the table. "'Tis simple, but perfect for working about the castle."

"Aye, 'tis."

"Try it on and make sure it fits properly."

Jocelyn undressed and slid the gown over her head, letting it settle over her chemise. It hung loosely on her body, especially about the waist. "'Tisn't quite right. You used the same measurements as you took yesterday?"

"Lady Helen said you requested a bigger dress, in the hopes of a baby."

Jocelyn rubbed her forehead, trying to process her words. Pulling off the dress, she handed it back to Matilda. "I'm sorry Lady Helen told you that, for 'tis not true. Would you take in the dress to the original measurements?"

"Of course, I am happy to do so."

"Then I shall take my leave. I've much to do." She left Matilda's hut, fuming at Helen's intrusion. Jocelyn could understand Helen forgetting her place after so many years of commanding Ramslea, but to interfere with her dressmaking? 'Twas no accident. It must stop.

Jocelyn returned to the kitchen, her steps determined. "Nelda, I require your aid."

The cook set down her spoon. "What can I do?"

"Spread word that everyone is to meet in the hall during the midday meal. That includes all the help." She'd have gathered the guards too, but Malcolm should converse with them.

"I will, m'lady."

"Good." Jocelyn clapped her hands together as she left the kitchens and returned to the solar. Looking out the window over the bailey, she breathed deep to calm her racing heart. Though ready to put a stop to Helen's schemes, her nerves tangled about like her hair during a fast run on Black. Helen's actions displacing Jocelyn's authority solidified Jocelyn's belief of Helen's proclivity toward subterfuge.

Dealing with Helen and all the anger she stirred within Jocelyn made it difficult to focus on her relationship with Malcolm. While she desperately wanted to work on her marriage, she needed to deal with her heart before she could proceed toward developing trust between her and Malcolm. Holding on to anger would stifle the honesty and love needed to build a strong bond with her husband. She would give clear boundaries and rules to the staff regarding her responsibility as chatelaine, hopefully putting a stop to Helen's interference and lessening the anger toward her stepmother.

Lord, I need Your help in dealing with Helen. Help me to make my directives clear while remaining calm and kind. Help me to temper my anger toward her.

Pushing away from the window, she pulled out her tapestry and embroidery thread. She thought better when her hands were busy. Sitting in one of the chairs, she stitched while putting together the speech she would give at the next meal. After poking herself for the tenth time, however, she set her work aside and went to the great hall to await the servants.

Not wanting to intimidate them, Jocelyn sat at one of the guards' tables as she waited. Men and women, young and old, began to fill the hall.

Once everyone was seated, Jocelyn stood in front of the head table and clasped her hands. "Thank you for your work here at Ramslea. You are invaluable to the running and safety of this estate, and I am proud to have returned to claim my place here."

Helen stood at the back of the hall, her arms folded across her chest. Jocelyn took a breath and continued, "There has been some confusion the past few days regarding who is in charge. While Lady Helen has been chatelaine these past four years, that role is now mine. I am married to the lord of Ramslea, giving me rights as chatelaine to run the castle as I see fit." The crowd murmured. "Please know that I am not angry with you over any miscommunication thus far." Only with Helen.

Love your enemy.

Faith, why remember that now? She glanced at Helen, a smirk resting on her stepmother's face.

"Lady Helen has done an excellent job at Ramslea, and I appreciate all of her hard work. I hope to continue to keep a grand home for all of us. Now, eat and drink, then return to your duties."

Jocelyn rounded the table and sat as the kitchen servants brought in platters of food. She straightened in her seat when Helen slid into the chair next to her. Jocelyn braced herself for Helen's reaction.

"That was quite impressive, Jocelyn. I admire your bravado."

"I only wanted to clear up any confusion."

Helen took a bite of cheese. "I hope you know what you are doing."

"I do."

"I daresay you don't."

Jocelyn drained her goblet. If she couldn't answer in love, then she wouldn't answer at all. She ate, then went to her room. Plopping onto the bed, she curled up under a blanket.

Her body bore the weight of a hundred iron shields as if she'd worked a whole day in the space of a few hours. She'd asserted herself and was kind in the process. 'Twas a good work thus far.

Closing her eyes, she relaxed, letting the tension of the morning drain from her limbs. If only Malcolm would attend the evening meal. They had much to discuss.

Malcolm returned late in the afternoon with two bucks, four boars, and several quail. The skilled hunters and productive hunt impressed him. There would be plenty of game to keep the people fed throughout the winter months. As he stabled Horse, the rest of the hunting party saw to their kill.

Malcolm's stomach rumbled, but he didn't care to be around Helen and Jocelyn and their combativeness. Instead, he headed for the bathhouse. A nice hot bath would at least ease his physical tension.

"My lord!"

A guard approached from across the bailey. "Aye?"

"A messenger has come. He is at the gate."

The guard led the way to where a man stood beside a lathered horse, missive in hand.

As Malcolm approached, the man bowed. "You have a message for me?"

The man handed him the paper, sealed with wax and stamped with a royal seal. "This is from the king?"

"From the king's official, my lord."

He broke the seal. Could this be word regarding Jocelyn's mystery? Or perhaps 'twas news of Helen's coming nuptials. The sooner she left, the sooner he'd gain some peace.

> *To Lord Malcolm Castillon, of Ramslea,*
>
> *When I arrived at Lomkirk Abbey to investigate the blackmail of the abbess, she was not here. She left the abbey four days after Lady Jocelyn ran away, refusing to tell of her destination. 'Tis said she headed north.*
>
> *I have discovered that Agatha is a sister to Lady Helen Ashburne, so I'm sending this missive by way of messenger to hopefully arrive before the abbess, should she be heading to Ramslea.*
>
> *Signed,*
> *Peter Williamson, official of King Richard*

Malcolm frowned. Helen had a connection with the abbess, giving Jocelyn's suspicions more weight. "How long since you left the abbey?"

"Two days. I rode straight through, changing horses as needed along the way."

Malcolm calculated the abbess's arrival if indeed she traveled to Ramslea. She could be here by tomorrow.

He folded the missive, nodding at the messenger. "Thank you for your swiftness. Guard, show this man to the stable, then take him to the hall and see he's fed well."

"Thank you, my lord."

His captain of the guard should be informed. While Malcolm knew the abbess didn't pose a physical threat, her connection with Helen bothered him. What if Jocelyn's suspicions were correct and Helen wanted her out of the way? He doubted Helen was truly malicious but, to be safe, he wanted Jocelyn guarded.

As Malcolm entered the gatehouse, Ian stood from the small table in the corner of the room. Beds lined the walls of the building that housed the guards.

Ian approached his lord, brows raised. "My lord, is all well?"

"I received a missive stating that the abbess at Lomkirk is related to Lady Helen. She's reported to be heading north, though no one knows her destination. I want Lady Jocelyn guarded at all times. No exceptions."

Ian nodded. "I shall assign one of our best guards."

"I prefer that you handle the task. Having been entrusted with Lady Jocelyn's care before, I want Ramslea's best for her safety."

"Thank you, my lord."

"Good. Now, after a long day in the saddle, I need a bath. I trust you will keep watch over our lady while I am occupied. Most likely I won't make it to supper."

"Aye, my lord."

They left the gatehouse, Ian to the hall and Malcolm to the bathhouse. The hot bath would give him time to consider his next steps. Somehow he must learn more about Helen and the abbess, for Jocelyn's sake—and his own peace of mind.

CHAPTER 24

Eyes crossing, Jocelyn laid aside the tapestry and leaned her head against the chair. Married four days and lonelier than she'd ever been.

Malcolm came to her each night, giving hope that he grew to love her, but each morning he left before the sun rose, then he stayed away until after dinner. He claimed much work had to be done, but she knew the truth. He desired her, but he still did not trust her, nor did he love her.

She understood that trust took time, but if he stayed away, how could she show him her trustworthiness? She ached for their easy camaraderie before their marriage.

Melancholy settled upon her like a heavy mantle of gloom, smothering her with hopelessness. While she knew love in a marriage was not a guarantee, she'd expected Malcolm to love her quickly after giving her body to him. Foolish thinking, to be sure. She'd been the dutiful wife—a loving wife—and God still hadn't blessed her marriage with even a hint of growth.

She'd never cultivated the virtue of patience, as evidenced not only in her poor tapestry skills but in her frustration at Malcolm's silence. Perhaps that was God's intention now. But hadn't she been patient enough? Hadn't she loved Malcolm well?

Love, as I have loved you.

Jocelyn bolted upright, her hands gripping the arms of the chair. "Who's there?" She glanced at the door, but it remained closed.

Rushing to it, she threw open the door and rushed into the hallway. Her face met the broad back of a guardsman. She yelped.

The guard turned and smiled.

"Ian, do not scare me thusly!"

He grunted, stepping to the side of the door. "You ran into *me*, m'lady."

"Did you see anyone just now?"

"Nay, my lady."

"Were you talking to yourself?"

Ian's brows rose. "Nay, my lady, I do not speak my thoughts out loud. Is something wrong?"

"Nay. I must have been dreaming." Jocelyn closed the door and leaned against the hard surface. Either God had spoken, or He had sent those words to her heart.

She'd heard tales of sisters who experienced such things, but Jocelyn did not feel qualified to hear from God. She knew her own dark thoughts too well to expect she had any special connection with God. And yet, what if He hoped to nudge her with those words?

Love, as I have loved you.

Why was it so easy to forget? Mayhap because 'twas difficult, sacrificing oneself for the sake of another. Was she up to the challenge?

Jocelyn walked to the small window and opened it wide. Gazing beyond the castle walls, she squinted against the sun high overhead. The land shimmered in the red-gold hues of autumn. She shivered in the crisp coolness. The beauty of God's creation brought a tangible sense of His presence, His creative power. His presence flowed through her like honey from a sun-drenched honeycomb.

Jocelyn drew in a shaky breath. She would be patient and earn Malcolm's trust. She'd love with no expectations. 'Twouldn't be easy for her needy heart.

Her stomach rumbled. She'd skipped breakfast in favor of solitude in the solar, now reaping the consequence. By the position of the sun, the noon meal should be served soon. She turned from the window and opened the door. Ian stood with his back to her.

"What are you doing here?"

"Keeping watch over you."

"Why?"

"Lord Malcolm commanded it."

"But why? I've had no guard since I returned home. Why now?"

Ian shrugged. "You should ask Lord Malcolm."

Jocelyn stepped past him. "Hmmm." She moved down the hallway, Ian following close behind.

In the hall, Helen once again sat in Malcolm's seat at the head table. Jocelyn lifted her chin against the smug smile greeting her.

Love, as I have loved you.

Perhaps those words applied to Helen as well as Malcolm. *Lord, forgive my anger and lack of desire to love her.*

Though Jocelyn must learn to love as God loved, she did not have to sit by Helen. Besides, she wanted to find out why Ian guarded her so closely. Walking past the table, she made her way to the bailey door.

Ian moved in front of her, walking backward as he pointed to the table laid out with trenchers of food. "My lady, won't you partake of the noonday meal?"

"Nay, I have something I must see to." She stepped around him.

"But—"

Jocelyn eyed the trenchers at the nearest table. She grabbed some bread and cheese, then continued on. "Stay and eat, Ian. I shall be fine on my own."

"Alas, I cannot. I must stay with you. I best be allowed to pound someone while protecting you if forced to forego meals."

Jocelyn laughed as she continued to the bailey. "I doubt I'll find any trouble today, so the pounding may have to wait."

"From what I've heard, you need a garrison of guards to keep you from harm's way."

Jocelyn stopped. Had Malcolm been sharing tales about her mishaps? Ian ran into her, jostling her forward.

"By the saints, my lady, you—"

"I don't know what you've heard, or who you've heard it from, but I do not need a keeper." Jocelyn took a breath, calming her defensive heart. She might not be a perfect lady, but that didn't mean she must be guarded. She wanted an explanation. "Do you know where Lord Malcolm is?"

"He is in the lists."

Jocelyn headed in that direction. Women weren't allowed in the lists, but if Malcolm would not come to her, she would go to him. Not only could she question him about Ian, she could ask him to question the guards about Helen. She'd also be able to watch him work—something that brought a smile to her face

"But Lady Jocelyn, you cannot think to go to the lists."

Jocelyn ignored him, taking a bite of her bread.

As she neared the lists, the clash of steel and men's shouts greeted her. At the gate, Ian moved in front of her, barring her entrance. "My lady, women are forbidden in the lists." He frowned and crossed his arms.

Jocelyn smiled and made to move around him. He shifted, not allowing her to pass. She raised an eyebrow. "I *shall* enter, and you *will* heed my command."

"My lady, please do not. My lord shall have my head for allowing his lady into the lists."

"I will not allow you to take the blame. I only wish to watch my husband do what he does best."

Ian grumbled, but he opened the gate and stepped aside.

The walled area opened to the sky, the sun bearing down upon Ramslea's guards. Many worked in pairs, practicing their swordplay. Ian pointed to a wooden bench near the door. She sat and spotted Malcolm walking through the lists, encouraging strong strokes, offering suggestions about technique, and pushing the men to work efficiently.

He stopped to watch two guards sparring, his arms crossed as their blades clashed. When one of the men stumbled, he raised a hand. "Cease!"

Both men stopped. Malcolm grabbed the nearest man's sword. "Place your hand just so, then swing through." He demonstrated the action. When he returned the sword, the guard did as Malcolm instructed. "Aye, 'tis good. Your strength is impressive."

Filled with pride, Jocelyn marveled at her husband's ability to balance criticism with compliments. The men responded to his instruction with gratitude. 'Twas evident they respected him, even liked him.

"You there, come work with me." Malcolm pointed at one of the guards. As the man approached, Malcolm drew his sword. The guard lunged, and the sparring ensued.

Jocelyn's heart skipped at the sight of her husband. His sure yet graceful footwork reminded her of a dance. Back and forth, give and take. His muscular arms swung his sword with power. He fought with such strength that she could not help but smile. Many of the men stopped their swordplay and gathered to watch the match.

Malcolm's opponent advanced, pushing him back. Jocelyn came to her feet. Malcolm lifted his sword high to deflect blow after blow. He faltered and backed into a water barrel. He stumbled, almost losing his sword with the next blow.

Jocelyn gasped.

Malcolm jerked, turning in her direction. His opponent took advantage, and Malcolm barely managed to twist away from another strike. "Cease!" He rose and stormed toward her, sword in hand, jaw clenched.

Twisting the edge of her sleeve, Jocelyn braced herself.

Ian walked toward Malcolm. "My lord, I allowed—"

Her husband strode around him to stand before Jocelyn and drove his blade into the ground "By the saints, what are you doing here?"

"I needed to speak with you and wanted to watch your swordplay."

He took her by the arm and escorted her through the gate, away from the sea of onlookers. Turning her to face him, his lips flattened. "This is not a place for women. You will have my men losing their heads and limbs at the distraction."

Once again, Jocelyn had succumbed to her impatience. Though needing to speak with her husband, she should have waited until he finished his exercise, no matter how much she wanted to be near him. She should have considered his needs before her own. Her eyes misted at her continued missteps. "I did not intend you harm."

She turned to go, not wanting him to see her tears, but Malcolm caught her hand. "Jocelyn, you must realize you cannot do the things you did when dressed as a lad."

She nodded, her throat thick. She had purposed to wait on God only a short while ago, yet here she stood before her angry husband, guilty as charged. "I am sorry. I promise 'twill not happen again," she whispered.

When he let go of her arm, she walked away. She hoped he would not come after her, for she did not think her heart could handle another lecture—even if he was in the right. Not wanting to return to the frustrating work of the needle, she wished for another distraction to ease her troubled mind.

As she approached the stable, a horse neighed. Black! She hadn't seen him since before the tournament. She altered her course.

Ian stopped beside the stable door. "I shall wait for you here."

She entered between the rows of stalls, dust dancing in the shafts of light streaming through the front and back doors. Horses whickered as she passed each one, looking for Black. He stood in the next to the last stall, his dark head looming above the gate.

"Black."

His ears perked forward, and he came to her. When she stepped into his stall, Black nodded his head. She stroked his forehead. "How good 'tis to see you," she whispered.

Jocelyn took her time stroking his smooth hide. Did he yearn to ride free as much as she did? Oh, to feel the weight of impossibility blow away in the wind. Closing her eyes, she leaned her forehead against his smooth mane and breathed in the scent of fresh hay and horse.

"Jocelyn."

She jerked back. Black tossed his head and snorted, prancing around nervously. His hoof stomped near her foot. Faith!

Strong arms yanked her from the stall. Heart racing and hair in disarray, she relaxed in the arms of her rescuer—saved once again by her husband.

Malcolm pushed the hair out of her face. "Are you hurt? I didn't mean to startle you."

Taking in a calming breath, she rested her hands against his broad chest. His heart beat beneath them, steady and strong. "Aye. Thank you for pulling me to safety."

Malcolm released her and stepped back. Her hands fell to her sides. He moved past her, grabbing a hold of Black's neck. He murmured into the horse's ear until Black settled. Once he did, Malcolm returned his attention to Jocelyn. "Were you wishing to ride?"

"Aye."

"Then ride you shall." He fetched Horse from his stall and saddled him, then led him out of the stable. Jocelyn followed, waiting for him to ready her horse.

Outside, three guardsmen stood with Ian. "I've men ready, my lord. We shall be right behind you."

Malcolm leaped onto Horse, then held his hand toward her.

Her brows rose. "You do not mean for me to ride with you?"

"Aye." Malcolm smiled. "I do indeed."

Jocelyn shivered. Such a small thing, his smile, but it melted her heart and eased its ache. She slid her hand into his, and he lifted her onto his lap.

Jocelyn struggled for breath, his nearness sending her heart into a thunderous beat. "Shouldn't I be behind you?"

Malcolm held her waist with a firm grasp. "While I would enjoy having your arms around me, due to your long skirt you will do better here where I can make sure you do not fall. If you were to do so, the castle would be in an uproar over my inability to see you safely about."

He spoke truth—riding astride in a dress would be most immodest—though she had hoped for a more intimate explanation. "If you insist." Nestled in his arms, warmth radiated through her. She rather liked riding in the front, even if only for practical reasons.

Malcolm walked Horse through the bailey. 'Twasn't long before guards rode up behind them. Jocelyn glanced over Malcolm's shoulder. They kept a discreet distance as Malcolm rode toward the barbican.

"I can understand having guards with us outside the castle, but why has Ian followed me around all morning?"

"I received word that the abbess was not at Lomkirk when the king's official arrived."

"What?" She turned her attention to her husband's face, looking for any sign of jest.

"I doubt the abbess will come near Ramslea, but the official discovered that she is Helen's sister."

"Nay!" Jocelyn's mind churned at the news. Helen *did* have ties to Agatha. If Helen was capable of blackmailing her own sister, she most certainly could have spread the rumor regarding Jocelyn's supposed death. Still, 'twasn't proof, but the new information secured Jocelyn's suspicions of her stepmother. "Do you think she will try to see Helen?"

"I doubt she would risk being caught, but I don't want to take a chance with your safety." He motioned behind them with his head. "Hence the guard. And you might want to keep your dagger at the ready."

Jocelyn swallowed.

"I jest. You are safe, I promise." He pulled her close, and she closed her eyes. He did care—another morsel of hope. They passed the castle gates, and Malcolm gripped her tighter, then coaxed Horse into a gallop. Jocelyn held his arm, thankful for the security he provided.

The musty smell of the damp terrain coupled with the crisp wind stole her breath as the warm sun overhead loosened the cords that had bound her in frustration. She laughed, exhilarated by the speed with which they flew.

Her home. Malcolm's land. 'Twas theirs as long as God saw fit.

They traveled the dusty road, passing copious trees that thinned until she spotted the village ahead. Malcolm slowed Horse to a walk while they navigated the streets, nodding at and greeting the residents who wished them well. They exited on the other side of the village, and farmland stretched as far as she could see. A handful of men tended the crops in the field to the left of the road.

Malcolm brushed her hair to the side, his mouth close to her ear. "I would like to stop and talk with the farmers a moment. Would that suit?"

"Aye." In that moment, with his hand on her neck, she would say aye to anything he asked of her. He'd gifted her his presence. 'Twas enough.

Malcolm veered in their direction. Once he reached the edge of the field, he dismounted, then held up his arms for Jocelyn.

Heat stole across her cheeks as his hands spread over her ribs. She hoped he hadn't noticed. When he released her waist, his lips quirked into a small smile before he moved toward the workers. Aye, he'd noticed.

The laborers drew near, using their hoes like walking sticks.

"Greetings. I am Malcolm Castillon, new lord of Ramslea, and this is the Lady Jocelyn. I would hear about your plantings."

"We are dealing with a new plant bug that eats the leaves of our barley fields. We've been killing them as we find them."

"How much damage have they done?"

"More than we would like. A sickness plagued the village the past week, and we haven't as many workers to help."

Malcolm looked at Jocelyn. "I promised you a ride, yet I would see the problems they speak of. Ian will take you home, and we shall ride another time." He motioned for Ian, but Jocelyn put a hand on his arm.

"Nay, I will stay."

"I fear I may be overlong."

"Please let me wait. There are trees nearby under which I can rest. I would dearly love to be out of doors on such a beautiful day. There won't be many left before winter sets in."

"If you are sure."

"Aye, 'twould be lovely."

He gave her a small bow before returning to the farmers. They walked through the fields, stopping now and then to examine different plants. As they did, Jocelyn walked toward the grove of timbers, loving the warmth of the sun on her face. She'd gather more spots across her nose, but 'twas worth it.

The trees provided a large expanse of shade, so she sat at the base of the largest one, taking in the view around her. To the west, the mountains nestled against the castle. A forest in the other direction crept across the rolling land like a mass of dark green moss. She knew from her father's stories that 'twas the best place for hunting.

Turning her attention back to the fields, she could make out Malcolm working alongside the men among the crops. What manner of lord worked with the serfs? She had expected him to be like her father, ruling from within the castle walls, set apart from the lower class. Malcolm didn't seem to mind working side by side with his serfs though, toiling in the sun.

Mayhap she'd been wrong in her assessment that he only cared about owning the land. 'Twould seem the new lord cared about the people as well. She could learn much from her new husband. 'Twould serve her well to help the servants with tasks around the castle instead of merely stitching tapestries and creating menus.

The jingle of tack drew her attention to the mounted guards spread out a good distance around her. Poor souls. They must be mindless with tedium, though she appreciated the level of security. The abbess's disappearance was disturbing.

As she watched her husband work, her heart filled with thankfulness. Even after her mistake in the lists earlier, Malcolm had sought her company. She didn't deserve it, but she'd treasure his company as often as he deigned to offer it. Time spent with Malcolm made for a wonderful day.

Shouts startled her. At the edge of the field, a lad lifted a pail off a cart, then carried it toward the workers.

Jocelyn rose, brushed off her gown, and headed toward the boy. Small in stature, he struggled with his load. Maybe she could offer aid. "Are you taking drink to the workers?"

"Aye, my lady." He set his pail down and bowed. "May I get you a drink?" He took a cup, dipped it into the pail, and handed it to her.

"Thank you. You are most kind."

After taking a long drink, she looked at Malcolm digging at the base of some plants. Damp hair clung to his face as he wiped the sweat from his brow.

I was thirsty, and you gave me drink.

Jocelyn handed the cup back to the boy. "May I take a drink to my husband?"

"Aye." The boy nodded so hard Jocelyn thought his head would ache. He filled another cup and handed it to her.

She drew close to Malcolm, and he looked up, squinting against the sun. He stuck the hoe into the ground, as she held out the cup.

"You must be thirsty."

"Aye." He wiped his hands on his tunic. "I am indeed."

Jocelyn's fingers tingled as his hand closed over hers.

The corners of his eyes crinkled. "Thank you, my lady."

She pulled her hand away and pushed her hair behind her ear. Taking the empty cup, she returned to the boy, refilling it and offering it to a worker nearby. She continued serving, nodding to each man.

By the time she had finished, Malcolm stood by the edge of the field with Horse, watching her walk toward him. She ducked her head, self-conscious at his perusal. Being admired in the daylight among guards and serfs was altogether different than under the cover of darkness in the privacy of their room.

When she drew close, he grasped her around the waist, lifted her upon Horse, then leaped up behind her. "You are quite the hostess, my lady."

"I could not very well give you drink and not the others." Her heart tumbled as his hand slid across her belly, then pulled her close.

"You could have allowed the water boy to do his duty."

"Aye, but then I would have missed the pleasure of seeing the look of astonishment cross your face."

His rumbling laughter brought a familiar comfort to her. She had missed his teasing.

Malcolm set his mount racing across the land. Jocelyn loved the surge of Horse's power beneath her. The trees blurred as they ran by, and it seemed they reached the castle in only a few minutes. She'd loved to have ridden longer but knew Malcolm must have duties to attend. They cantered to the stable where Malcolm slid off Horse.

With the attention Malcolm had given her today, would he attend the evening meal? Jocelyn did not want to seem as if she begged, yet she had missed his presence and wanted him to know she had noticed his absence. "Will you be at supper, my lord?"

Helping her down, he did not release his grip on her waist. Instead, he gazed into her eyes. "Do you want me there?"

"I do, though you need not come if you find it tedious."

Malcolm leaned down, his lips hovering over hers. Heart hammering in her chest, she struggled for air, waiting for his kiss. His roughened cheek brushed hers as those lips—which should have claimed her own—brushed against her ear. "You, my lady, are anything but tedious." He pressed a kiss beneath her ear. Her breath hitched.

Malcolm stepped back and gave her a small bow. Bereft of the warmth of his hands, Jocelyn swallowed hard. "I thank you for a most enjoyable ride."

With a wink, he left the stables.

She sucked in a deep breath as Malcolm's tall, broad form swaggered through the bailey. My, but he muddled her head. He hadn't said he'd be at supper, yet his attention today spoke of his interest.

Someone snorted behind her, and she twisted around. Ian handed the reins of his horse to a stable lad and walked toward her. He couldn't have heard all of their conversation—at least not the whispered words in her ear.

Jocelyn's hands settled on her hips. "What do you find so humorous?"

"Only the dance of love." Ian crossed his arms and smirked.

"Humph." Jocelyn punched him in the arm. "The dance of love, indeed. What do you know of such things?"

"I have eyes. And I have some experience with women, I assure you."

"I'll wager you do." She shook her head with a smile as she left the stable.

"Where do you go?" Ian fell in step beside her.

"My belly is so loud, I'm near deaf. Nelda will have some tasty morsels to tide me over until the evening." As Jocelyn neared the kitchen, her mouth watered at the aromas emanating from the ovens. Inside, fresh-baked bread cooled on the table while the pot on the fire bubbled with a delicious-smelling brew.

"Well, look at wha' come in me kitchen." Nelda wiped her hands on her apron. "Ye must be a mite starved, I imagine. Ye missed the meal if I'm not mistaken. Ye *and* the master."

Jocelyn ducked her head, a sheepish smile tugging at her lips. "Aye, we observed the crops today. Malco—uh, my lord even worked the fields."

"Ye don't say?"

"Aye. He did."

"I never heard such a thing. Most unusual." Nelda cut a large portion of bread and handed it to Jocelyn. "'Twould seem he has the makings of a fine lord."

Jocelyn bit into the warm treat and nodded. "Aye, 'twas most impressive."

"'Tis happy I am for you and the master. A good union, to be sure."

The bread stuck in Jocelyn's throat. "I am happy enough. My life is better now that I am home, though I miss Father."

Nelda handed her a cup of milk. "Aye, things have not been the same since his passing."

Lisbet burst through the back door. "Nelda, you need to come—" She stopped, noticing Jocelyn. "Sorry to disturb, but something has happened to the greens in the garden."

"Och, my lady, I must see to the garden and choose something else for the meal."

Nelda left with Lisbet as Jocelyn downed her milk. Ian entered the kitchen, ducking his head through the doorway

"I wondered where you had gone," she said.

"I had something to attend to."

"Here, food will do you good." She handed him a slice of the bread.

"I thank you, my lady. I am famished." Ian ate it in one bite. "We mustn't skip the breaking of our fast thusly. 'Tisn't good for a man's strength."

Jocelyn rolled her eyes. "You don't look to be wasting away."

"I should think not." He stood straighter.

Jocelyn laughed. "I'm not questioning your brawn, Ian. My thought was you would not perish by missing one meal." Her laughter turned into a yawn. "I don't know why I am so weary. You may go about your manly affairs while I take a nap in my chamber. I shall be safe enough."

"I shall escort you, my lady, else my lord have my head." He grabbed another piece of bread and followed her out of the kitchen.

Once in the bedroom, she stoked the fire, remembering Malcolm's example in the field. No use calling a maid when she could do the job herself. It wasn't expected of her, but she rather enjoyed caring for herself. She chuckled. She had grumbled about her chores at the abbey, and now she missed the work. Mayhap blending her different lives would be just the thing to bring purpose and fulfillment to daily life.

With the fire crackling, she crawled onto the bed. Stuffed with feathers, the mattress wrapped about her like a cocoon.

Watching her husband work and seeing his care over the land and its people revealed his noble heart to her in a new way. Now if only she could cease pondering about him, she might claim a lovely nap.

CHAPTER 25

Bathed and dressed for the occasion, Malcolm left for the great hall. His stomach knotted, but he wouldn't admit to his nervousness. He was a warrior, not an inexperienced youth. Blowing out a breath, he wiped his sweaty palms on his tunic.

His wife wanted him at supper—the woman who didn't grow angry when he spent time in the fields, leaving her to herself. The woman who gave of herself to serve the workers. The woman who desired his attention. The protective wall he'd built around his heart crumbled piece by piece as he discovered more of Jocelyn's character. Perhaps 'twas time to let her within the walls of his heart.

Once inside the hall, he scanned the room for his wife. Helen stood by the fire, hands outstretched, but Jocelyn was not present. He made his way to the main table to await her.

As he sat, Jocelyn appeared at the bottom of the stairs. Before he could stop himself, Malcolm walked around the table to meet her. The blue of her eyes was deepened by the sapphire of her gown. Her curls gleamed about her shoulders. Even with the fading bruises, she was most becoming. Her countenance bloomed as he approached, and when she welcomed him with a smile, his knees all but buckled.

"You are lovely, Jocelyn."

"I know I should cover my hair since I am now a married woman. I cannot bring myself to do so just yet. It feels good to be free of the veil I had to wear at the abbey."

Malcolm wrapped a curl around his finger. "'Tis fetching. Leave it undone, for I enjoy the view."

A tinge of pink touched Jocelyn's cheeks. He took her by the hand and led her to the table. Settling her beside him, he pulled the trencher between them.

"Thank you for joining me tonight," she said, choosing a piece of fowl.

"How could I refuse my lady's request?" He handed her a chunk of bread and took a large portion of the fowl for himself.

"I am still hungry, even though I sampled Nelda's bread before I napped."

"Did you? I too snatched a loaf while she wasn't looking. I didn't realize how long we had been absent. You complained not once while waiting for me to finish with the workers."

Jocelyn frowned. "You think me impatient?"

"'Twould seem you have a short memory, my dear lady." He smiled as she straightened her spine. So predictable. "You forget how you moaned at the slowness of your sword lessons."

"I did no—"

Malcolm put a finger to her full lips. He leaned in close and watched with satisfaction as her eyes grew wide. "Today, however, you surprised me. You said not a word about having to wait on me. And you brought me water."

His finger moved from her lips, and he gave in to the temptation to caress her smooth, rosy cheek. "I have been thirsty of late." How he wanted to drink from those lips again. Captivated, he watched her mouth part.

"'Twould seem the two of you are getting along." Helen sat in the chair beside Malcolm.

He pulled his hand back and reached for his drink. "Lady Helen, I trust you are well."

"Not as well as you, apparently."

Malcolm nodded but didn't respond. He almost felt sorry for the woman, having lost so much in such a short time. But knowing her and the abbess were sisters added a layer of caution. What if she had the power to hurt Jocelyn?

As they ate, musicians set up in the corner and struck up a lively tune. He turned to Jocelyn. "Did you request music this evening?"

"They play every night. 'Tis a custom my parents started when I was young. They believed merriment was good for morale. Dancing is a favorite pastime at Ramslea."

"Your favorite?"

"One of my favorites."

Malcolm envisioned dancing with Jocelyn in their middle-aged years, hope spurring his heart into a rapid cadence. Trusting Jocelyn would be such an easy thing to give in to, but his heart remained safe behind the barrier he'd built. He pushed aside the doubt, choosing to enjoy Jocelyn.

Helen sipped her wine. "I enjoy the dance as well."

Malcolm turned his attention to Helen. "I seem to recall you did not enjoy dancing with me."

"Sir Rolland is a better dancer."

"Now that he is gone, I will suffice?"

"There are plenty of men in the room who can dance with Helen," said Jocelyn.

Malcolm smiled at her assertiveness. "Helen, tonight I dance with my wife."

"If you must," she said. "I shall not want for partners."

Malcolm did not doubt her words. After they'd finished their meal, he rose and held out his hand to Jocelyn. She paused before putting her hand in his.

"You hesitate. Do you not wish to dance with me, my lady?" Uncertainty rose within him. Had he been wrong about his wife's attentions?

"Aye, I do." She let Malcolm lead her to the middle of the hall. She curtsied, dipping low. "Shall we perform for your men?"

Malcolm looked over at his crew, many still sitting at tables off to the side, merry from their ale. "I can manage quite a performance." He bowed, taking her hand and bringing it to his lips, kissing each small knuckle. She shivered.

Malcolm enjoyed this kind of performance.

Moving with grace and a lilt to her steps, Jocelyn laughed as they moved across the hall. Song after song they danced until the musicians begged for release. By the time they stopped, the hall had emptied of people, save for Ian and a few guardsmen standing along the wall.

"I'm parched, and my feet ache." Jocelyn sat on a bench and pushed back her hair.

"I shall obtain something to ease our thirst."

Before he could move, a young maid appeared with two goblets of mead. She curtsied. "Would you care for a drink after your entertainment, my lord?"

"Indeed, I would."

Taking the drinks, he handed one to Jocelyn before downing his own. "I know you must be weary. Why don't we retire so I can ease the pain in your feet?"

"How do you propose to do that?"

"I could rub them for you. Though if you care not for that idea, I could bring you wine to make you forget the ache."

Jocelyn pursed her full lips. "I suppose you might be able to relieve my pain." She tilted her head. "Have you ever performed such a task before?"

"Nay, but I am up to learning a new chore." He offered his hand. This time she took it with no hesitation.

"My lord!" Lisbet rushed into the hall. "You are needed in the stables. There is something amiss with Horse. Come quickly!"

"Is it something the stable hand can manage?" The last thing Malcolm wanted to do was leave Jocelyn.

"Nay, he said to fetch you straight away."

Jocelyn squeezed his hand. "You must see to your horse. It sounds important."

"I will not be long. I promise you."

"All is well. Go."

Malcolm lifted Jocelyn's hand and kissed the inside of her wrist. His gaze met hers. "I would hear of your other favorite pastimes.

We may have a few in common."

She laughed. "Indeed."

Malcolm grabbed a torch before striding from the hall. He had a beautiful wife to rush back to.

Jocelyn leaned against the wall and sighed. Her attentive husband had melted her heart with his lingering looks and soft caresses. She looked forward to his return. A smile on her face, she headed for the kitchens to snitch some honeyed cakes and mead to share with Malcolm later.

"Where do you go, my lady?"

Jocelyn looked over her shoulder at the ever-present Ian. "Only the kitchens."

"I shall enjoy following you there."

She laughed. "Are you saying you do not care to follow me *everywhere*?"

Ian came up beside her. "I will put forth that the kitchen is my favorite place you go."

"Then let us see what Nelda has for us."

They stepped into a dark kitchen. The only light came from the smoldering embers in the fireplace.

Ian retrieved a torch from the hall and held it high as Jocelyn walked to a small table in the back. A wooden chest sat upon it. She lifted the lid, peering inside.

"Here we are." She pulled out several cakes. Finding a towel on the side table, she wrapped the cakes in it. "Now for drink."

"There." Ian pointed to the jugs on the other side of the kitchen.

Jocelyn went to them, smelling each one until the spiced aroma of mead filled her nose. She picked it up and handed it to Ian. "What else?"

"Cups?"

"Aye, of course!" She grabbed two cups off the shelves, then headed for their chambers.

Ian followed her across the hall and up the stairs. She looked forward to getting off her achy feet. As she neared the top, her foot missed a step. She dropped the cakes and mugs as she reached out to brace her fall. Her ankle twisted and her shin hit the edge of the stone stair.

"My lady!" Ian rushed to her, setting the jug on one of the steps. "How do you fare?"

"I think 'tis only my ankle." Her shin pained her, but she couldn't look to see the damage with Ian present.

"Can you walk?"

"I believe so." With Ian's help, she stood. When she put weight on the foot, pain like fiery needles shot all the way to her toes. "I think I can make it down the hall."

"Let me get the healer."

"Nay, I am well enough." She took a step and faltered, grabbing hold of Ian.

"You are not." Ian picked her up and carried her to her room.

"I could have made it on my own."

Ian laughed. "That would have been painful for the both of us—you with your foot and me with the tedium of watching you."

"Malcolm is blessed to have you in his garrison."

Ian's neck reddened, and he pushed open the door. "I shall see you comfortable, then fetch the healer." He laid Jocelyn upon the bed.

Jocelyn placed a hand on his arm. "Thank you for—"

"What is the meaning of this?" Malcolm stood in the doorway, hands clenched.

Ian straightened and faced Malcolm. Jocelyn smiled. "You are back early. Is Horse well?"

Malcolm strode across the room and grabbed Ian by the neck of his tunic. "How dare you touch my wife in *my* bedroom?"

"Malcolm! Nay! He was only helping me."

Malcolm pulled Ian across the room and pushed him to the door. "I would see you gone on the morrow."

"But my lord—"

"Send another guard! I do not want to see your face again."

Ian nodded, the color draining from his face. He left the room, head up and shoulders back.

"Malcolm, he was only giving me aid." Jocelyn's heart sank at his anger, knowing he didn't want to hear her words.

"I saw enough." Malcolm crossed his arms, his feet planted wide. A vein pulsed in his neck.

"If you truly saw, then you would have seen a chivalrous knight carrying a hurt woman to a place to rest her foot."

Malcolm's jaw clenched, and his brows furrowed. "You are hurt?"

"Aye, I tripped on the stairs."

His eye twitched. "You speak the truth?"

"Aye. Please, trust me."

"Therein lies the difficulty." He turned and strode to the door.

"Wait!" Jocelyn hobbled after him. "You can trust me, I am not like her."

Malcolm stopped at the door. He stared at her for a long moment, then shook his head and stormed away.

"Wait!" Jocelyn limped into the hallway, fear driving her forward—fear that she'd ruined the chance to heal their relationship, fear that she'd never gain his trust. "Malcolm, come back!" She peered down the hall, tears streaming down her face. She had ruined their burgeoning relationship by a mere slip of appearances.

Footsteps pounded upon the stairs, and Jocelyn held her breath. A guard rounded the corner. Ian's replacement.

"My lady, I am Erwan." He gave a slight bow. "May I be of service?"

Her lips quivered. "Nay, thank you," she whispered. Backing into her room, she shut the door. Her shoulders shook as she swiped at her eyes. She stumbled to the bed, throwing herself upon the covers as she gave in to the tears. The day had been special— his attentiveness, his conversation, the touch of his fingers in the dance, the sweet kiss on her wrist.

All gone with the twist of an ankle. Could it ever be made right? Only God knew. She blew out a breath. Aye, God knew.

Oh Lord, help me to trust in You to make right this situation. Help Malcolm to see the truth. Ease his pain. Through every storm, You are there. In the darkness, You shine the brightest. Give us the peace only You can bring. I trust You.

CHAPTER 26

Malcolm sat on the edge of the bed and rubbed his hands over his face. A morning breeze blew through the room, stirring the ash in the fireplace. Bare of Jocelyn's decorative touch, this room contained only a bed, nothing more. He'd tossed all night, reliving the scene from last eve. By the saints, his blood churned at the remembrance.

The chapel bells rang, and Malcolm rose, going to the small window. Throwing open the shutters, he peered out over the bailey where people made their way toward the chapel.

He desired the lists, not the chapel. Crawling back in bed would suit him even better. Laughter below drew his attention. Two children held hands, skipping behind their parents. To be carefree like that …

He pushed away from the window and headed out the door. He needed peace, and the best place to find 'twould be in the chapel.

Entering the familiar building, he searched the room, spotting Jocelyn on the front bench. As lord, Malcolm would be expected to sit by her. Though 'twas the last thing he wanted to do, he walked to the front and slid onto the bench, leaving a handbreadth between them, then focused on the priest.

The early morning sunlight streaming through the stained glass decorated the room in a rainbow of colors. The sweet aroma of incense and the flickering flames of the candles lent an atmosphere of sacredness.

The priest opened the tome on the pedestal in front of him. "God's Word instructs that we who are strong ought to bear with the failings of the weak. We ought not to please ourselves."

Malcolm doubted his strength when it came to his feelings regarding Jocelyn.

"Everything that was written in the past, preserved here for our reading, was given to teach us. Everything in the Scriptures is to encourage and provide us a hope."

He needed hope—hope for a marriage with a foundation of trust, a lifetime of joy and companionship.

"May the God who gives us both endurance and encouragement give you the same attitude toward each other as Christ Jesus had—"

Aye, he needed the same attitude as Christ.

"Christ accepted you as you are. Now accept one another, the weaker and the stronger both."

Malcolm sighed. 'Twas difficult to accept her. To trust her. How could he when every time she smiled at a man he burned with jealousy thinking the worst? He wrestled with his thoughts while the priest continued to read and pray.

"Malcolm." Jocelyn touched his arm.

He stiffened and raised his head. The service had ended.

"Are you well?" The place between her brows crinkled.

He stood, her hand falling away. "Aye."

She rose and grabbed his hand. "Malcolm, please don't send Ian away. He did nothing wrong. He is a loyal knight. You know this to be true."

Deep down he—aye—he knew she spoke truth. 'Twould be foolish to lose him over a bout of jealousy.

"I may have been hasty in my dealings with Ian, but"—he pulled his hand from hers —"I cannot trust you." He left the chapel, squinting against the sunlight.

Halfway across the bailey, a man on a chestnut horse emerged from the stables. Malcolm lifted a hand over his eyes. 'Twas Ian. Full saddlebags hung around his horse. He was leaving Ramslea as ordered.

Pushing aside his pride, Malcolm jogged toward Ian, intercepting his departure. "I would speak with you."

Ian quirked a brow.

"What are your intentions toward my wife?"

"To protect her, as my lord ordered."

"And last evening?"

"Carrying an injured woman to safety, my lord. No more."

The same as Jocelyn explained. Malcolm pursed his lips. "I want you to stay and continue as captain of the guard."

"Thank you. 'Tis my wish to stay."

"Though you are the best knight, I shall better utilize your abilities than guarding Lady Jocelyn."

"I understand." A weight lifted off Malcolm. While the vision of last night still stung, he'd been wrong in his quick judgment. "Put your gear away, then meet me at the stable. I'm inspecting the western crops today and want you with me."

"Aye, my lord."

Ian returned to the guardhouse, so Malcolm turned toward the stables. As he did, Jocelyn left the chapel, her hand resting on Erwan's arm as he led her across the bailey. She smiled at the knight, then laughed at something he said. Malcolm ground his teeth. How easy 'twas for her to be around other men.

And how easily his jealousy sparked into flame. He knew it to be irrational. Even with her hand on Erwan, she limped. Still Malcolm struggled. She desired him, but did she love him? Saying the words didn't mean she spoke truth. His past taught him that. Never had she spoken of love.

Neither had he. Could he love her if he could not trust her? He would have to come to terms with the issue. But for now, he needed time to shed the heavy cloak of his troubled feelings.

He continued to the stables. A hard ride would clear his mind and ease his heart. Perhaps he could come to accept Jocelyn as the priest instructed. To accept and to love.

'Twould take a miracle.

Jocelyn clung to Erwan, her ankle throbbing with each step. 'Twas better than yesterday, but she was thankful for his assistance as she hobbled to the keep. She'd hoped Malcolm would give her aid but, alas, he was still angry with her. She understood his reaction, but it saddened her to know he still wrestled with his past hurt.

"Would you like me to carry you, my lady?" Erwan's gentle voice interrupted Jocelyn's maudlin thoughts.

"Nay, I shall walk."

"I could get a cart and pull you."

Jocelyn laughed. "Nay, I need no more attention brought my way." She glanced around the bailey and spotted Malcolm near the stables, watching her with a frown. Before she could acknowledge him, he spun around and walked into the stables.

Let him be angry. She refused to feel guilty for walking with Erwan. 'Twas nothing untoward. If she and Malcolm were going to have a good marriage, he needed to learn to trust her. She'd make every effort to be circumspect, but at some point, he needed faith. Faith in God and faith in her.

Erwan escorted her to the solar and eased her into a chair near one of the windows. A fire crackled, providing warmth to the room. He brought another chair close to elevate her ankle, then left the room. Assumedly, he stood outside the door as Ian had done.

Jocelyn sighed. She should have asked Erwan to bring her the basket of needlework. It sat against the far wall. She limped to the basket and pulled out the tapestry she'd been working on. A dead mouse fell at her feet, and she screamed.

Erwan burst through the door.

"Mouse! Mouse!" Jocelyn pointed to the floor and shivered. She hated mice!

"Sit and I will remove the vermin." Erwan helped her back to her chair, then searched the basket. "'Tis safe." He handed her the basket, then threw the mouse into the fire.

"Thank you. 'Tis foolish to be so frightened of mice, I know."

Fingers shaking, she pulled thread from the basket.

"Do not feel foolish. If you speak of this, I shall deny it, but I am afeared of lizards." Erwan nodded, then returned to his post.

Jocelyn smiled, watching the broad back of the knight walk away. A knight afraid of lizards. She giggled, the tension of the morning leaving her. Picking up her tapestry, she worked the needle for quite some time, praying and thinking of things to be done around the castle.

Her mother used to take food and clothing to the serfs. Jocelyn could take stock of the food stores and see what they could spare. 'Twould keep her hands busy and her mind off of Malcolm—as if that were possible.

"I hear things are not well between you and your lord."

Jocelyn startled. Helen strode into the solar. Ignoring the bait, Jocelyn turned her attention back to her work.

"Ah, your silence speaks." Helen took a slow turn around the room. She stopped behind Jocelyn and whispered in her ear. "'Tisn't easy keeping a man's attention."

"I don't believe my marriage is any of your concern."

"Everything about Ramslea is my concern."

"It shouldn't be."

Helen laughed. "You poor dear." She walked across the room and out the door, laughing all the way.

Jocelyn jammed her needle into the fabric. How she disliked that woman! Such self-importance. Such unkindness. "Ouch!" Jocelyn dropped the tapestry, grasping her finger as a drop of blood pooled at its tip. She swiped at the blood, flustered and ready to be free of Helen. She limped to the chest along the far wall. She'd find a game and make Erwan play with her to bide the time.

Opening the lid, Jocelyn reached in. A snake coiled, ready to strike. She screamed, scrambling back.

Erwan pulled her away, his sword drawn. Jocelyn climbed on a chair as he used his sword as a stick, flicking the snake over the side of the chest and onto the floor. He chopped off its head, then disposed of it as he had the mouse.

Jocelyn climbed off the chair and sat, her nerves frayed. How had a snake gotten into the chest?

"I shall stand inside the solar now." Erwan took his position beside the door, sword unsheathed. "You require more guarding than I originally thought."

Jocelyn frowned, remembering Helen's laughter. "'Twould seem so."

CHAPTER 27

Jocelyn piled the clothing into Erwan's arms. She chuckled at his stoic face peering above the mound. "You are ever so chivalrous."

"'Tis my duty to help those in need."

She took the last tunic from the seamstress. "Thank you for sewing these so quickly. I cannot believe it took only three days to finish."

"I sew extra clothes in my spare time, so some were simply awaiting a home."

"Your work will bring a smile to someone's face today." Jocelyn left the seamstress's hut with Erwan behind her.

The past three days had been spent preparing food and clothing to give to the poor. She'd enjoyed the work, though it had not distracted her from thoughts of Malcolm. He stayed away both day and night now, and she missed him dreadfully.

She pushed away the dreary thoughts and strode to the stables, her ankle almost fully recovered. As instructed, two pack horses stood outside carrying bundles of food and clothing. Black was saddled, as well as Erwan's horse. Three mounted guards awaited them.

Once she reached the horses, Jocelyn and Erwan bundled the last of the clothing, securing it to one of the pack horses. He helped her mount, then swung onto his own horse.

"Let's be off." She motioned to Erwan, who took the lead. She didn't bother to leave word for Malcolm, as he stayed informed about all that went on at Ramslea.

Once outside the gate, the crisp wind invigorated her. When they neared the village, Erwan raised a hand. They walked their horses through town. People came out of their homes and businesses to watch.

Jocelyn waved. "Come! We've brought gifts!"

A crowd followed them to the town center. The open space supplied room to vendors selling produce, drink, and various supplies. Small thatched homes lined the road on the other side of the market.

Erwan stopped at the edge of the market near the tavern, and Jocelyn slid off Black. With his aide, she opened the bundles. Children and women gathered close.

A woman pushed her small daughter forward. "Might you have a wee dress for my Anne?" The girl pushed stringy blonde hair from her eyes. Her tattered clothes hung loose on her small frame.

Jocelyn's heart ached. She wished she had a whole trunk full of dresses for the child. "I'm sure we have something that will fit." She searched through the bundle until she found a small dress in a pale blue. "Here we are. 'Twill match Anne's lovely blue eyes."

The woman took the garment, clutching it to her chest. "M'lady, thank ye. My Anne has never had anything so nice."

Jocelyn handed her a loaf of bread. "I wish it could be more."

As the goods were passed out, the people's excitement fed Jocelyn's joy. She laughed and chatted with them, enjoying herself more than she had since dancing in Malcolm's arms several nights past. 'Twas such a simple thing to give of her excess. As she watched the villagers smile and accepted their gratitude, she vowed never to forget the privilege into which she'd been born.

When all the food and clothes had been passed out, Jocelyn put a hand to the small of her back and stretched. "Erwan, perhaps I could train with you to work out my stiffness."

Erwan frowned. "Women do not train."

"I trained with Lord Malcolm."

"I am not he."

Nay, he was not. Not even close to being like her husband. While attentive to her needs, Erwan remained aloof. She missed the easy camaraderie she had shared with Malcolm and even Ian. Jocelyn moved toward Black, her step faltering. Several lengths away, Malcolm sat atop Horse. He watched her.

Jocelyn straightened, then walked toward him. How long had he been there? She stopped a few paces away from him. "I brought food and clothes to the villagers."

"So I see."

"I brought four guards with me." Surely, he'd be pleased with that.

"Aye. A good thing, though you should have consulted me about going outside the castle."

"I have hardly seen you these past three days." She tilted her head. "Though I suppose I could have sent you a messenger pigeon."

Malcolm's brow drew together. "You can send word by way of a servant."

"True. I'm sure most lords and ladies communicate as such. I shall do better next time." His white knuckles gripped the reins. She knew the answer but wanted to probe. "You are angry with me still?"

Horse stomped his front hoof, and Malcolm patted the animal's neck. "I am busy with the work of the castle."

"Even after dark?"

"I am weary after all my work, wanting only peace and quiet."

"I could be quiet for you. I would not speak, should you prefer that."

Malcolm ran a hand through his hair. "I prefer being alone for now."

For now. Jocelyn smiled at her handsome husband. *For now* implied at some point in the future there would be a time when he wouldn't want to be alone. It was enough—for now. "As you wish. I shall be ready when you are."

Malcolm moved Horse toward her, his eyes upon her. Her heart fluttered like a bird caught in a net. "You shall know when I am ready." He kneed Horse and moved on.

Faith, Jocelyn wanted to sit and fan herself. As she watched him gallop to the other side of the village, she grinned. He hadn't completely turned her away. 'Twas only *for now*.

Malcolm attacked the day like a warrior facing his greatest enemy, pushing forward with swift focus. He'd inspected the guardhouse and the smithy, making note of several needed repairs. As he neared the healer's hut, he marked the crumbling mortar and rotting thatched roof. He circled the building, spying a small hole near the ground. Probably a mouse hole. No need to inspect the inside. He'd seen enough of the dwelling.

The sun nearing the middle of the sky, he drew close to the chapel. While he knew the chapel required work, he didn't care to make conversation with the priest. Nay, he would visit the armory instead. Malcolm changed course, hurrying away.

"My lord!"

By the saints, 'twas the priest himself. Malcolm slowed his pace as the robed man approached him. "Good day, Father."

"Good day, my lord. I heard you were examining the buildings today."

"Aye, that I am."

"I have much to show you. Come." The priest walked toward the chapel.

Malcolm resisted a sigh and followed.

"These windows here"—the priest pointed at two stained-glass windows on the east wall—"need daubing." A leak in the roof and a hole in the wall of the priest's quarters also needed repairs.

After the inspection, the priest led Malcolm back to the bailey. "Thank you for taking an interest in Ramslea. 'Tis much appreciated by all."

Malcolm's shoulders eased, relieved the priest hadn't asked about Jocelyn. "I want to do right by all those under my care. I vow to be a good lord and to make a good home for all here."

The priest clasped his hands in front of him. "How is your wife? Has it turned out as you expected?"

Malcolm cringed. "Nay, but I am working on it."

"How so?"

"I am giving her room while she earns back my trust."

"Earns it back? Has she taken it away?"

Malcolm frowned. "Aye, though 'twas a misunderstanding on my part."

"How did she break your trust?"

The priest's gentle voice cracked a fissure in Malcolm's defenses. He could use a listening ear. "Her circumstance looked as if she were unfaithful. I know now that she wasn't, but it reminded me how easily she could be."

"My lord, if I may. Jocelyn cannot earn your trust without interacting with you. Avoiding her because you fear what might happen only makes your fear stronger. Let God help you to trust. Let Him ease your fear."

Malcolm heaved a sigh. It sounded so simple when the priest gave him directions, but he knew 'twasn't an easy task. Yet the hope of the suggestion gave him pause. "Your words are comforting to me, Father. I thank you."

"Seek the Father above, my lord. He will guide you."

Malcolm nodded. He entered the armory still mulling over the priest's words. Malcolm prided himself on his courage. To be called out for his fear … well, it chafed against his pride.

But the priest was right. Jocelyn couldn't earn his trust if they were never together. He'd observed her from afar the past three days since seeing her in the village. She'd been so kind to the people. So joyful. Back at the castle, she'd sent food and drink to his room every evening, making sure he was taken care of. She'd even had a new tunic made for him. Her thoughtfulness flooded him with shame at his treatment of her.

Could God truly give him the courage to face his fear of

rejection?

I don't want to avoid this anymore. God, make me brave enough to fully give Jocelyn my heart.

A weight lifted from his chest as he gave silent voice to his fear. He'd never admit it out loud, to be sure.

Now, he wished for her company. To have more days like the one in the fields. To talk. To hold. To kiss. But she had taken more food and clothing to the village. Very well. That would give him time to bathe and dress in his new clothes before she returned home.

Home. In his mind, home always meant peace and quiet—no trouble, no discord. It was what he'd dreamed of for the past several years. But now that he'd kept his distance, having the solitude he thought he wanted, he found he disliked all the quiet. He missed his wife's chatter.

When had his lady become the whisper of home?

CHAPTER 28

The sun neared its peak as Jocelyn followed Erwan out Ramslea's gate. Several guards rode behind, leading several pack horses carrying food and clothing for the villagers. She drew Black alongside Erwan.

"Thank you for helping pack all the supplies. I know it has only been three days since we last visited, but I don't want anyone to be without." The disappointed faces when they ran out of supplies last time tore her heart asunder.

"'Tis a good thing you do."

Jocelyn shook her head. "'Tis a good thing *we* do." She'd been grateful to have something to occupy her time, as well as her thoughts, while Malcolm remained angry. She hoped the solitude was helping him work through his feelings.

Though she had determined to wait on God to sort out her marriage, three days with only glimpses of her husband seemed an eternity. Would that He saw fit to hurry along the process.

Erwan urged his horse into a trot. The group matched his gait as they moved through the countryside. When they rounded the bend in the road, a company of men—fifty or more—fanned across it. Jocelyn's pulse quickened, taking in their weapons. She gripped the reins, her body tensed.

Rolland sat atop his steed at the front of the group.

Nay! God save us!

Erwan drew his sword. "Jocelyn! Flee!"

She spun Black around toward Ramslea and kicked his side, sending him racing. Fear coursed through her, her limbs tingling. Could they outrun Rolland's men? Was Black fast enough? If they made it within sight of the castle, they might stand a chance.

Erwan drew beside her. "Hasten!"

Horses thundered behind them.

A guard's anguished cry spurred her on. She bent low over Black, the trees along the road a blur. She couldn't fall into Rolland's grasp. One of his men drew close to Erwan. Her protector swung his sword. The man veered away. Another man pushed forward, coming alongside Jocelyn.

"Faster, my lady!" Erwan raised his sword as another man appeared. He deflected a powerful blow, the clash of steel loud in her ears. Erwan swung at the man, his blade connecting true. "Nay!" Erwan dropped his sword. An arrow pierced his arm.

Dread struck Jocelyn's heart. She glanced over her shoulder. Rolland's men gained on her. Where were the rest of her guards? "Go, Black, go!" She bent lower still, Black's mane whipping in her face.

A rider approached Erwan. How could he defend himself, maimed and unarmed? "Erwan! Behind you!"

He glanced over his shoulder. The rider thrust his sword forward, piercing Erwan's back and through his chest. "Aargh!" He slumped forward, then fell.

"Nay!" She must get to Ramslea. To Malcolm.

Jocelyn kicked Black harder, but another rider came alongside. She reached for her dagger and struck at the man, but to no avail. He grabbed her wrist and twisted. She cried out and dropped the knife. Snatching her reins, he pulled, slowing her horse. Jocelyn pounded the man's hand, trying to get control of the reins. Reaching across, she clawed at his face. He grunted, then shoved his elbow into her face. Pain blinded her and blood ran from her nose. She ignored her throbbing face and pushed at the man as he jerked the reins until they stopped.

Nay! She would not surrender. Not for all the king's gold would she willingly give in to Rolland. Jocelyn jumped down and ran toward Ramslea once more. Futile—perhaps daft—but she wouldn't stop.

Rolland's men surrounded her, horses breathing hard, their hooves stirring dust from the road. With nowhere left to run, she pushed her shoulders back. *Have courage. God is with you.* Two men dismounted and grabbed her arms.

"Lady Jocelyn." Rolland rode his horse toward her. "I need your services."

Jocelyn snorted. "I shall never do your bidding." As if she would acquiesce to his requests ... or demands.

"You do not have a choice." He nodded to the man on his left. "Bind her."

She struggled to pull free as the man slid from his horse, grabbed a rope off his saddle, then bound Jocelyn's hands in front of her. Would Rolland take her to his land? Use her ... abuse her? She shuddered.

The man jerked her forward toward Rolland. When the man put his hand on her waist to lift her up, Jocelyn reared her head back, then forward against the man's face. Spots scattered across her vision, and she blinked against the pain.

The man cursed. He raised his hand as if to strike her.

"Nay! Do not touch her. I need her conscious." Rolland glared at his man.

Jocelyn's head pounded, but the man's curse gave her satisfaction. She would not go willingly.

Jocelyn kicked at him when he tried to lift her, but he merely grunted and pushed her up to Rolland. Grabbing her around the waist, Rolland pulled her to him and pressed a knife against her throat. Jocelyn stilled, the blade cold against her skin.

"There now," said Rolland. "Cease your fight and all will be well."

'Twould not end well, no matter what he said. As Rolland's blade paralyzed her movements, his man tied her bound hands to the pommel.

"Regroup!" Rolland lowered his knife but held it in front of her, the glint from the sun a reminder of its deadly presence. Kicking his horse, they broke into a run, Rolland's men following close behind.

They headed for the castle. Was she to be used for bargaining?

Jocelyn struggled to loosen the ropes as they sped down the road. 'Twasn't an easy task, the knife a constant threat, but if her hands were free from the pommel, she might could grab the knife.

The group topped the hill, and the castle rose before them. As they approached, the porticullis lowered, barring their entrance. Rolland halted his horse thirty paces away. Voices rang from within the castle walls. Jocelyn continued to dig at the rope, pulse hammering in her ears. If she could create a distraction, perhaps Malcolm and his men could gain the upper hand.

"Raise the porticullis! I have your lady!" Once again, Rolland pressed his knife to Jocelyn's throat.

The guards on the parapet raised their bows, notching their arrows.

"If you value your lady's life, you will raise the porticullis!" Rolland pressed the knife harder against her skin. Jocelyn sucked in a breath, trying to remain still. "Fools," he muttered.

"What is it you want, Rolland?" Malcolm appeared atop the parapet, arms by his side, fists clenched.

Jocelyn drank in the visage of her husband, powerful and in control. He looked and sounded every bit the lord he should be. His anger was palpable from the rigid lines of his body to his clenched fists, but she trusted his ability to think clearly. He'd proven himself many times.

"I want Ramslea and Helen."

"Helen you can have, but Ramslea is mine."

"Then you shall lose your lady. Let me in, and I will let both of you go."

"Nay, he lies!" Jocelyn cried out as Rolland's knife pressed into her skin, warmth trickling down her neck.

"Jocelyn, do not speak!" Malcolm took a step forward, his

hands outstretched. He ran a hand through his hair. "If I let you in, you will let Jocelyn go free?"

"Aye."

What was Malcolm thinking? He couldn't give up Ramslea. Not without a fight.

"So be it." Malcolm left the parapet.

Nay! Ramslea left to Rolland? Surely Malcolm had a plan. Her fingers continued to loosen the ropes. If she were free, she could help.

The clank of chain signaled the porticullis opening. Rolland lifted the dagger into the air, and his men drew their swords. The scrape of steel announced the battle to come. Jocelyn's pulse raced as Rolland led his men through the barbican.

Malcolm stood in the center of the bailey, sword in hand. Knights surrounded him, swords drawn and shields in place. Jocelyn's breath hitched. *Lord, protect him. Protect them all.*

Riding into the bailey, Rolland's men surged forward. Swords raised, they charged. Their battle cry pebbled Jocelyn's skin. Arrows flew from the parapet.

Malcolm ran toward them as she frantically pulled on her bindings. The rope slackened. With all of her strength, she jerked free of the pommel, forcing her elbow up and into Rolland's chin. He grunted and loosened his grip. In that second, Jocelyn twisted, falling to the ground. Horse hooves stomped around her. She rolled and struggled to her feet, her bound hands and long skirts impeding her progress.

Malcolm pulled her upright, then sliced the ropes from her wrists. He pushed her behind him. "Go to the hall!" He rushed forward, sword raised.

Jocelyn ran.

Men battled all around her. She dodged past them, running toward the keep. Rushing up the steps, her mind raced. She needed a knife! Gaining the door, she glanced back at Malcolm.

With every heavy stroke of Rolland's blade, Malcolm fell back, deflecting the blows with sword in both hands. Jocelyn held her breath. *Fight, Malcolm, fight!* He planted his feet, swiftly striking Rolland's sword. He continued his assault, blow after blow, until Rolland stepped back.

Relieved, Jocelyn turned and made for her room. If she was to help Malcolm defend their home, she needed a weapon.

Lord, save us!

Rage spurred Malcolm on. Rage at Rolland. Rage at himself for not better protecting Jocelyn.

Malcolm tried to watch Jocelyn as he deflected Rolland's strikes. He allowed Rolland the upper hand until she gained the door.

With Jocelyn safely ensconced within the keep, Malcolm focused on the enemy before him, ignoring the knights fighting on every side. Rolland's sword bore down upon him. Malcolm brought up his blade. The clash reverberated through his arm.

Rolland thrust his sword toward Malcolm's chest. "You will die this day!"

"I doubt that." With renewed vigor, Malcolm arched his sword, bringing it down toward Rolland's head.

Rolland backhanded, then brought his sword across Malcolm's middle. Malcolm curled his back, jumping out of the blade's path. He lunged, his sword nearing Rolland's chest. Rolland pivoted, sweeping his blade horizontally, connecting with Malcolm's.

Malcolm's grip on his blade loosened with the blow. *By the saints, focus!* Tightening his hold, he surged ahead, raining blow after blow upon Rolland, sending him back one step at a time. Rolland grunted with each stroke, echoing each heavy clang of steel.

"You shall never have Ramslea." With both hands, Malcolm raised his sword above his head and swiftly sliced downward upon Rolland.

Rolland met his blow, keeping his sword aloft. He took a step forward, and the two stood locked together, face-to-face.

"I shall, with Jocelyn as an added prize."

The picture of Rolland with Jocelyn sent a wave of anger pulsing through Malcolm's veins. With a roar, he pounded his blade upon Rolland. Rolland stumbled as his foot met the steps to the keep. He fell.

Malcolm thrust his sword toward the man's chest. Rolland twisted and rolled over. Malcolm's blade glanced off the stone steps. Rolland's blade caught Malcolm's thigh, pain shooting through his leg. Saints, would he ever manage to fell the man?

Rolland scrambled to his feet. Malcolm ignored the throb in his leg.

"Jocelyn will make a tempting mistress."

"And what of Helen?"

"Helen can kill Jocelyn when I tire of her."

Malcolm charged Rolland, fury consuming him. Fueled by fear for Jocelyn, his blows sent Rolland rearward. Malcolm changed the angle of his press, pushing Rolland into the path of a fallen man. He drove Rolland back until he tripped over the dead body.

Malcolm lunged, pressing the tip of his blade to Rolland's neck. "Yield!" He kicked Rolland's sword out of reach.

"Never." Rolland rolled twice and gained his feet. He pulled a dagger from his belt. Blood trickled down his neck.

"You are no match for me armed as you are. Yield!"

"I will never yield to you."

"So be it. You shall die at my sword." Malcolm charged.

Rolland pulled back his arm. A guard tackled him as the knife flew from his hands. The knife nicked Malcolm's ear as it hurtled past. By the saints, that was close!

Rolland and the guard wrestled. Malcolm seized the opportunity. Adjusting his grip, he thrust the hilt of his sword against Rolland's head. The man went limp.

"See that Rolland is bound and taken to the dungeon." Malcolm ran to the keep. To Jocelyn.

Jocelyn raced to Malcolm's chest in their room. She had thought it odd he kept extra knives there, but now she knew the wisdom of it.

"Stop!"

Jocelyn halted, foreboding seeping through her.

She turned as Helen stepped through the doorway, one of Ramslea's male servants behind her holding a piece of rope. She lifted a dagger, pointing it at Jocelyn. "Finally, you shall be removed from Ramslea forever."

Jocelyn's pulse quickened. "Why do you hate me so much?"

"You took my future."

"The king will find you a rich husband."

"I do not want a rich husband! I want Rolland and Ramslea. I had it until you came back and ruined my plans."

Jocelyn inched toward the bed. "You blackmailed the abbess, didn't you? Your own sister?"

"I dare say Agatha's hiding in Scotland by now. She thinks she's out of my reach there. Foolish woman. I warned her what would happen if she failed me."

"But why?"

"I did whatever was necessary to reclaim Ramslea."

"Reclaim?"

Helen threw back her head and laughed. "You fool. My grandfather held Ramslea until he died, then the king decided to hand it over to your father instead of mine. For *grand exploits in battle and service to the king*, I believe was the reason."

Jocelyn swallowed. She didn't have to wonder why Helen's

bitterness ran deep.

Helen motioned to the servant. "Seize her."

The man moved around the bed, cornering Jocelyn. She leaped onto the bed, scrambling to the other side. Helen stood between her and the door. The servant leaped over the bed. Jocelyn grabbed the jug sitting on the table and rushed toward Helen. Startled, the woman froze. Jocelyn swung the jug, hitting her in the shoulder.

Helen grunted. The dagger fell.

Jocelyn ran out the door.

"Get her, you fool!"

Jocelyn sprinted down the hall. If she made it to the kitchens, she could snatch a knife. Footsteps pounded behind her.

Something hit her in the back, and the floor rushed up to meet her. Pain shot through her knee and shoulder. The servant hauled her to her feet, twisting her arms behind her.

Never would she give up without a fight. She stomped on the man's foot. He cursed and bent her hands backward until she cried out. Jocelyn ceased her struggle, at least for a time.

Helen strode toward them, dagger and rope in hand. She snatched Jocelyn's hair, pulled her head back, and placed the knife against her skin. "Now bind her with the rope."

The servant bound Jocelyn's wrists. 'Twould make it difficult to run—or do anything—with her hands behind her back.

Helen whispered in Jocelyn's ear. "Soon I shall add to the blood already staining your neck."

"Why wait?" Jocelyn winced as Helen jerked her head back further.

"I want all of Ramslea to see you die at the hands of the rightful heir."

"You aren't the heir unless the king deems it so."

"With Rolland's help, we shall retain Ramslea. He has many allies opposed to the king." Helen released her. "Take her to the parapet."

The servant hefted Jocelyn over his shoulder and carried her up the stairs, Helen following close behind. He pushed open the door and walked onto the parapet, setting her on her feet.

Helen pointed her dagger toward the bailey. "Take her to the edge and hold her there."

Not for the first time, Jocelyn wished her father had added a railing to the parapet. While the thick outer wall rose five feet, no wall stood between her and the bailey. Between her and death. Her pulse raced as the servant pushed her forward.

Helen stood beside her. The battle raged below them and along the parapet. Malcolm fought one of Rolland's men.

"Nay," whispered Helen. "He lives." She searched the bailey, her breath becoming erratic. "Where is Rolland?" She brought a hand to her brow, peering across the castle. She growled and pointed her dagger at Jocelyn.

"Malcolm Castillon!" Helen's voice pierced the air.

Malcolm ran his opponent through, then looked for the voice.

"Killing Rolland was a mistake! You shall now watch your wife di—"

"Rolland lives!" Malcolm threw down his sword and ran toward them, coming to stand near the edge. "Rolland lives!"

Helen swayed. The servant holding Jocelyn grabbed Helen's arm with one hand. His movement threw Jocelyn off balance. She pushed backward and gained half a foot of space from the edge, but he blocked her from moving further. Her limbs quivered.

"Cease, fool." Helen shook off the servant's hand. "If Rolland is truly alive, then release him!"

"Let go of Jocelyn, and I will bring him out."

"Release him now or Jocelyn dies!"

The servant pushed Jocelyn forward, losing the precious space she had gained.

"Stop! I will—" Malcolm took a step forward.

"Aargh!" Jocelyn's captor loosened his grip. She twisted, spinning away from the edge as the servant pitched forward, a dagger in his back.

Jocelyn ran, but Helen grabbed her by the hair, yanking her close. She pressed the point of the dagger between Jocelyn's ribs. They faced one of Ramslea's guards standing twenty paces away. "Drop your sword or she dies."

The man set his blade on the floor and backed away.

"Leave the parapet." As the guard made his way to the stairway, Helen turned Jocelyn to face the bailey.

"Release Rolland immediately!" Helen gripped Jocelyn's hair tighter, pulling her head back.

"Aye! Do not hurt her."

Helen screamed and dropped her dagger. Still gripping Jocelyn's hair, she clutched the arrow protruding from her leg and crumpled to the ground.

Jocelyn fell back. Her feet slipped out from under her and dangled over the edge. She pulled her knees up and tried to push away from the ledge. Helen moaned, cursing Jocelyn and cursing Malcolm. "You shall never have Ramslea. Never!" Helen shoved Jocelyn. "Die!"

Jocelyn slid forward. "Nay!" Her calves moved past the edge, then her thighs. "Malcolm!"

His wife's scream rent the air.

"Jocelyn!" Malcolm ran toward the bailey wall as Jocelyn's legs swung over the edge of the parapet. Fear fueled his stride as he pumped his legs, arms outstretched. He bellowed, straining to reach her.

Jocelyn's legs disappeared, and Malcolm stopped, chest heaving. What happened? He backed away from the wall, searching.

Ian pulled Jocelyn to her feet and cut the ropes around her wrists. Malcolm's shoulders sagged, relief rushing through him. She rubbed her wrists and looked at him, a trembling smile on her lips. By the saints, he wanted to weep!

Helen rose to her knees, clutching a dagger.

"Behind you, Ian!"

His guard twisted, but Helen was too close. She stabbed him in the back of the leg. Ian stumbled, and Helen stabbed him again. She yelled and swung the knife toward Jocelyn.

"Jocelyn, the ledge!" Malcolm's heart hammered as she jumped back, missing the knife. The heel of one foot landed off the edge. Her arms waved in the air as she struggled for balance. Malcolm ran toward the wall.

Jocelyn threw herself forward, but couldn't regain her footing. She fell, grasping for the edge. Malcolm reached the wall, ready to catch her. She caught the edge with one hand.

"Malcolm!" She swung, trying to grab hold with her other hand.

Ian and Helen's yells sounded from above him.

Malcolm stretched out his arms. "Let go! I will catch you."

She grasped the edge with her other hand.

"Jocelyn! Trust me!" Even as he said the words, their full weight struck him hard. *Trust me*. Hadn't she spoken those very words? She'd asked him to trust her, and he'd refused. She'd asked him to let her in, and he'd closed her off. Trust didn't guarantee not getting hurt. Trust was faith that all would work out in the end.

He believed 'twould.

"Malcolm!" Jocelyn gripped the edge tighter.

"Jocelyn, let go. I am here."

She glanced over her shoulder. "I'm afraid!"

"I know, but you can trust me." She could. He would catch her. And he would never let her go.

Jocelyn opened her fingers and fell, her cry reverberating in his heart.

He caught her, bending his knees, and rolling back to break the fall. They landed sided by side on the ground. Before the dust settled, Malcolm leaned over her. "Are you hurt?"

She put a hand to her forehead, gasping for breath. "Nay." She touched his cheek. "But you saved me."

Malcolm put his hand over hers. "'Tis what I do best."

Jocelyn briefly closed her eyes, the corner of her lips tilting upward.

He helped her to her feet, then crushed her to him. "I thought I'd lost you," he whispered, clutching her tighter.

"I thought you'd lost me too." Arms wrapped around his waist, she pressed her face against his neck.

Malcolm reveled in her embrace. Her trust in him humbled him as he realized he hadn't had the courage to do the same. Scooping her into his arms, he gazed into her eyes, amazed at her calm. "I have much to say to you, but first I must get you to safety and send for the healer."

Ian leaned over the parapet, a smirk on his face. "I am unharmed. I know you worried for my safety."

"I had no doubt. And Helen?"

"Unconscious." Ian shrugged a shoulder. "She is insane, that one."

Jocelyn trembled in Malcolm's arms, so he tightened his grip. "Bind her and take her to the tower." He paused. How did one thank the man who rescued his wife? "And Ian, thank you. I owe you many times over."

Jocelyn put a hand over her heart. "Aye, thank you. I owe you as well."

Ian nodded. "'Tis my honor to serve."

"Come with me, and the healer can tend your leg after seeing to my lady."

"I shall make sure the castle is secure, then find the healer."

"Very well." Malcolm strode across the bailey, moving around the bodies scattered across the yard. A handful of Rolland's men sat on the ground near the guardhouse, bound and awaiting transfer to the dungeon. Malcolm's men stood tall and at the ready.

Malcolm glanced at his wife. She watched him, and heat crept up his neck. He cleared his throat. "Ramslea's guards did well against the attack."

"They have a good leader."

He grunted, pleased at her words. They gained the stairs to the keep, and Malcolm stopped one of the guards. "Send the healer to my lady's room."

She pressed a hand to his shoulder. "I can walk. Go see to the castle. I will await the healer."

"You come first." Malcolm meant the words. Though he never thought anything could be more important than land, Jocelyn had thrust herself into his life—and his heart.

She wrapped her arm around his neck and laid her head on his shoulder. By the saints, his eyes misted at the sweetness of his wife. This wouldn't do at all.

He climbed the stairs, entered the bedchamber, and laid Jocelyn upon the bed. He opened the shutters wide, letting in light from the afternoon sun.

"I shall be fine, Malcolm." Jocelyn looked at him and smiled. He loved it when she said his name, especially when accompanied by such a smile.

Seated on the edge of the bed, he took her hand in his. "I will not leave you unguarded."

She placed her other hand on top of his. "You are very thoughtful."

Malcolm cleared his throat and shook his head.

"But you are."

"I haven't been. In fact, I've treated you shamefully this past week." Malcolm brushed a curl away from her face. "I must admit to you that I have been afraid."

"Of me?"

"Aye. Nay. I mean, I'm not afraid of you. I'm afraid of loving you."

"But—"

Malcolm put a finger up to her lips, sliding it over their velvety softness. Her eyes crinkled at the corners, and he pulled his hand away. "I've been a fool keeping myself away from you. Not trusting you. You are nothing like the woman who betrayed me before. You are kind to others, helpful, and generous." A grin tugged at his lips. "You even put on a brave face in the midst of my ignoring you, sending food to my room." He took a deep breath. "Please forgive me and forget my foolish behavior."

Jocelyn's eyes glistened, but she smiled. She placed a hand on his cheek and rubbed her thumb over the stubble. "There is nothing to forgive. After the many untruths I told, I understand your reluctance to trust me. I prayed that, in time, you could learn to trust me ... to love me. And here you are, loving me well already."

Malcolm leaned forward and pressed his forehead to hers. "I do love you, Jocelyn."

"And I love you, Malcolm, Lord of Ramslea and lord of my heart."

Malcolm slipped his hand through her hair. The silky curls slid over his fingers. He angled his head and tasted her lips. Softly. Gently. Teasing her with his kiss, until Jocelyn grabbed his tunic and pulled him closer.

By the saints! Malcolm smiled against her lips, wrapping her in his embrace. While peace and quiet had been his goal, he held the ultimate prize in his arms.

EPILOGUE

Ramslea, England, 1203 AD

From the top of the parapet, Jocelyn reveled in the warm breeze. After a hard winter, the spring winds blew from the south, and she couldn't get enough of the sun and its warmth. She put a hand over her eyes as she looked to the western forest. Varying shades of green dotted the land, the trees in full bloom.

She hooked her arm through Sister Mary's. They continued their slow walk around the castle, enjoying the sights inside and outside of the castle walls. "I am so thankful you were able to come for a visit. Five years is too long not to see your friendly face."

Mary placed her hand over Jocelyn's. "I agree. While I enjoy your missives, to hear your stories from your own mouth thrills me more than I can say."

Laughter rang out in the bailey. Jocelyn and Mary stopped.

"Look at your handsome husband and son."

Jocelyn's heart nearly burst with pride. At only three years of age, little John held his wooden sword high, hitting Malcolm's wood sword with fervor. Malcolm dropped his blade, then fell over yelling. John tackled Malcolm, his laughter tickling Jocelyn's ears. As Malcolm came to his feet, he scooped up John and seated him on his shoulders. They walked from the keep toward the stables—the stables situated below where she and Mary stood.

"Faith, I can't be caught up here again."

"What do you mean?" Mary's brow puckered.

"Jocelyn!" Malcolm's voice thundered from below.

Jocelyn sighed. "Alas, I've been seen." She turned to Mary. "I am not supposed to be up here without him."

"That seems—"

"Overprotective? Irrational?"

Mary smiled but didn't reply.

Jocelyn looked down at Malcolm. He shook his head. Pulling John from his shoulders, he handed the boy to Ian, who stood a few steps away. Malcolm jogged to the stairs, bounding up them two at a time. He drew near, a frown creasing his brow.

Jocelyn took the offensive. "I have Mary to see to my safety."

Malcolm glanced at Mary, then back at Jocelyn. "You will pardon me when I say that wee Mary is not fit to catch you should you fall. You are twice her size."

Jocelyn gasped.

Mary choked on a laugh.

Putting a hand on her overlarge belly, Jocelyn lifted her chin. "I won't be bigger than her much longer."

"Aye." A smile spread across Malcolm's face. "What think you, Mary? A girl this time?"

Mary shook her head. "I believe another boy for John."

The smile slid from Malcolm's face. "Truly? I was hoping for a girl."

Jocelyn laughed and took Malcolm's hand. "Mary jests. There is no way to know for sure, love."

Malcolm grunted. "I knew that."

"Of course you did." She pulled on his hand. "Shall you stroll with us?"

Malcolm pulled her toward him, then lifted her in his arms. "Nay, you and Mary will walk on the dirt while I continue John's lessons." He strode to the stairs.

Jocelyn looked over his shoulder. "Mary, our merriment has ended."

"I don't know but that our merriment has only begun." Mary chuckled. "'Tis so much better than your missives."

Jocelyn mused over Mary's words. *Our merriment has only begun.* Life with Malcolm had exceeded all her expectations. She'd prayed for a loving marriage, and God did not disappoint. Malcolm spent time with her, sharing his heart fully. He cherished her and loved her well. Their family continued to grow, as did their faith in the Lord—the foundation for a joy-filled marriage.

Aye, their merriment had only begun.

CPSIA information can be obtained
at www.ICGtesting.com
Printed in the USA
BVHW080948070519
547592BV00002B/381/P